MIND HOW YOU GO

By the same author

Roaring Boys
A Cackhanded War
The Outside Contributor
The Penny World

Edward Blishen

MIND HOW YOU GO

Constable · London

First published in Great Britain 1997
by Constable and Company Limited
3 The Lanchesters, 162 Fulham Palace Road
London W6 9ER
Copyright © The Estate of Edward Blishen
ISBN 0 09 477460 9

Set in Linotron Sabon by
CentraCet Ltd, Saffron Walden
Printed in Great Britain by
St Edmundsbury Press Ltd
Bury St Edmunds, Suffolk

A CIP catalogue record for this book
is available from the British Library

For Sim and Arnold Rattenbury
and for Nick Tucker

Yes, sir, being over seventy is a bore, for one is marked for execution, and is daily awaiting the death warrant.

Sydney Smith

How should I complain, who am still able to wonder?

Henry David Thoreau

'Why are people proud of expecting to die soon?' said Dudley to Mark. 'I think it is humiliating to have so little life left.'

'They are triumphant at having made sure of more life than other people. And they don't really think they will die.'

'No, of course, they have got into the way of living. I see it is a lifelong habit.'

Ivy Compton-Burnett, *A Family and a Fortune*

I find being old very interesting. I wish I had tried it before.

John Snowling

Prologue

'I don't know if you have any idea,' he said, 'how your bladder works?' He didn't pause for a reply, having already a sheet of paper in his hand: he was sketching eagerly. 'This sort of thing,' he said. It was the Aswan Dam, I thought: a prodigious reservoir, prodigiously contained. And *that* – a quick scribbling – was what he was declaring to be an average amount of urine, although it seemed to me as much as would turn any of us into a walking rainbutt. And here were the taps and sluices and the general system of hydraulics by means of which this flood could be voided. 'You are having to wait for it to begin?' he asked. Well, I understood now why I had to wait – even in my prime I'd have been hard put to it to pump up, and eject to a suitable distance, half of the accumulation the doctor's artwork suggested.

Having to wait for it to begin was certainly one of the embarrassments that had brought me to the surgery. You'd be in a public convenience, a creature from a world of slow motion marooned in a world of the speeded-up. You would wait and wait, and younger men would arrive, disadjust their clothing, noisily discharge themselves (sometimes insolently humming), zip themselves respectable again, and vanish, to be succeeded by others, and others, while you continued to wait, and wait. You were ready to be officially questioned about this dilatoriness. DO NOT LOITER IN THESE TOILETS said a notice I'd seen on Paddington station. For me, now, doing what between roughly 1922 and 1929 I was encouraged to call Number One was synonymous with loitering.

[3]

'How would you do against a wall?' the doctor asked. For a moment I was surprised by the question. It had a schoolboyish sound about it. Then I thought that this old playground measure of one's vigour must be a perfectly good criterion to appeal to. As it happened, not a hundred yards from this surgery, at numerous moments in the 1920s, I might have been seen making boastful use of a wall with three or four others from Barley Road School. The wall was still extant: in those days it marked the limit of the territory owned by the P.S.A. – a gentle religious body offering Pleasant Sunday Afternoons. I don't think we took the competition seriously, or even bothered much to note the result. We'd reach the wall together and obey an easy noisy common impulse and, having effected our swift splashes, would shout our claims and clatter onwards. We had these built-in water-pistols, and they must be brandished.

'Badly,' I told the doctor.

He was boyish, now I thought of it, young Dr Rowe. He had this admirable intention that a patient should understand what was going on, and set out to ensure it was so with his diagrams. Sometimes I would wish that he'd taken a crash course in drawing. Amateur illustrations of one's innards, meant to pacify, could appal. Last year I'd come to him with a cough that wouldn't go away and that was led up to by a curious helpless upward-bubbling and gasping of breath, as if you were seized by laughter: the laughter didn't come, but the cough did. Delighted always by an account of a problem – it was as if you had asked his help with a crossword clue – he cried, helplessly beaming: 'That's bronchial asthma!' And he snatched up a sheet of paper. At the top he wrote MR BLISHEN'S LUNGS: and below this drew what he declared were my bronchial tubes, dripping uncontrollable fluid: but for all the world it was as if Macbeth, having his vision of the air-drawn dagger, on its blade and dudgeon gouts of blood, had seen double. That had been when I was condemned to twice daily use of an inhaler, with another for emergencies.

Pollution, Dr Rowe said, was the culprit. I'd been in the presence of cars too long: had been unwisely, if unconsciously, dining on carbon monoxide. It occurred to me that almost my first practical memory of the car followed from an event in the street outside, somewhere between the P.S.A. and the surgery. It was 1928, perhaps. I'd stepped out, maybe dashing to join friends at the wall, had seen a car coming out of the terrified tail of an eye, and had leapt back onto the pavement in what was even more nerve-racking than the nick of time. To this day part of me is still leaping out of the way of that car. In 1928 we spent much of our time in the road. Union Street, where all this happened, was on the way to Barton Market, and cattle would be driven along it: smaller animals being transported by horse and cart. We shared the road with the rich droppings that resulted. It wasn't carbon monoxide that was dominant in Union Street in 1928.

But there I was, doomed to gasp for the rest of my days. The question: how many of those days will there be? had been thrust upon my attention on the very morning of this raffishly illustrated lecture on the bladder. It had come through the letter box – one of those messages from corporate strangers who address you, courtesy of their computer, by your name. WHO, MR BLISHEN, inquired the headline, WILL CARRY THE FINANCIAL BURDEN OF YOUR FUNERAL?

I took it that those behind this document must have glanced at the idea that I'd be reading it at the sink, in my overlarge dressing-gown, at that frail hinge of awareness between night, aswamp with silly dreams, and day, to which (the task made more difficult by those dreams) one had to reconnect oneself. The naivest understanding of human nature would suggest that such a question (*personalised* with one's name or not) at such a moment would amount to a macabre slap in the still half-asleep face. Making half a turn the recipient, groaning, would thrust the document into the piggy bin.

But there was this huge new trade, a fruit of the frightful years since 1979, springing from the view that life was all a shuffling and shifting (and shiftiness) of money: the trade in financial advice. And one of the effects of pursuing it was severance from the most simple grasp of the ordinary human scene. So (in this case) my advisers chorused:

'Not many of us, Mr Blishen, like to spend too much time thinking about our own funeral. Nevertheless, funerals are expensive affairs which can sometimes impose a heavy burden on those left behind.

'Today even the simplest arrangements can cost between £1500 and

£2000, and should your spouse or family want to be able to give you a more memorable tribute, then £5000 plus is not unusual . . .'

How heavily each delicate step these fellows took landed on the early-morning toes of their personalised victims! Having been obliged to think of a funeral groaningly assessed as costing £x, you found yourself face to face with the insinuation that a halfways decent spouse or family would aim at a less perfunctory tribute, and that you should strain to provide for this ambition of theirs by setting aside for it something in the order of £3x. Such a tumult of miserable thoughts, there in the still night-haunted kitchen! That your nearest and dearest might be among those not near or dear enough to want to see you disposed of in any but the most frugal fashion! Then, the curious difficulty of knowing for whom this superior act of riddance was meant to be memorable. Somehow the prose, the whole address, suggested that your financial advisers had *you* in mind: and that made you aware that the occasion in question would be the first major event at which you would demonstrate your inability to find anything, whatever, memorable.

Add to all that, this notion that the memorability of your departure rested on the amount spent on it. What did they have in mind as a mark of that increased memorableness? I could think, waiting for the kettle to boil, only of trumpets. Did they mean trumpets?

No, bugger them, they meant a better class of coffin: perhaps a parson who had been at the computer, and would know how to personalise you. They meant some morbid form of keeping up with the Joneses.

Healingly then (as I warmed the pot) I seemed to see the face of my friend Harry Frost, on a recent Saturday-morning encounter in the Friar's Holt. In his early seventies, Harry was part of a confederacy I'd lately become aware of – a loose union of the ageing, astonished, indignant, rueful: some, as in Harry's case, actually becoming, as they grew older, unmistakably younger. In 1946 he'd found himself, somehow, having snatched at unfamiliar and perplexing opportunities of the kind that were around when you were demobbed, a lecturer in carpentry. For a long busy time it had been a plain matter of woodwork, he said, until with the approach of retirement came a growing curiosity about the edges of his craft that took him into design: and design took him into a hundred other things, that now were in serious and energising danger of becoming a thousand other things. He was always pouncing on ideas, if they were not pouncing on him, and reading had become a form of chain reaction, any one book making it necessary to read two or three others, so that he was involved in a widening explosion of borrowings from the library and purchases from our incoherent local bookshop: he had always with him, in a carrier bag, an astonishing mixture of books. With all this, he was a perfectly unpretentious man, amused by his own seriousness: and on that occasion in the Friar's Holt, when he'd been talking about his recent package trip to Russia – which had caused him to be interested in lacquered miniatures, and to begin reading Gogol, and to feel restless because he knew barely anything (yet) about the history of underground railways (and how to find time to satisfy his curiosity about Peter the Great?) – he'd said, with a grinning twitch of the shoulders: 'I find being old very interesting. I wish I had tried it before.'

Dr Rowe was communing with his computer. He smiled at me absently as the screen offered, as I guessed, news of the latest state of play with respect to bladders. I recalled fleetingly the coarse laughter Harry Frost and I had surrendered to, again in the Friar's Holt, when I'd happened to mention Samuel Pepys's friend, Captain Cocke. We'd laughed because of the shared thought (Harry having cried '*Captain Cocke?*' and raised an eyebrow) that it was unusual for a Cocke to be promoted above the lowest rank. I'd been talking of Covent Garden, for which I'd had a long-smouldering passion, knowing it in a twice-weekly way when I'd worked for the BBC at Bush House. Pepys was among its astounding ghosts: he had strolled with the Captain in the Great Square of Venus, as they'd called it, 'among all the bawdy houses'. And it was on a visit to Cocke that (perhaps because the Captain on his arrival was still in bed) Pepys had recalled his last night's dream: that he had my Lady Castlemaine in his arms and was admitted to use all the dalliance he desired with her, and then dreamed that this could not be awake but that it was only a dream. And he'd reflected that since it was a dream and he'd taken so much pleasure in it, what a happy thing it would be if when we were in our graves we could dream, and dream but such dreams as this: for then we need not be so fearful of death.

Somehow my concern with Covent Garden had impregnated Harry (so easily fertilised) with a delight in the Embankment and then in its statuary: his favourite example at the moment being the memorial to Sir Arthur Sullivan in the Embankment Gardens. Here was the profile of this substantially moustached Englishman, staring with severe eschewal of emotion in the direction of Fleet Street: and against the plinth a young woman in black marble had dashed herself, in the worst extremes of grief. In her anguish she had snatched up a stray sheet, but it was ill-chosen, could never have seemed large enough: it revealed what it made an inefficient profession of concealing. Among other aspects of this disarray, Harry was struck by the fact that it involved a detail of nakedness more often associated, nowadays, with plumbers. He was impressed altogether by the distance between the sobriety of the representation of the hero of this monument, in his Victorian tweed, collar and cravat, and the quite other convention in which the distraught young woman was cast: that of a confusion of sorrow with sly nudity.

It expressed, surely, though in a decadent form, Pepys's thought that death, against all probability, might turn out to represent yet another erotic opportunity.

Dr Rowe turned from the computer with a murmur of impatience. There was a blood test now, he said, that addressed itself entirely to the prostate and the associated lumber. But he couldn't remember how it was identified. He turned back to his spread of gadgets, pressed a button and spoke to a colleague. The colleague couldn't remember, either. He tried two more, drawing rueful blanks. A last call was successful. 'Just one among my partners knew the code,' said Dr Rowe. I'd no right to feel superior, I said. I was engaged nowadays in forgetting on a massive scale. 'No doubt about it,' I said. 'After seventy, it gets worse . . .'

'Varies . . . varies . . .' said Dr Rowe, beginning to scribble his way furiously through a sequence of forms. I and my deranged bladder were becoming part of the archives.

[8]

Well, it didn't vary all that much, I thought. That confederacy of those who'd turned a corner and found themselves ancient were united in their nervous desire at once to monitor and not to monitor the frequency of their forgettings. Even my oldest friend, Ben, had recently confessed that he was torn between anxiously noting, and anxiously ignoring, the moments when, for example, a word wouldn't come to him.

Since our sixth form days Ben had been against the whole idea of our not lasting for ever. At school he'd been a notable scrum half, and he'd always seemed to feel that to discuss any symptom of one's own or any other person's mortality was to betray to the Fates the exact whereabouts of the ball in the scrum. Four or five years ago he'd have said nothing about words slipping out of his memory. We'd met once, about that time, by arrangement, in a pub. 'You'll have a drink?' he'd demanded on my appearance. I thought: he can't have imagined that I'd have agreed to this meeting place if I'd wished to avoid drinking. Then it struck me that of course he'd wanted to rule out all possibility of his asking, and being asked, how one was. But now Ben too seemed to need such comfort as the confederacy had to offer.

'How long do you think we've got? Ten years?' he'd asked at our last meeting: with the jauntiness that had always marked those moments when, with a great show of not doing so, he was admitting to a weakness. I told him of my prostate trouble, conjoined with recent constipation. I couldn't stop one thing, and couldn't start the other. And we laughed into our glasses. The drift of our talk had demanded whisky. Ben said he had these cancers that periodically had to be burned off his head. That was a consequence of combining baldness with sunbathing. We remembered the lawn at 1 East Drive, Barley Wood, a house we'd shared when we were young men with young families, and how we'd lain on it on gloriously uninformed summer afternoons in the 'fifties, incurring cancers. He had, he said, abandoning himself to the swell of laughter this discussion was causing, a massive irritation on his belly that he was convinced was malignant. By now he had begun to weep: extremes of laughter, often caused by some sort of accountancy of this sort, piling up the odds against ourselves, had always brought him to helpless tears. He'd wept in such a manner in 1939, when we were talking of the unlikelihood that we would outlive 1940. My own laughter made me cough. I mentioned my bronchial asthma. Then, of course, there'd been the blotting out of my eyes, in turn, by rapid cataracts . . .

Having wiped his own eyes, Ben refilled our glasses. It was for this sort of thing that whisky was distilled.

There were going to be lots of funerals, he took the opportunity of saying, and he hoped no one expected him to attend any of them. And he'd like it to be clear that his own was included.

Sixty years ago (though it seemed like five minutes) he'd been against marriage, too, and spreading yourself over an entire house. Like Diogenes, he'd said at one of those sixth form discussions, he'd live in a tub. And here he was, in the latest of his tubs, a smart single room that allowed, in the gaps between the houses opposite, a glimpse of Hampstead Heath. In his newest move, as in all previous moves, he'd virtually discarded what he'd had before. Though he did seem to have rather more books than usual: surprising, for I'd never known a man obsessed with literature whose shelves were so spartan. But, rebelliously retired, he was recognisably as he had been c1936, rebelliously not yet started. He was studying with the Open University, and was engaged in systematically dismaying a range of tutors. Ben had long had a taste for embarking on academic courses with the declared intention of making life miserable for the academics involved. He thought he might have inherited the need to do this from his mother, a memorably powerful woman, who like Ben was enraged by the claim of anyone whatever to be an authority on any matter whatever. A definition of the other person was that he or she was setting out to humiliate you by superior knowledge, superior ability to understand a situation, superior powers of action. Jessie's path, like Ben's, had been littered with officials and others whose ears had been randomly and rudely boxed. Now Ben was reading Descartes: he was reading William Morris: he was in love with Elizabeth Siddall, for the following reasons: he was, for what seemed much the same reasons, out of love with Elizabeth Siddall. ('One must beware of redheads!' From the beginning he'd had this habit of turning the ups and downs of his admirations into slightly menacing admonishments.) No longer for him, he'd said in one of the abrupt poems that now took the place of letters, the long legs of young girls, or smooth skin of any kind. Only this queer passion we both suffered from, for putting words together.

And staring out towards the Heath, he said how unenriched our childhoods had been. We'd come from that working-class world, in his case, that lower-middle-class world, in mine, that had simply known nothing of most of what made life worth living: ideas, books, music, art. Perhaps it had meant we were more excited than those who'd always had access to these things? But might it not have been better, I wondered, to have had access to them and still be excited?

And I thought of Harry Frost, who in his seventies was shouldering his way into that richer world, having lived so much of his life out of sight and sound of it.

Harry had lately been found to have high blood pressure. He'd done some reading, and somehow had attended a lecture in one of the teaching hospitals. (He had become a practised raider of the educational opportunities the capital offered, finding one could often ignore the official restrictions on attendance: he was inclined to think he might take part in the next meeting of the inner council of the Royal Society. 'They don't really notice,' he said.) He'd dieted himself into a slight gauntness, and brought the pressure down: but not before he'd been given a drug the taking of which precluded the consumption of alcohol. How on earth, asked Harry, was one to go to Italy, as he intended to do almost immediately for a fortnight, if one couldn't drink? He asked this question soberly, as one might ask how you could hope to dig the garden without a spade. There were some countries a teetotaller might be in a position to appraise, but Italy was not among them.

'Well,' said Dr Rowe, glancing through the forms he had filled in and signed with the frown of someone who couldn't believe what he saw, 'the blood test is what must come first. And we'll go from there.' I took from him the now familiar form to be presented at the hospital. Lately I seemed to have done little but have blood tests. There were times when I suspected commercial use was being made of me: lorries were waiting outside pathology labs to thunder this way and that through the night with my blood. It was like the requirement to give one's date of birth. Everywhere medical computers were choked with mine. Mysteriously, it seemed even more powerful an identifier than one's name. I was rapidly slipping into being 29.4.20. There'd been the young woman, one in the chain of inquisitors, all asking the same questions (beginning with the date of birth), who'd supervised my admission to hospital for my first cataract operation: 'You're *not*,' she'd said, busily. 'I'm sorry?' 'You're not seventy-one.' It sounded like a compliment (or, of course, the reverse), but it was impossible to smile (or, of course, to scowl) because there was on her face no expression as of one intending to give pleasure (or offence). Fleetingly and flatly she was stating a view of her own, which happened to be contrary to mine: and she went straight on to this other vital matter of my postal code. For a few days I'd allowed myself to feel that perhaps I looked as I felt, about twenty-three: but such cautious, half-ashamed exhilarations never lasted. Though it was odd how little perception of age there was from within. It was rather as if you were baffled to find yourself on a train you'd obviously been unwise to travel by. The rolling stock was old, there were problems arising from rust and lack of oil: this was a line where stops occurred at every station, and at an increasing number of points in between. You, the passenger, were as moved to be buoyant as you'd ever been: but the suddenly ponderous and mechanically doubtful vehicle you were travelling in was no setting for the bright, light activity you had in mind. And all the carriage doors were locked.

Dr Rowe said: 'Writing anything?' A question always difficult to answer. When it was part of the politely busy final exchange in a surgery, there was really no way of answering it at all. I had this absurd uneasiness about being superficial which would lead me naturally to reply in depth, trying to convey the untidy truth as to my work – how much of it consisted of broadcasting, and how that couldn't usually be counted as writing, though a little writing did come into it. Then I would fear that I was being solemn, and would make a number of statements about the unimportance of what I was describing. I would then say that as far as I could make out, I was being prevented by the loss of energy that came with ageing from writing a book that would be about being prevented from writing a book by the loss of energy that came with ageing. I could probably contrive to say all that in a decently short space of time, by a modest prodigy of precis: but being aware of all the others waiting for Dr Rowe's attention would make me stammer, aim at a phrase and miss it, perhaps tie myself into knots that resulted from the entanglement of the attempt to be exact with the attempt to be brief.

But in the end, it was a matter of being nervous of doctors. They were of the order of people I'd never been wholly at ease with: among the attitudes I'd acquired when young, awe of doctors remaining powerful. They were gentlemen (not a lady among them then), they were copiously, swaggeringly educated, and they had what I'd taken to be a scornful and capricious power over one's physical well-being. Their knowing how to make you well seemed close to an ability to leave you as you were, unwell. And there was a depth of unease below that, arising, for example, from the fact that, uncertain of access to medicine, my mother had put her faith in a gasometer.

That was in New Barton. Nowadays Kate and I would walk on some Sundays through Barley Woods to the Carpenter's Arms. You crossed the railway by a bridge that continued above the gas company's main depot. The bridge had become a gallery of sprayed graffiti, immense scrolls in thick fierce colour, a sort of sweating sullenness of paint. Every three or four years the council painted them out: within days they were back. Lesser artists added plain messages of mostly generalised derision. And so you stepped into Albert Recreation Ground. As long as I'd known it, and that was seventy years, it had had a desultory spirit. Typically, a slow cyclist, perhaps two, made sad circles, trying for that moment when a bicycle will topple, and fall sideways. Cycling was against the byelaws that ruled the Rec, but the Rec had no particular air of being ruled.

And beyond a wire fence bloomed the gasometer. I'd walk with my mother alongside that fence, she pushing a pram that would have had my brother in it (who died on his first birthday through a misdiagnosis of his condition): the year would have been 1923, and we were there to sniff the air with our noses as close to the gasometer as we could get. There was gas in that air, I thought of it as smelling grey, the colour of the gasometer: and my mother held that gas sniffed out of doors, close to its origin, was a cure for several conditions. I'd been marked out as a particular plaything of those conditions, from colds through mumps to measles and beyond. I can't think this therapy of exposure to a gasometer made me any less liable to be stricken down by one or other of these distresses: but that wouldn't have deterred my mother, who needed to believe in the odd kindly freak of magic.

Once born, we were steered away from the perilous starting line and through the shaky early laps by various of her fetishes: in respect of cotton being good for this and disastrous for that, and wool having certain efficacies, and it being a good or bad thing to do this or that at such and such a time. It was a world, after all, in which access to rational medicine was something to be had by way of a *letter*. 'She's been given a *letter*,' they'd say: it was a letter to a hospital, and being given it was like being granted a visa to a country difficult to enter. It was also, in itself, a sort of magic. During the war a neighbour, who'd herself as a child been brought to sniff that gasometer, worked as a nurse and reported on letters that had not been used as intended: instead they'd been slipped under pillows in unblessed beds, their magic held to be contraceptive.

It suddenly struck me that Ben's mother must have boxed the ears of a doctor or two, in her time. She knew an excluder of the poor when she met one. The phrase was Ben's, in one of his recent poetic letters:

> Nowadays
> It sometimes seems to me
> That the various Greens
> Of the almond tree,
> Mountain ash
> And ancient lime,
> Seen from my window
> Are more acceptable
> Than the sharply political
> Red and Blue.
>
> How about you?

And yet the pleb in me
Still finds
The simpering
Excluders of the poor
And feckless
Fit to be spat upon –
Even shat upon!

You too?

P.S.

Today
A long-tailed bird,
Magnificently pied,
Tapped at my window
Soon after dawn.
'Yes,'
I believe he was saying,
'Let's avoid all temporising,
Safely polite
Shades of Grey:
Say it in Black and White!'

OK?

I smiled at Dr Rowe, whose parents might well not have been born
when I'd gone sniffing alongside that fence, in awe of the immense
grey barrel beyond it, and said oh I was writing this and that – when I
wasn't sleeping. 'Too much sleeping,' I said, as if he might call me
back from where I stood at the door to his room. 'Too much sleeping?
Take this prescription. I guarantee it will protect you from being
withdrawn from circulation after lunch.' 'And after nine o'clock in the
evening?' 'Particularly after nine o'clock in the evening.' The time for
reading, writing, walking, gazing, thinking was becoming so appal-
lingly pinched . . .

*

And there I was, stepping out of the surgery and into Union Street. Still the street I'd run through six decades earlier: but no longer a place for children to run in. Cars seeking to park crept between cars parked. I looked for our own cause of bronchial asthma and worse, thinking Kate might have managed to lodge it here: but it was plain she must have taken it to the multi-storey car park. There too I'd peed *en passant*, when the site was part of a semi-wasteland called the Barracks. I walked in that direction: Kate would be coming to meet me. Across the road, at the junction with The Drive, was the front door I'd played my part in knocking at, and running at once round the corner: something I seemed to remember us doing four times a day, coming to school morning and afternoon and coming home from it – but I guess in that case there'd have been traps set. We must have done it often but erratically. The door seemed unchanged, and on the fanlight above it appeared the same gilded name: BALMORAL. That was a common style locally: in The Avenue there was a SANDRINGHAM. We walked or ran to school between modest houses with immodest names: ST RONAN'S, MALMSMEAD, LANGHOLM, IVY HOUSE, NORFOLK LODGE, CLYDE VILLA. Here, alongside me now, was DUNGIVEN: which I'd recently found was a Scottish placename, though in later years I'd thought it might mark the home of a retired philanthropist. On the gate someone had scrawled a felt pen assertion: BEST SUCK YOU EVER HAD.

Oh dear. Here I was, inwardly all sighs because the shabby world of my childhood had been made sophisticatedly shabbier: as well as being made tormentingly less convenient by some of the most ambitious of apparent improvements in convenience. I thought of the lady on the tomb Kate and I had revisited at the weekend, in the village three or four miles away, where she'd lain on her back, frugally laced and staring at the ceiling, for 423 years. We often took visitors to see her, as the stillest thing we knew. The lines of her were cut into alabaster, and made clearer by black wax. She was in the furthest corner of the church from the door we entered by, and was subject to a dubious amount of morning sunshine. She always astonished me: for having been there so long, of course, but also for being so plainly rendered, and for seeming so strongly to exist within a mere outline.

This quietness of hers had been at the heart of a net of quiet lanes, once. An arterial had been thrust through them in the 'thirties, and that counted then as a disturbance and touch of the modern ruffian. But the arterial had become a motorway, and the memory of that old rowdiness, a matter of stuttering, coughing, humming, the now-forgotten sound of tyres *pottering along*, caused almost as much nostalgia as the lady's handsome silence and immobility – she with her hands pressed together, waiting at worst for some blast of doomsday trumpets. The motorway was a solid injury to ear and mind: with its unceasing suggestion of an immense ripping, it made literal the idea of that quiet net being torn. When I woke in the night I could hear it, a hollow sullen unceasing sub-thunder. I tried to be sensible about it but, once on the bridge that crossed the motorway from one modest severed vein to another, I found it difficult to contain my amazement and grief. Amazement because this was what the logic of evolving existence seemed to cause us to do to ourselves – to make roaring channels through our own quietest places: and grief because I couldn't believe a tolerable future for human beings – such ruffians, but such delicate ruffians! – could lie at the end of a furiously mounting series of insults to the nerves.

But here was Kate. For her, as a child, this hadn't been the most familiar quarter of the town, as it had been for me. She'd gone largely between one end of the High Street, where as manager of a garage her father had innocently tended to the amiable motorcars of the day, and the girls' grammar school at the other end. I had probably been one of those who'd walked behind her with the specific intention of observing the gyrations of her bottom. That was what at the boys' grammar school we believed the girls' bottoms were trained to do: to revolve, to spin from step to step through 360 degrees. It was an illusion, but so strong that we saw it happen. We had managed never consciously to meet: she at the Sunday School over the Co-op: I at the Methodist Sunday School followed by Crusaders: she among rather flighty friends, I among flightless, earnest ones. We'd had, it turned out, one vague friend in common: Brian Hatt, whom we both chiefly remembered for the extraordinary pallor of his legs. I recalled them bearing their generally ashen owner into action on the rugger field. Ugh! that intimacy we had with each other's skin, and smell, and uncompleted shape! Both boys and girls, Kate and I discovered when exchanging memories, had responded to Brian's lack of even a trace of colour as if it had been an aspect of character. Even now I couldn't be sure that it wasn't. The girls, said Kate, puzzled him by giggling whenever he appeared among them to play tennis. It was something I'd never seen him play, tennis being a pursuit of a posher sort of people. Kate hadn't been posh herself, but had tended to move among the posh. She said he was plainly unable to relate their giggles to questions of pigment. He started obstinately from the premise that he was attractive, and so was prevented from considering the idea that he was not.

I remembered it had been the same in the classroom: he had imagined himself able, and was not swayed from this view by his low position in almost every subject. Yet you couldn't say he was conceited: rather, he was unrealistic. Oh, the simple fashion in which we'd assessed one another! The elaborate human creatures we were had been turned into thumbnail sketches. So there'd been (in this sort of reductive view) the comically self-deluding Brian Hatt, whose skin was unforgivably white, and who believed he was bright when he wasn't. And suddenly, before he could have found time to take breath after leaving school, he'd been married to another vague friend of Kate's. It had been the first marriage among us: and there was a general feeling that the headmaster disapproved: because, I now guess, Brian was a prefect, and, if the timetabling of following events was to be taken as evidence, might have committed a prematurely adult act whilst wearing his prefect's cap: or perhaps having laid down his prefect's blazer and taken up an unprefectly position on it. There'd been a crop of these young marriages, a yoking of thumbnail sketch to thumbnail sketch. Brian and his wife were still together, multiple grandparents, and we were on smiling terms. I'd wondered sometimes about his legs, which old age must surely have made whiter yet, though there seemed no likely white beyond that original white of his. When we did speak, what sprang out of that old lack of realism in him was a general obtuseness of assessment: in the most good-natured fashion he was always, sometimes breathtakingly, wide of the mark.

Kate asked now: 'What did he say?' I told her of Dr Rowe's sketch

of my bladder, wanting to make her laugh; but she remained anxious.
It was what happened between you, on this last lap. One or the other,
unbearable thought, was to be left alone: the leaving and the being left
equally gross and unthinkable events. So you watched over each other,
weren't quite able to be relaxed about each other's misfortunes, no
matter what amounts of comedy accompanied them. (And in the midst
of our tragedies, how comic we were!) Still, I guessed Kate must
welcome anything the doctor might have proposed that would limit
the number of occasions I got up in the night. She was a deep sleeper,
and I had perfected the silentest exit and return, had made myself an
absolute master of doorhandles and floorboards: but from time to time
this very creeping about must have woken her. And I had to say that
another effect of ageing would appear: a failure of balance, so that I'd
find myself falling against a cupboard door, or an insubordinate knee
would crumple and throw me against the bed. She'd be glad for that
to stop: but the difficulty of smiling at my jokes about Dr Rowe's
draughtsmanship lay rather in the general difficulty of believing that a
manageable threat might not develop into an unmanageable one. It
might be an overgrown prostate, but it might also be a cancerous one.

Old age was a sustained process of injury. You were being very
distinctly shot at. Kate's arm in mine said: Please duck! Please let it
turn out that you kept your head below the parapet!

I remembered my father – well, no more than two or three minutes
ago – saying: 'I hope you grow old, and know what it's like!' Alas, it
was always the turn his anger took: not calling for your sympathy, but
wishing upon you what had descended upon him. He'd forbidden
himself to feel any regret that my generation was plunged into the
second world war, because his generation had been plunged into the
first. According to his sad sense of the justice of things, an injury done
to him was made curiously less intolerable if it was also done to you.
So he'd be glad, I had to think, that I'd entered the seventies, and was
breaking up: though I knew that, if it had been possible to imagine
him returned to the scene, he'd have been much concerned about my
bladder. Long ago he had given it its first training. I had sat on the
potty for what at this distance seemed days on end, so that the point
was thoroughly made: that was the place for Number One, and it was

[19]

also the place for Number Two. I think sitting on the potty was the setting for some of the most comfortable reveries I've ever had. I seem to recall having taken it that this was a way of side-stepping (or side-squatting) the action for a decent length of time. You sat and pensively waited for the machinery to catch your drift. I remember a Christmas morning: there I sat, my back warm from a neighbouring fire, and, as a perfect match for the leisurely performance of bladder or bowel, played with a new toy: a violinist, of tin, the halves of him held together by tabs uniting, I remember, among other features (a watch chain?), a copious musical moustache. You pulled on a wire, and the arms moved, and the moving arms moved the bow, across and across: a tiny hiccup of sound.

My father wouldn't have cared for that early bladder's becoming this recalcitrant late one. And he'd really have worried about my elderly mishaps. Confronted with our actual illness, he was always solicitous, helpful, anxious. He had lost a child by way of that misdiagnosis – which had led him to punish his tiny son for resistance to potty-training, when in fact he was physically incapable of being obedient to it – and he was always terrified of losing another.

And anyway, by now I'd have stopped infuriating him, as I did, by being young, and having working parts that ... worked. I'd have removed almost all the offence I'd given him by being, not him, but me.

Kate turned me in the direction of the High Street. We must think, she said, of all the positive things that had happened, and were happening, to us. Good Lord, we were rather tremendously alive! She took by way of demonstration several large gulps of air: I was about to tell her of my thoughts about the current atmosphere of Union Street, but decided not to. Walking, she said. Reading – Sleeping, I said. Of course, though we rebelled against it, there was this ageing infatuation with the pleasure of sleep. Not long ago, waking up, I'd called across the room: 'Oh good, we're going to bed again tonight!' – And travelling. Östendorf. Malcesine, which offered for sale more leather belts than you'd think there were human beings to wear them: Gargnano, where we'd tried, and failed, to follow in the footsteps of D. H. Lawrence: whose chest, in 1912, was in a bad way, but still let him climb higher than we turned out to be able to climb, eighty years later. And realising an old dream of walking down the Nevsky Prospekt, in St Petersburg, as I'd done that year, arm-in-arm with our son Tom – And being with friends. And being on our own. And going to look at pictures – those extraordinary windows opening onto amazing scenes! And being among the derivatives of our original acts of procreation: those grandchildren who in relation to us were small parodies, travesties, comic footnotes, alarming glosses!

Good Lord, yes, I said. And Covent Garden. And even the clown in Covent Garden. And even that extraordinary man who was part of the radio programme I was going to record on the morning when I encountered the clown in Covent Garden.

Part One

I

As I came out of the central arcade that morning I found myself part of a crowd, oddly intent. I looked where they were all looking and saw, under the portico of St Paul's, two men walking. They were followed, though they were clearly unaware of it, by a young man in a tilted top-hat. For a moment I couldn't make out what was happening, or why this scene commanded such attention. Then I saw the young man was imitating the others, exaggerating their small private gestures. One of the men shrugged: the young man turned the shrug into a monstrous convulsion of his shoulders. 'Ah,' signalled a hand of the other man, raised with fingers curled, 'but – ' The clown's hand rose into the air like a floundering bird. One of the men, as if pleased with some conclusion they had come to, drove his hands deep into his trousers pockets. Their shadow thrust his hands into pockets that seemed unfathomable: they were lost there, and frantically sought to escape. The crowd laughed. The men were absorbed and had no interest in the laughter. They turned into Henrietta Street, and at once the clown attached himself to a plump woman crossing the space in front of the crowd. Her obliviousness had a worried quality, and the clown made himself short, stout, anxiously rapt. From an inside pocket he took a wooden measure: held it to the woman's bottom, and declared the width of it by holding the measure above his head. The laughter curved round the edge of this long, famous space. They made a solid mass there, as if they were occupying an actual grandstand, and it seemed extraordinary that such a demonstration of breathless interest should not alert the clown's victims.

But it might do so, I thought. And at once I realised that it wasn't only laughter that came from the crowd, but a sense of terror. At any moment a victim might turn round and react to the clown's behaviour for what it was: unforgivably intrusive and insulting. In this comedy there were no intentions but those of furtive intrusion, and insult. The crowd was waiting for his luck to fail. Their attention tightened now as he moved across to the entrance to the men's lavatory at one side of the church. A man had just gone down the steps that led to the urinal, and the clown leaned against a wall and bent his head back and to one side, pretending to follow the man's progress. He communicated a sense of it with quick birdlike bulletins offered by his eyes. He'd gone in, yes. He'd found a stall, yes. The clown made something coarsely beautiful out of the idea of a man's, very privately, undertaking the little drama of unzipping his flies. Extraction: and then the jet beginning, strengthening, in mid-flow (the clown exaggerating, having difficulty in keeping control of some immense hosepipe with a life of its own), slowing, finishing. The appearance of a sort of milking, followed by a rapid shaking. The clown suggested all the routine severity these actions might have for a man, wanting no nonsense of belated dripping. Then the zipping: and the clown telegraphed the progress of the man as he returned up the steps. It had all been done with his eyes, with small writhings of his body. And here the man was, stepping into the open, all eyes on him. He was half-struck by the atmosphere and looked about him fleetingly: concluded that whatever was happening need be no business of his: and rapidly walked away. The crowd laughed again: at the joke of a man having been so intimately travestied, and being unaware of it.

It was about the biggest distance, I thought, that could be established between the conviction that you were private, secret, uninspected, of little interest to others, and the truth that you were not.

Then there was a clatter and something . . . a piece of wood . . . flew across the cobbled space. It was on the other side from where I was standing, and it wasn't immediately obvious what had happened. I saw the clown throw down his hat and become at once a young man in jeans, the impertinent shadow gone. Now he was standing angrily close to a man at the edge of the crowd. There was anger on both sides. The clown turned, strode to the centre of the space and began to address the crowd.

I could catch only the odd word, a tone, but it was clear that the clown had been enraged by the throwing of the piece of wood, and was consulting the crowd. Did they agree with what was implied by its being thrown? Did they. too. hate what he was doing? Should he pack up?

'Get on! Get on!' people shouted. But it wasn't approval of the clown, I thought, so much as impatient dislike of his stepping out of his role. If he had been shocked, they'd been more shocked by the throwing down of the top-hat, the surrender of his status of clown. They'd been appalled by his appealing to them. Well, surely, it was a curious cowardice, that asking for support. Such a clown, engaged in such clowning, should take whatever came of it: and somehow the crowd needed him to be valiant in his insolence, to have the courage of it. They felt let down.

Oh dammit, I thought, making myself walk away. I'd have taken all that in my stride if I'd been in my forties: but for anyone in his seventies, the occasion must seem only too pointedly laid on. That play with the belief that we were private and unsuspected, and the powerful probability that we were not! Behind each of us, a troupe of clowns, derisively imitative! And the problem of our being given at once to effrontery, and to the longing to be forgiven for it. Our boldness, yoked to our timidity!

It was a moment for walking briskly away, not looking back.

2

I thought as I walked how often Covent Garden seemed to offer images that were only just decent, respectable, controllable. Even its everyday clowns and jugglers, those with no intention of insult, had something anarchic about them; they offered brazen tricks and illusions. It was magic all right, but the magicians, perhaps as a result of what appeared to be their amateurishness, were uncertain of their skill. They were sorcerers' apprentices, who'd never make it to the top, and meanwhile practised a magic somehow more worrying than successful magic could ever be. It didn't stay on its own side of the fence, safely inexplicable. It got muddled up with real life. They seemed to come from nowhere, these illusionists and tumblers, from some large tribe of lurking entertainers, and return to nowhere. I'd seen them, before they set up on their patch of cobbles, laughing, nervously loud in corners, unimpressively practising their wizardry. There'd been a stout man once who simply borrowed things and, twice perhaps in every three attempts, made them disappear. They might turn up ten yards away. 'He could have the knickers off you and you'd never know it,' said a woman to another standing at my elbow. Well, perhaps he could: but his success in having *your* knickers, and not, by a fault in his art, the knickers of some murderously offended passerby, would astonish him more than it astonished you.

I remembered how close I'd been to that sort of mishap when an eye had been blotted out by that quick cataract. You saw what the point was of having two eyes. Placing a pint of beer confidently on the table enormously visible a few inches to my left, I'd seen it fall into the space between that and me. I'd felt amazement that one-eyed persons ever did anything but let pints of beer fall to the floor. Nelson: would he not, intending to lay a loving secret hand on an intimate part of Emma Hamilton, have found he'd laid a loving secret hand on an intimate part of her husband, Sir George? Judging distances correctly was a two-eyed virtue. Might it not be sufficient magic to make sure that glasses arrived securely on tables, the correct person was surreptitiously caressed? Have an eye cloud over, suffer some small displacement in the system of nerves, and the magic of doing what we think of as everyday would become, suddenly, beyond us.

In the nick of time not stepping into the road (that instinct planted in Union Street in 1928 seemed still to operate), I thought how much more difficult it was to cross Cambridge Circus than it used to be. I had this practice of walking in London, when I could, partly because it was always better than being underground, but largely because it was a very old habit, that I was unlikely ever to shake off. I still thought of myself as walking through the London of the 'fifties and 'sixties, when there was half the amount of traffic: and, surely, half the number of people. They talked of traffic jams but nowadays there were people jams, with occasions when entire armies bore down upon you, twenty abreast, laughing, scowling, shouting, grimly pre-occupied, not one of them looking where he was going. Though perhaps that sensation was another effect of ageing. It was one more mark of being old – realising that to get comfortably through a crowd depended on a youthful skill, on instantnesses of reaction, and the ability to change direction at speed and at once to change direction again: a general capacity to make a path for yourself where, strictly speaking, there was none. Old, you were simply too slow and unsupple.

This was a bruising, half-phantom London I moved through, full of public conveniences that had ceased to exist, and of old short cuts that had become new long ones. But inside me there must have been some quiet genius of navigation – some magician of better-than-Covent Garden quality. Through the years he'd adjusted my timing, and my choice of streets to walk by, so that today, for example, he would undoubtedly deliver me at Broadcasting House between 10.45, when I wasn't expected, and 10.50, when I was.

Manet Street. I wondered, not for the first time, if that sensation of mine about Covent Garden, feeling it was . . . attractively dangerous, a wanton place, a place full of old styles of wickedness, followed or preceded my reading in its history. Surely I'd always sensed the ghostly lust it was thick with. It had been the home of a Bishop of Durham at whose door, they said, every foundling of the parish was laid, with reason. And if you looked a little further in the direction from which that piece of wood had been thrown this morning, you were staring at where those establishments known as Little Hummuns and Great Hummuns had been, places that must have left a great deal of sweating salacity in the air: they were based frankly on the availability of body to body offered by the Turkish bath: providing an opportunity for men and women to meet in circumstances of ready-made steam. Take

[29]

a step or two and you'd be where the young woman had accosted Dr Johnson and he had said: 'No, my dear, it will not do!'

That corner of London, I'd thought at times, might have been the very headquarters of my own fleshly clowns.

Well, I meant of course that you had this tyrannical department of yourself. You were set on leading a life of a thoughtful kind, quietly and not at all puritanically going about your business, exercising your senses in a manner that didn't exclude passion: and still this anarchical office within you, staffed by persons of unrecognisable grossness, insisted on intervening, throwing its shocking weight about, crossing your sane intentions with madly coarse objectives of its own.

At times, sitting in Covent Garden, I'd caught myself reacting into the familiar longing to be a monk, and seen at once that this was no escape from the flesh (with the thrilling oppression of which the place was heavy), but only an alternative exaltation of it: resulting from what might be called lust fatigue.

D'Arblay Street. Tracking me through life, travestying my gestures, measuring my bottom and perhaps worse and holding up the measure for the amusement of the crowd, was not, it seemed to me, a single erotic clown, but a pair of clowns: one naked, the other wearing a monastic robe.

Bother it, I thought (Poland Street), surely in my seventies I might claim exemption from this war between flesh and mind, between the clown who performed in front of you, and the clown who trod at your heels?

I thought of a moment in, perhaps, 1938. Ben and I had been to the Old Vic, to see *A Midsummer Night's Dream*. We'd been alarmed by the use of Mendelssohn's music. 'It turns those Elizabethan fairies into ... ugh ... Victorian fairies, doesn't it?' said Ben. Victorian, for us, then, was unspeakable. The human race had never sunk lower than in being Victorian. Ben had lately discovered that the composer had been taken to Victoria's bosom. Ben's dislike of the Queen was passionate. 'They write books about her,' he'd said in a sixth form discussion, when we were waiting for the arrival of our Latin master, who never came because he was devoting himself to his preferred interest, games, 'but she wasn't half as honest or useful as my old grandmother.' As

we came home from the theatre we'd talked about John Donne. Ben
had been reading 'To his Mistris: On going to Bed' and said it made
him uncomfortable. 'Well, I mean, I don't suppose you could write
much better about lust ... What do you think? Trouble is I don't
know what to do about lust. Have you worked out anything?'

Ben was always likely to make some inquiry along these lines, as
though he expected me to have put together some helpful handbook
of advice in respect of our adolescent tempests. I thought of the storms
of phenomenally indecent desire in which I was being blown from one
nocturnal melodrama to another: and said no, I hadn't.

And then, just before we parted, Ben in the direction of East Barton
and I in the direction of High Barton, he said: 'The real trouble is that
I don't know what happens, what you do. Have you got round to
that?' It was another statement of his reliance on me as a sort of
research assistant. With great nervousness, for there had been a
striking tension about Ben as he asked this question, I said I could only
offer a phrase I'd read somewhere recently, about a sword and a
scabbard.

And Ben had taken to his heels. It was something I'd never forgotten:
my formidable friend, intent on out-tubbing Diogenes. running
through the empty suburban night, in flight from a mere, diffidently
offered image.

Regent Street. Through my mind as I walked there was this constant
replay of the scene in Covent Garden: the crowd so nervously rapt,
that very young, sour clown so impudent. If it came to images, here
was one that wouldn't go away. No need to think of pursuit by ghostly
clowns: it seemed only too likely that at any moment we should find
we were being sized up satirically, our rumps measured, our intimate
performances the subject of a fearful comedy of exaggeration. Exag-
gerate what we did by nothing worse than a doubling of the size of
our gestures, and we became absurd. Oh dear. Meanwhile, here I was,
about to encounter a clown of another order, with whom I had to
record a programme. Here was Broadcasting House: it was 10.47.

3

He was cold, as I'd expected. I wasn't sure why he'd agreed to take part. This was in essence a warm programme devoted to the praise of books. Myself as presenter: and two others, each of whom chose two books, available in paperback, that in their opinion might be described by the programme title: *Couldn't Put it Down*. Of course, some contributors said, a good book *could* be put down – it might require you to put it down, to get your breath back – but the phrase generally would do. There were occasions of dispraise, when the choice of one contributor was horrifying or baffling to the other – or to me. But it was all warm, driven by the hope of having stumbled upon a good book: and the chemistry of each programme was never to be guessed at in advance as, given two chance people, four chance books, it hardly could be. When people talk about books, more goes on than talk about books. There was a manic comedian who'd made his choice with great seriousness, and recommended it earnestly: except that his whole nature was excitement, astonishment, eyes amazingly increasing in size as his voice turned from clarinet to oboe to flute: he piled words on words, he hinged what he had to say on some very rare form of punctuation: every sentence was a firework, and each firework was more breathtaking than the one before it. He was astounded by the book, and astounded by his own reaction to it: and came to a halt on the point of personal explosion. And I turned to the other, also an entertainer, whose gift was to make glumness comic: and with perfect flatness, and after a pause filled with the glitter of sparks from those fireworks still descending, he said: 'I hated it.'

My companions this morning were a novelist and a children's writer. The first wrote dark wicked stories that had, I thought, an odd quietness about them. The second was a Pied Piper of a man, whose short stories for adults were largely concerned with ingenious kinds of cruelty: as a writer for children, he was wonderfully successful, having the storyteller's gift absolutely. He mesmerised. I had complex feelings about him: for it seemed to me that part of the spell he bound children with rested on his being himself an unregenerate child: he was drawn, as they were easily drawn, to injustice, unkindness, delight in the idea of the downfall of others. I thought Piggy, sad victim of *Lord of the Flies*, had he strayed into this man's stories, would have undergone a second and worse martyrdom. He'd written a book about werewolves, that had an introduction suggesting to the reader that the most admired and trusted person you knew might well be a werewolf: your beloved father, a favourite uncle, that best of your teachers. I thought he mesmerised, often, in order to undermine.

He'd objected at once to both the novelist's choices: and challenged the producer to defend herself, being in charge of a programme with the title it had, for allowing contributors to choose such *crap*. He was firm about this word. Both books chosen by the novelist were *crap*. The producer would have sent him away, there never having been any thought that one contributor might veto the choices of the other: but it was the last programme to be recorded in the series, and the transmission date was treading on her heels: so she half-gave in. The novelist was persuaded to change her mind about one title, but clung to the other. He with his (as I thought of it) ducking and weaving malice allowed that. He made his own choices. One was a novel about a serial murderer, more awful by far than the ghastliest werewolf, who flayed his victims, in the interest of providing himself with a perfect patchwork cover of female skin. Reading it, both the producer and I felt we were in that curious region (where some of the work of the children's writer was itself situated) in which *couldn't put it down* was close to *wishing you'd never taken it up*. And not out of a desire to evade an awful reality: but because there seemed to be at work a relish in the violence involved. 'What did you think of it?' asked the children's writer on the phone to the producer. 'I didn't care for it,' she said. 'Oh come,' he said. 'That's not true. It excited you. You don't want to admit how much you loved it.' To her it was clear that a novel about someone who wanted to make himself a perfect pelt out of favoured fragments from the flayed skin of his victims was not something she *loved*. And it was infamous of him to propose that we

all secretly adored the dreadful, and that he had only to challenge us
to cause us to cry: Yes, you are right: we are thrilled by cruel tales. I
thought: He really does believe that what's important in us is an
undeclared lust for violence! And then: He is a manipulator of moods.
He has set out to create fury, and uncertainty, and dismay, and
indignation: and when it came to the recording, he'd perhaps take the
game a step further by being equable, making us stumble out of shame
that we'd ever become agitated.

But no, that wasn't the game he was playing. As we seated ourselves
round the table, there were the beginnings of chatter. You naturally
talked yourself warmly ready for a recording. He was against our
becoming warm, and said: 'Can't we start! Let's start!'

And so we began: with the first of the novelist's choices: the one
she'd clung to, despite his attempt at a veto. It was Mary Kingsley's
Travels in West Africa. This must be one of the wittiest of all travel
books: the account of the visits to those alarming lands, in 1893 and
1895, of a woman who'd been on course for the life, or half-life, of a
gentlelady of the time, required to devote herself to ailing parents. And
then the parents died, and she was free: making herself, in the context
of those days, *stupendously* free. At such a moment such a lady
couldn't have claimed a greater liberty than that of going 'to learn her
tropics', as she put it. She said she felt like a boy with a new half-
crown. (I remembered being a boy with a new half-crown, that
uniquely substantial coin: no one's first million was ever as thrilling as
my own first half-crown.) Referred to the missionary literature, she
said that 'these good people wrote their reports not to tell you how
the country they resided in was, but how it was getting on towards
being what it ought to be.' Mary Kingsley was not easily fooled: she
had what Bernard Shaw called the rarest thing, the ability to see what
was in front of her: and she made this masterpiece of clear-sighted
pioneer observation as comic as it was serious.

The children's writer would have nothing to do with her. He hadn't
brought himself to read it. It was a fat book, and it was published by
a feminist publisher: and he clearly did not care for self-possessed
women. Mary Kingsley was a frump in a long skirt. He made much of
what was plainly to him the damning fact that her skirt was long.

[34]

'Boring woman,' he said. We countered with quotations. There was what she had to say about her first voyage out, when she didn't know the Coast and the Coast didn't know her, and they terrified each other. 'I fully expected to get killed by the local nobility and gentry: they thought I was connected with the World's Women's Temperance Association, and collecting shocking details for subsequent magic-lantern lectures on the liquor traffic: so fearful misunderstandings arose, but we gradually educated each other, and I had the best of the affair; for all I had got to teach them was that I was only a beetle and fetish hunter, and so forth, while they had to teach me a new world, and a very fascinating course of study I found it.' 'You think that's well-written?' he cried. I had to ask him not to drum his fingers impatiently on the table: to a listener it might have sounded like incidental effects, perhaps misrepresenting Mary Kingsley as being welcomed by war-drums. I read a passage in which she told of a missionary who arrived in a village late one day and announced his intention of making his home there and vigorously converting the villagers. When he woke next morning the entire village had dis-mantled itself and vanished. 'You think that funny?'

It wasn't ordinary critical dissent. I thought that behind it lay a need to torment: and that with him one of the main instruments of torment was to set out to lower spirits all round. The temperature in the studio fell phenomenally.

We came to his first choice: which was Damon Runyon. There was no argument about that: we loved him, had long loved him. He was impatient with our delight. Well, yes. Express your pleasure in some warm fashion, if you must. He was content with a few cold laconic commendations. Let's get on. I'd stopped him drumming his fingers on the table, but that sort of drumming, of a scornful impatience, was still in the air. I saw that we were creatures in one of his short stories. Our intent: enthusiasm. His intent: to flay – yes – to strip the skin off those expressions of delight. Even of the delight he shared.

And so we came to the novelist's second book: the one she'd been prevailed upon to suggest instead of her first choice. It was another travel book: by a journeyman writer popular in the 1930s. As a priggish schoolboy I'd taken against him. Someone who wrote so

[35]

much so readily about anything that offered could have no value. In the school library he occupied half a shelf: and he was noisily recommended by our headmaster, Percy Chew. 'A thoroughly sound writer, gentlemen! Worth a dozen Aldous Huxleys!' It was the form in which Percy Chew commonly cast his critical views: writers he admired, and peremptorily required us to admire, were estimated in terms of their being rather better than a hundred Bernard Shaws, or a thousand D.H. Lawrences. Reading this writer again now, I was surprised. He wrote with an effect of obligatory wonderment that was the general tone of travel writing at the time: 'wonderment' being absolutely the word. I seemed to have spent my youth in the midst of books that urged on us the wonder of things: the first big book I ever recall, one whose pages I sprawled on the floor to turn, being *The Wonder Book of the Great War*. But now the tone had floated free, and under it you could feel how he cared for his subject matter, what a diligent love he had for the visible world, how interestingly shrewd he often was.

So I came to this occasion half-penitent. I couldn't have offered myself more neatly for flaying. 'You're trying to be nice!' the children's writer cried. The novelist, attempting to explain her affection for the book, got nowhere against his perfectly contemptuous refusal to be interested. And suddenly, his evident goal was reached. She broke off in mid-sentence. 'I am dashed,' she said, and fell silent.

It was a gentle word, I thought, but an accurate one, for what he did: he *dashed*. As a word for contriving to bring about depression it had a long history. 'This hath a little dashed your spirits,' says Iago, having allowed himself to be discerned to be short of enthusiasm when the talk turned to Desdemona.

The discussion was becalmed almost beyond hope of its being started up again: but somehow we came to his thriller: which he introduced by saying it was a hundred times better than those novels that were fashionably praised. (He suddenly sounded like Percy Chew: the worth of this book could be measured in crateful of Martin Amises, whole warehouses crammed with Kazuo Ishiguros.) It told its story mercilessly, and addressed itself to the honest guts. On a sheet of paper I'd noted words I must use whatever else I said: 'I couldn't put it down but was relieved when I did so. A repulsive story.' But I didn't quite use those words: or not with that clarity. He had us where his cruel mischief wanted us: aware that the mood of the programme had plunged from moment to moment, and thinking therefore – in our spinelessly concerned way, as he'd conclude – that it had somehow to be lifted. On top of all that nay-saying, it seemed impossible to utter a crushing, crowning nay of our own. Instead, we expressed some sort of miserable, pale, cowardly interest.

The recording came to an end, and the clown had triumphed. He'd never fling his hat to the ground and call on the crowd for support.

In my introduction I'd said we were fairly exact contemporaries. He now asked, an unexpected anxiety appearing, if that was so. I looked well, he said – much better than he felt. He had . . . some sort of anaemia that wouldn't let go. Was I certain we were of much the same age?

He was the last man I'd ever have thought would be of the confederacy of the aged: yet I knew that tone. He was hoping for reassurance. In a moment he had recovered, and was speaking unsympathetically of the plight of Salman Rushdie: whose novels, he said, were *crap*.

Well, I said, I had a galloping cataract.

4

I'd noticed the problem when doing the crossword in the bath.

This habit sprang from love of lying long in the water, but dislike of doing that only. Somehow I'd come to think of merely bathing as a matter of strangely choosing to get wet and then having tediously to get dry again. And I seemed to be averse to the idea of being both wet and vacant-minded. So, the crossword: which must be finished or despaired of, before I got out. It was a perfect arrangement, setting a time limit for bath and crossword. But of late I'd found I had to squint to read the clues: they seemed to be rising grey above, or falling grey below, the point of focus. I had to hunt after them: and being able to make them out at all depended on angles of head and newsprint.

I thought the bathroom light was inadequate. By the same light I'd read crossword clues without difficulty for years, but I didn't carry my thoughts as far as that. Personal decay is no one's first notion of the cause of anything.

Then there was the night I'd spent in an extraordinary bedroom. I'd been giving a talk, and the secretary of the literary society that had invited me to do so had offered me lodging: in a house that had been not so much furnished as methodically pampered. The lavatory was amazing: everything in it wore a muff. The bedroom when I was released into it turned out to be on several levels, with a bed on a platform, and various profoundly carpeted wells that led to other platforms on which furniture stood. In a raised corner, behind an ambush of curtains, as I later discovered, was a bathroom, itself on more than one level, with the bath sunk almost out of sight and the washbasin raised so high that it looked as if it were made for praying rather than washing at. I had a confused sense of many things draped: and almost at once, gazing round me as I moved into the room, found myself stumbling from a platform into a well. I made myself stand stockstill: this was a place in which not a step must be taken without thought. It seemed to be laid out according to some notion of there being great charm in uncertainty of flooring: but in truth it was simply perilous. Here were tremendous possibilities of falling headlong in the small hours, waking the whole household. I'd been offered a night's sleep in a room that was no better than a heavily carpeted sequence of elephant traps.

Yet, as I made my way muttering around it, I was aware that to the bizarreness of its layout was added another problem: and that arose from some mysterious uncertainty – I'd shake my head in the hope of dispelling it – as to what lay to my left, and a general tendency for the details of this dreadful room to sidle in and out of vision.

Well, I thought, in such a plight anyone might become uncertain of any or all of his senses.

And then in the Saturday morning High Street, Georgie Wicks, a boy now inexplicably bald and white-stubbled whom I'd been at

Barley Road School with sixty years earlier, caught my arm and said: 'I say!' I knew it meant he had something to tell me that would consolidate some displeasure. All those years ago, in the Barley Road playground, you'd have a mishap and Wicks would be gleefully at your elbow, spelling it out for you. 'You fell over!' 'That'll be bleeding for a long time!' Now he said: 'Noticed you walking along, winking. You were *winking*!' From bloody knees I'd come, he'd have concluded, to the onset of insanity. In him, spiteful satisfactions had always had the quality of a tic, something he was helplessly subject to.

I hadn't been winking. I'd been closing one eye: inspecting the world: opening that eye and closing the other. I was checking on an increasing suspicion that the left eye wasn't what it had been. There was some element about it of . . . a wearisome smudge: alongside an impression, more and more difficult to dislodge, that my eyes had moved apart. I had to strain – surely? – to bring them together. The left one was always about to desert me, simply to move off.

So I'd shut the left eye and look down the High Street. Three cars and a bus. Then I'd shut the right eye and look down the High Street. Two cars.

I went to see the oculist. He lowered the blinds in his surgery and frowned over his notes in such a fashion that I said: 'You were expecting me.' 'No,' he said. 'Well, yes. But not, to tell the truth, for another two or three years. Maybe more. But let me carry out my tests before I say what I'd thought you might come and see me about.'

It was a cataract. It was a bad one, and had advanced and was still advancing at speed: for it had been only minimally present when Bernard had seen me six months earlier for a regular check. 'Now I'm free to confess,' I said, 'that I feel all the time as if I'd been hit in that eye by a ball.' In fact I'd dismissed this notion again and again, as a nervous illusion: but suddenly I saw it was as true as it would have been if straightforward observation had told me I was a leg short. 'Thank heavens for my good right eye,' I said. It *was* a very fine eye, as all that winking had convinced me. 'I'm afraid,' said Bernard, 'that I've just detected the beginnings of a cataract in that.'

It was ridiculous. Cataracts were what Kate had. Hers had been ripening for twenty years: and not long before she had had one of

them dealt with by way of a lens implant. I realised that under the
sympathy I felt for her had lain a complacent sense of immunity:
cataracts were not for me. And now, good Lord, they gallopingly
were.

Much was explained. Physical clumsiness, for example.

I had a long history of subjecting Kate to inconvenient embraces:
when she was carrying crockery, or wet from washing up, or between
one cosmetic condition and another. It had struck me that I couldn't
have been alone in these faults of romantic timing – the surge of
passion coinciding with some awkward conjunction of activities – and
that their absence from fiction and film was an example of the failure
of these media to reflect reality. Now I was regularly treading on
Kate's toes: or bringing about clashes of our reading glasses. The
intention had been delight: the result was distress and even tears. In so
far as there was anything to be happy about, I was glad the cause was
not a runaway decline in judgement.

But the conversion of one eye into an increasing fog brought about,
not only difficulties of sight, but a general dislodgement of confidence.
You weren't sure of anything.

And the problems of looking at pictures on the walls of galleries
were explained, too.

We'd been in the Courtauld recently, in its new home in Somerset
House. The light there was low: but that didn't explain the tendency
of pictures to dodge out of reach of my eyes. They'd do so sometimes
by retreating, sometimes by moving to new positions. Even as I
worried about this, I had no real belief in it. Pictures in reputable
galleries do not retreat, and they don't take up new positions. But here
were (or almost were) Cranach's 'Adam and Eve', anorexic ado-
lescents, under the perfection of an apple tree, the sort I'd dreamed of
as a juvenile scrumper, and I seemed to be on the point of registering
that this ideal tree was crammed with round unruptured reds. Eve was
– I was almost able to establish that she was, before the picture drifted
sideways – handing over the fatal apple: and Adam was scratching his
curled head, in what seemed a naive indication of his uncertainty.

Leaves (as the picture fled from me into the fluctuating distance) sprang from the ground, masking the laps of the pair as they stood there, silvery, pale: and Adam's hidden genitals appeared to be offered support by a stag's Y-fronted antlers. I knuckled my eyes and blinked and the painting rehung itself. Across the room there was Domenico Potti, who'd been on the scene not much later: the couple, turfed out of Eden (the very leaves failing them) had instantly invented seventeenth-century dress. I closed my right eye and the picture abolished itself. It could be retrieved only by opening my right eye and closing my left.

I felt tired: my head ached. Well, said Bernard, when I mentioned such distresses: I must remember that the true organ of vision was not the eye but the brain. For seventy years my brain had been accustomed to receiving a reliable flow of evidence from two outposts three inches apart. Now from one of those outposts came plain contradiction of what was offered by the other: two cars instead of three cars and a bus: together with a growing amount of plain fog. The brain was livid. It expressed its anger by the chief means available to it: it went in for dramatic fatigue, and it ached.

From such confusions, we'd take occasional refuge in the local pubs. But here, too, as in that dire bedroom, the eye might have problems, even without a cataract. The pubs had all become marked lately (with the sturdy exception of the Friar's Holt) by a frantic anxiety to vary their decor.

The idea seemed to be that if things looked the same for longer than six months, drinkers, unable to endure such aesthetic monotony, would desert in droves. The Duke of Lancaster, for example, had been modest, friendly, easefully shabby: and the first of its transformations set out, successfully, to be immodest, unwelcoming, and uncomfortably smart. Almost at once someone was seized by the idea that what ought to be aimed at was modesty, friendliness and easeful shabbiness: the attempt being made largely in terms of threatening canopies built out over the tables at which patrons sat, these canopies bearing an immense weight of old casks, irrationally large tankards, and muddled copperware. At some point the walls and other surfaces were thickly armoured with old advertisements on tinplate, many of them rashly

[41]

drawing attention to the fact that before the evolution of our current Utopia, beer cost as little as 1s 3d a pint. At each transformation the position of the bar tended to be changed, so that all but the most regular of regulars could be seen advancing towards what turned out to be a blank wall, or an unfamiliar outburst of horse brasses. It was no place for the one-eyed.

The most recent rearrangements revolved round what came to me as a not very comfortable surprise, being based on the notion that, shelved on purpose-built mantelpieces and fake windowsills, books that had perhaps not been read when they were new ought to be laid out with the aim of making sure that they were not read when they were old. As a writer I'd known the dismay of being remaindered: but worse by far than that was the thought of having one's wretched work converted into a ridiculous item of decor. What was it believed that these listless rows of books would suggest? Nothing, surely, but that the Duke was abreast of the latest fashion, which was (though no one could remember how the idea had first arisen) to fill the nooks and corners of pubs by emptying the nooks and corners of secondhand bookshops.

About these books I came to have much the feeling that the Scarlet Pimpernel had about condemned French aristocrats. I wanted to rescue them. Many in the Duke turned out to be nineteenth-century children's books, some with astonishingly vivid, or charmingly absurd, coloured illustrations. Kate, coming across a pleasant, early two-volume edition of *Middlemarch*, felt as I did: that she wished she had the boldness of a straightforward thief: and that she was certain taking the books down and opening them made us, to eyes behind the bar, not perfectly suitable patrons of the Duke.

But it lay at the obvious turning point of a favourite local walk. So we'd found ourselves there from time to time, less and less able to imagine the comfortably relaxed Duke that had occupied this space before the mad modern quest for constant renewal took charge. It was here that we talked once of the world of things you gathered round you as you lived, and of which you grew nervously aware as the end approached: this awareness being sharpened on this occasion by the recent death of an ancient cousin of Kate's. There was such slightness about what he'd left behind him. A dozen books: no pictures – he'd never gone in for them. Of papers, letters, mementoes, photographs, only what a small bureau held. And of this meagreness, Kate had the disposal. Few as Cousin Dennis's effects were, we had the feeling, as of people brutally laying hands on the sensitive substance of a life, that we'd had when we hurried through the disposal of what our parents had left. And we realised how impossible it was to think without ridiculous resentment of what would be done with our own leavings by survivors greatly loved. The tenderest dismantling by these would be vandalism. Something built into the human plight: the inevitability that the burdensome and often deeply worried scattering, burning, ripping, selling, giving away of the objects that had been dear to the dead – or, if not dear, part of that complex mesh of familiar things almost as vital to existence as blood or breath – would be dreaded by those about to die, and cause them to regard their executors, if only marginally, or at the worst moments of the night as . . .

Mongol hordes. I remember our old headmaster, passionate about those barbarians, and ready to suggest that they had lately been reincarnated – in Ben and me, for example. There was civilisation, at the heart of it a headmaster's study: and there was barbarism, a sort of playground.

In a horrible sense, he was right. Every life was the making of a minute civilisation: every death was devastation by Mongol hordes.

5

Dennis was complicatedly a cousin of Kate's: his family and hers had rather often intermarried – always, it seemed, to their own surprise: the general effect was of aunts being also nieces, together with a pervasive uncertainty as to grandparents. It must have been on the verge of, but gave an impression of steering confidently clear of, impropriety. Dennis was tall, mild, perfectly dull, and querulous. All his life he had thought ill of neighbours, shopkeepers, local councillors, the government (guilty of governing) and the opposition (guilty of wishing to govern). He reminded me of my father in this general habit of disgruntlement. It was an effect of being lower-middle-class: you had no power at all, so gave yourself the illusion of power that comes from withholding your approval from virtually everything. Out of this condition my father made something dark, venomous and half-tragic: but in Dennis there wasn't a trace of such passion. He was simply, growsingly dissatisfied.

His wife (an aunt who was also a niece) had died at eighty, leaving Dennis (they'd been childless) to grumble on alone. They'd retired to Somerset, to a fragile bungalow in a clumsy estate on the edge of the country town (in so far as any notion of town or country had lately been left intact), and they'd been much less than friendly to their neighbours: who were guilty of having children, making offensively amiable overtures, filling their front gardens with vans, motorcycles, and cars that might or might not be capable of reanimation. Dennis, widower, kept up his attitude of separateness, but was no match for the simple good nature of the family over the road, the family next door. He had this forlornness edged with ill-nature, but there was some other element in him, that grew stronger now he was alone: he was murmuringly responsive to the goodwill on offer. No one would ever be able to rely on his thinking well of them: but he ceased to resent being visited, and came to mix his habitual distrust of things with what he clearly didn't recognise as long stretches of simple trust.

Though exasperated by his inability to enjoy the world, Kate had always loved him, from the memory of his being able, when she was a child, to make a sort of comedy of his captiousness. So he'd claim that her hair was no better than rats' tails, or that her legs would serve perfectly well as matchsticks, and the manner of it made her almost as happy as if he'd praised these features. I remembered that delight in the crabbiness of relatives: my uncles being satirical about my being at the grammar school, and wondering, beyond my understanding, what any young woman would do who became associated with me, having to rely for amusement entirely on my brains. So, now that Dennis was in his eighties, and widowed, Kate took seriously the obligations she thought were hers, regularly making her way to Somerset to see how he was managing. She had always been doomed to a sense of commitment. She herself pointed out that this was a suspect kindness: going down to see Cousin Dennis enabled her to escape alone, for a few days to be free of the pattern of our shared life. Somerset was on the way to a further county where her oldest friend now lived. You were invited to think that Kate was kind to Dennis out of blatant selfishness. As it happened, any visit involved long sessions of Scrabble. Dennis, who rarely opened a book and had no apparent interest in language, was a master Scrabbler. One could only say he had some sort of quite random lexicographical cunning. Kate groaned a little at the prospect of Scrabble, whilst looking forward to another apparent opportunity of overturning this, as it always emerged, unoverturnable, ancient cousin.

And Dennis became older and older, and ancientness seized him by the throat – or, principally, by the heart and the legs. His heart simply had enormous intermissions, which he somehow survived. His legs became the stiffest of obstacles to perambulation. It was awful, having legs and being so incapable of using them. The unusefulness of Dennis's legs became the core of his general dissatisfaction. You'd warred with intolerable neighbours, and shopkeepers, and local councillors, and governments and would-be governments, and in the end what made you most apoplectic was having legs, purportedly designed to make movement possible, that made movement impossible.

We'd ring Dennis, with a long wait for the call to be answered, and ask how he was, and he'd always say: 'Can't grumble': which was his way of saying 'Can grumble.' 'These legs,' he'd say, disgustedly. He'd been sold this pair of legs, the salesman couldn't speak too highly of them: a cheat, as so often. If Dennis could have returned his legs, he'd have done so. In time his large frame became a shrunken frame, and his trousers, sold to him as a good fit, became a blatantly bad fit. 'This belt!' The belt, claimed to be suitable for his waist, had become absurdly unsuitable. 'Mustn't grumble,' he'd say: meaning, as the phrase had always meant to him, that he must grumble.

He was twitchily amiable about my being a writer: though if I'd not been married to Kate this might have been held against me. To her having (when young) hair like rats' tails she had added the possession of a husband unnaturally occupied. I think he may always have felt at a loss, when there seemed a demand for conversation. He was, at any rate, very much given to humming. He would hum extensively when I was around: expecting me, perhaps, to be exacting in this matter of conversation. His humming was orchestral: he made a distinction in it between instruments. There'd be recognisable trumpets: an odd humming through the teeth that suggested violins: a beating of the lips together for percussion.

With the notion, gently presented to him, that his heart might give out, and that it was essential he had a device for summoning neighbours, he was simply cross. He assented, gloomily humming, to the installation of the device: but made it clear to the neighbours that, if found half-gone, he shouldn't be restored. He didn't want the bother of it. He didn't want the prying interference that, to him, medicine always was. A neighbour, not alerted by the device but simply anxious, went in and found Dennis half-dead in the bedroom. She said she couldn't help it: she called for an ambulance. Dennis, grumpily moribund, allowed himself to be taken aboard. But as the ambulance was about to be driven away, he came surprisingly, typically, to indignant life. 'Razor!' he cried, through the oxygen mask he'd been clapped into. 'Razor!' His razor was hunted down and they started off again. We found him in hospital, his face a condemnation of everything that was happening. Where were his pyjama bottoms? He was freezing. Where was his watch? Where was anything whatever? He had, his gloom granted, a sort of sardonic valour. What would they dream up next, he was asking, to bother him with? He was being enormously bothered by the slow bureaucratic processes of death. From the final town hall the final abominable buff envelopes had begun to arrive.

Kate remembered the young cousin's face, and could hardly bear the face of the dying cousin: which, for all that grumbling courage, looked so deeply hurt. Approaching death, I noted again, seemed always to lead to that bruised, deeply injured look. And I recalled that Dennis had been overborne, rather, by his wife, a woman almost dementedly domestic. Calling on them once, we'd been invited to take tea, it being absolutely four o'clock. Dennis began such a complication of humming as was remarkable even for him. There was an orchestra and a half in it. Then: 'Time to get out the silver teapot, Hobson,' I heard him murmur. I thought then that he'd always had this satirical overview of himself. In the midst of that quite unattractive surliness, this younger inhabitant of his flesh made fun of his plight. Looking into Dennis's dying eyes, I saw the satirist, aged about nineteen, faintly but insistently present. 'You're staying at 34?' he asked. That was the number of the house. 'I'm afraid I'll have to charge you for it.' Then the brightness faded, and he resumed the business of dying.

On our last journey to see Dennis, I noted little failures of language of my own that filled me with instantly suppressed alarm. I talked of our turning off the road into a layabout and described someone we knew, a timid-natured friend who appeared unable to allow himself a moment of leisure, as a workshop. BLIND SUMMIT shouted a sign as we neared the hospital: followed almost at once by RUMBLE STRIP. The very roadside seemed to be playing a surrealistic sort of Scrabble. Thinking of Dennis – infected perhaps by the long-drawn-out distress of his dying, and also by that expectation of his that the worst you could imagine would always have something even more unpleasant coming up behind it – I'd been seized lately by one of the most bizarre fears I'd ever inflicted upon myself: that the moment of dying might go on forever. You'd be buried alive in the unendable moment of your extinction.

And other thoughts filled my head, and Kate's, that we were uncomfortable at finding there. Dennis had made so little of life: from his teens onwards in the same clerkly job: a tremendous absence of general curiosity. He was naturally suspicious of anything even mildly grand, bright, aspiring. He'd been a quite uneager traveller. Once only he and his wife had left the country: they'd gone to Switzerland, which they'd decided had been made uncomfortable by having more mountains than was sensible. There was some acceptable limit as to the ratio of elevated ground to flat ground that Switzerland had exceeded. They'd not known about meals on planes, and had taken their own sandwiches. On top of their habit of scarcely ever allowing themselves a lapse into satisfaction, there was this curious gaucherie that I understood very well: it's what came of being lower-middle-class, of never cottoning on, of having made a habit of living in the smallest scene possible. My father, invited to stretch himself across a political thought, would ask what was the use of his doing that: since no one could have any interest in his opinion. 'Do you imagine Mr Chamberlain will come knocking at the door and ask: "Mr Blishen, what do you think?"' he replied once to some fervent adolescent challenge of mine. My upbringing had left me with a residual tendency to be, and even to seek to be, small, naive in that fashion: not knowing that they provided meals on airplanes.

Dennis had been the cousin Kate had a child's fondness for; and he was also the baroque hummer who gently mocked himself under his breath. But what case – we miserably found we were driven to ask – could be made for anyone taking ninety years to taste so little of life and find most of what he'd tasted undelightful?

Oh, he'd arrived on this spectacular scene and had simply made a sour face at it!

But then we came to the hospital and found we were half an hour too late. Dennis had said: 'I hate this damned lemon and barley water', and had instantly died. And those guilty thoughts about the value of his existence were displaced by helpless affection and sadness, together with a kind of admiration. Damn it, it was rather fine to have ended it all in such a doggedly characteristic manner: to have gone out with denunciation of a soft drink!

The little hospital gave us a thoughtful leaflet it had prepared, offering advice on grappling with sudden bereavement. The sister in charge of the ward and several nurses said how much they'd miss Mr Hobson. His grumpy jokes had won their hearts.

And Kate had a sudden memory, of a tale that had been scarcely believed in the family. It was of an early moment in Dennis's marriage. What they said was that he'd been observed chasing his wife round a kitchen. He'd been brandishing an uncooked kipper. And they had both been laughing, wildly.

6

Ben wrote to say he'd been thinking about me – how I'd been a diffident schoolboy chewing his tie out of shyness and embarrassment. That would have been, I thought, in a corner of a room in which he, an unshy schoolboy, would have been orchestrating some urgent discussion. Now, he wrote, I was the comfortable literary burgher, mastering his paunch. It was a typical Bennish phrase, causing in me typical admiration laced with familiar affectionate rage. I wrote in reply that I was not comfortable (if I seemed to be sitting down, it was on the edge of my seat), and that any legitimate burgher (always Ben's term for someone socially acquiescent) would laugh at the idea of my being one.

He called in at once. It had been an exploratory formulation. And I thought how odd it was that Ben must view things (and often valuably) in hostile terms, whilst I was doomed to look at the world in a helplessly amiable fashion: and that on the basis of this, one would think, fatal incompatibility we had for nearly sixty years enjoyed a mysterious unity.

It hadn't been easy, for I'd done things for which Ben in his nature could not help giving me the lowest of marks. With Kate I'd persisted with marriage (nought out of ten). I'd lived in the same house for thirty years (if less than nought out of ten was possible, then less than nought out of ten). I sometimes thought of Ben's unwillingness to attach to a stationary object any idea but that of sluggish conformity in terms of his particular dislike of occasional tables. He'd said once of an acquaintance that even his occasional tables were permanent. Permanence had always irked him. And now that I thought of it, he'd often expressed his distaste for it by references to furniture. He'd begun by not wanting any himself beyond a tub, but had later concentrated his disgust, so that there was no crustier enemy of chests of drawers, wardrobes and sideboards. He *had* furniture, certainly, at the moment of choice and purchase much admired: but never clung to. There had been times when he'd been brutally frank about our furnishing, Kate's and mine. I'd found him at a party of ours once drawing the attention of a fellow-guest to (of course) an occasional table. This one had an associated usefulness: you slid the top back and there was a box for Kate's wools and cottons and needles. 'Admire this splendid bourgeois object,' Ben was saying. 'Bastard!' I said, going past. 'I was inviting an opinion,' said Ben. 'Bastard!' I insisted.

The fact was that among the achievements I could look back at with absolute pleasure was that of being one of a duo described once by someone as Mr Chalk and Mr Cheese.

The question of furniture was typical of the questions over which, through the years, we'd frowned at each other. Long ago I'd come to the conclusion that, if you didn't have too much of it, furniture was an enemy only to the man or woman who was opposed to sitting on anything, eating at anything, storing anything in anything. Ben, who gave his dislike of it some plausibility by having a lot of it but rarely hanging on to any item for long, felt that persistence of possession amounted to acceptance of imprisonment. He had a dread of being ever tied down, and was constantly scaling prison walls, each of his abodes being a gaol from which he arranged, in due course, and as spectacularly as possible, an escape.

It was where we collided: this notion of his that the extent to which you were to be seen as one who'd held out his wrists for the manacles was to be measured by your accepting forms of persistence. As a boy I'd been in awe of this attitude of his, and had been ready to decry myself as a coward when my habits were compared with his of ruthlessly throwing things (and people) overboard. But I'd grown to think that you needed a subtler measure of conformity: and that, in any case, what appeared to be our philosophies (Ben's view of furniture, for example) were really effects of the way we'd been made. The recipe that produced a Mr Chalk was not one that would produce a Mr Cheese. The recipe by which Ben was made had included, for example, a powerful pinch of distaste for the idea of adjusting his existence to that of anyone else. His unwillingness to do so could be turned into a stunning argument in favour of freedom. You could not be free without forbidding yourself to lean on others, and others to lean on you. The recipe by which I was made drew me to a little leaning, and being leant on. It seemed to me that if our value rested inflexibly on our being non-leaners rather than leaners, then huge numbers of people were doomed to inferiority by a single quirk out of the legion of quirks from which human character was created.

Well, I said in that reply to Ben's letter, *he* hadn't changed: I rather thought that, in remaining essentially what he'd always been, he'd gone in for more persistence than I had. *His* end was not at odds with his beginning. He was still the boy he'd been all those decades ago, looking for bureaucrats whose heads he could knock together on behalf of helpless people.

In the last years of his official life he'd been responsible, five thousand miles away, for the welfare of villagers displaced by a great new industrial development. He cared for them doggedly, cussedly, intransigently, giving lazy and unimaginative local officials a bad time: pushing through humane schemes of his own for the building of new villages, and new schools, and for what went on in the schools. His was, as it had always been, a concern for individuals: he knew hundreds of his villagers by name. His passion for being particular about people, and never thinking of them easily as quantities, had been something, as it seemed to me, that the government departments he worked in had endured with uneasy scowls. Ben had made piratical use of stolid and cautious institutions. Nearly ten years after retirement, he was still concerned for his villagers: still went back to see them, still kept a watchful eye on the conduct of local bureaucrats.

But the impulse behind all this, besides genuine sympathy for those who were easily trampled on, had its roots in something else: and this other force had also overawed me when we were boys growing up intellectually together, and it overawed me still. Ben was drawn to the world in which power is exercised, and in which those who exercise it are everlastingly locked in conflict. I didn't, and never would, understand any of that: and was astonished, since we were such close friends, that there should be in him this intense love and need of power, and in me a complete absence of it, so that in this respect we were utter strangers.

I simply couldn't understand what it was like – how it felt – to have such an appetite as Ben had for contention and for devising schemes to outflank other schemes. Whenever I visited him nowadays in his flat – on entry pausing in the doorway as we looked at each other and digested the dreadful joke of our being septuagenarians – there was always some struggle, small or large, here or a long way away, that made him narrow-eyed, pale, absentminded.

Odd, I'd think of myself – odd to have no idea what it could be like to wish to be, and to work towards being, say, Prime Minister: or even Mayor of Barton.

I remembered an occasion when (although I don't think I understood I was doing it at the time) I first observed the strength of Ben's ambition to make his way into some environment in which power could be sought and wielded. It was the summer of 1942: Ben was on leave, a sailor, red and swollen of face from Atlantic winds as experienced on the deck of a destroyer. I was less dramatically coloured, from work on the land as a conscientious objector: and I had promised to take Ben to see Williams, our old English teacher.

In those days, when the war had barely allowed us to stop being schoolboys, my admiration for Ben, for the readiness and crispness of his thought and his capacity to manage the world – even then there was an impression that he might have been the impresario behind it all – caused in me horrible unnecessary shynesses. Didn't anything happen in Barton? he'd ask after an hour of my throttled company. I feared my account of anything whatever would be lame and silly alongside his trenchant confidences. 'After the Atlantic, which is grey from end to end, you want bright things,' he said. 'I suppose that's why the sailor likes coloured parrots – and coloured women, too.' I thought I couldn't say anything about work on the land and my fellow-ditchers that measured up to the brisk vividness of that. He glancingly mentioned the young woman he would go on to marry. 'You may perhaps remember that tall girl I know?' There was no possibility of my having the faintest difficulty in recalling her: she was a major resident of my imagination – no one less than Juliet to his Romeo.

Though I'd never have let him guess I thought of them in those terms: Ben was impatient with Romeo, as someone ignominiously insistent on appraising a woman in terms entirely favourable to her.

We made our way through a small park not far from Williams's house, and Ben talked of the fate of a selection of D.H. Lawrence's stories, essays and poems that I'd lent him. It had travelled, he said, from one of his shipmates to another. Always when it was returned he asked: 'You liked it, didn't you?' and the answer was, to him puzzlingly, usually a variation of such a comment as: 'Isn't he conceited!' I said it was perhaps because of Lawrence's exhilarating confidence in whatever he wrote – he offered ideas and observations and perceptions with thrilling conviction, as if he'd been a swordsman taking on the world single-handed. There was this air of his constantly striking weapons out of the hands of feebler persons. Then I thought how odd it was that I should be saying this, who was among the hesitant and doubtful whom Lawrence would have disarmed with the most scornful briskness. But then, when it came to an exchange of general thoughts between Ben and me, or comments on books, my shyness loosened its grip. We'd always sparked each other off. It was at the level of what we were as persons that the sense of inferiority fastened itself on me, springing from the knowledge that I hadn't his boldness, his determination to lay hands on life. And, of course, my simply entertaining the idea that I was inferior was profoundly unBennish. Moving in full battle-rig through the world, he'd not have dreamed of embracing the self-disarmament involved in thinking yourself damagingly lesser than someone else.

I said I remembered walking through this park on the way to school, when as a prefect (soon to be de-capped for bringing Hamlet-like hesitations to the doing of the punitive things a prefect was supposed to do) I could take this route because it led directly to the playing fields surrounding the school. Prefects were allowed to enter by way of those fields. Oh, I said, what I'd liked about being, so briefly, a prefect, was having been able to make this green approach to the school day. Ben had come by bike from another part of the town and hadn't made use of this privilege. Now he said: Yes: but when he was a prefect, his mind was already beginning to decay.

[53]

And I laughed helplessly. Because Ben's giving a date, as he fairly often did, to the decline and collapse of his mental powers, wasn't at all a piece of self-disarmament: it was a grand mark of his belief in himself. He could allude to this process of decay as confidently as the governor of a besieged medieval city deploring his governorship whilst standing on his triumphantly unbreached walls. What was the joke? Ben asked; and I told him: and our laughter, which brought on one of his fits of tears, took us to Williams's house.

Williams had married while Ben was away at sea, and Ben hadn't seen the house he'd settled in. Now we stood in front of it, a conventional small villa, with neatly banal arrangements of doors and windows, and Ben didn't believe what he saw. 'That can't be it!' There was a National Savings poster in the window. 'That *can't* be it!' But it was. Mrs Williams answered the bell. She too was neat, and had an Oxford voice, and was polite: and so to Ben was subject to much the same suspicions with which he regarded Juliet. Williams was working, at school, she said: but she rang, and he said he'd be with us in half an hour. She made tea for us: another black mark, for the elegance of the cups and saucers, and a damning daintiness of biscuits. But she was teaching at the school too, French and German. and she spoke with amusing dryness about being Williams's brand-new wife, and about the hope the boys clearly had that, giving some helpless hint of the improprieties for which they had formed their union, they might disgrace themselves in classrooms, or, more wonderfully, at morning assembly.

I was ready now for Ben's judgement on Mrs Williams: 'Why does she have to make it so difficult to like her? That *polished* voice?' he'd say (and he did): 'But she's probably all right, don't you think? as far, of course, as you can be sure about anybody.'

And now Williams came in. He was a tiny man, who'd taken Ben and me under his not entirely competent but warm wing, and recognised our love of language, and, at a low point in our lives, had provided us with a summer holiday in his native Wales. His defects, of which I'd not yet become aware – at this stage I wouldn't have dreamed of thinking of him in terms of defects – included a love of talk that swallowed everything: being eloquent on any matter convinced him that he had had a forcible practical effect on that matter. He was doomed to talk his life away. He also had a passion for providing plots and plans for other people's lives. Now he was being amusing, in the style that had brightened our sixth form existence, about a colleague, the school's almost officially recognised sadist. It might have been in the prospectus: Head of Sadism: W. Batty, BA(Lond). Everyone knew why Batty thought no weakness or remissness in a boy could be dealt with by anything less than flogging. He had a flogger's purple face. Being a sadist, Williams now said, he sought power by depriving others of what they needed: and being in charge of the school's copier, had devised a fiendish set of rules designed to make it virtually impossible for anyone to use it as they wished. But he'd been absent that afternoon – thus Williams's own absence from home: he'd been copying material for the National Union of Teachers, a use of the machine that Batty particularly disallowed.

And now Williams turned to the matter of our being there, and the question of what we were doing, and what we might go on to do. And at once I felt a change in Ben as if he'd gone into another gear, was driving in another lane. There had been times enough in our relationship when he'd become, in a moment and in this fashion, unrecognisable: fuelled by some suddenly superior propellant. It happened when he played games, and it happened whenever he found himself talking to anyone who had, or seemed to have, an effective hand in any enterprise at all. One of Williams's own passions was for the discussion of the way power was exercised. With him, as I was to come sadly to see, it was a kind of intoxicant, that at the same time helped him to hide from the truth that, a great talker about powerful action, he was doomed by his nature to loquacious inaction.

And now Ben was saying how much he wished not to return to the civil service, where he'd been a clerk in the Board of Education: and Williams was talking about the Board, and how a Tory minister had naively allowed the National Union of Teachers to carry him away for an entire weekend of persuasions and exposure to advanced ideas: and how within days the minister had been hoisted out of office and into the House of Lords. Ben spoke of the inner workings of the Board, and Williams of the union's cunning connections with it, and there was talk of the country's director of education, and of his being a dull reactionary: and Ben was proposing ways by which, drawing on his acquaintance with the Board, he could help to frustrate the man's dismal aims. And the excitement grew: and Ben said intensely that he wished he'd had a father who could have kept him at school and saved him from the civil service: and Williams proposed other possibilities for him, which included becoming, by some process not too closely looked at, director of a research institute And I saw Ben halt a moment, become blank, exasperated by this proposal: there were few roles I could less easily imagine my friend playing than that of director of a research institute. Williams turned to ask what I thought Ben might do. I said I could no more answer that than I could say how I was to escape from becoming again the local newspaper reporter I'd been before the war. 'But Ben and I had thought of simply wandering together round the world.' That had been intermittently a dream of ours, growing partly from an earlier ambition of Ben's to be a tramp. But laying out prospectuses for our eventual arrival at the status of vagrants did not attract Williams, who began to slot Ben into the educational system at various focal points. Ben frowned again and impatiently widened the talk. The mood and pace of our walk through Barton and the little park were left behind. Ben's eyes narrowed: he pounced upon a point before it was made, and instantly had two or three other points growing out of it. Williams having made a political reference, Ben laughed with what sounded to me like instant excited understanding and – in the manner of a conjuror whose hand had seemed to be empty – made a flourish out of providing a complete flush of related allusions. And here he was, conjuring up the postwar world: the British Empire gone, the Japanese stronger than ever, America and Russia quarrelling with Britain over markets. 'We want a Lenin,' said Ben, 'or three or four of them.' Williams uttered a laugh of wary agreement. They concluded, on the exhilarated wing, that the Labour Party was merely an echo of the Conservative Party.

Ben talked a little about being at sea: causing cries of 'Ah! Ah!' from Williams, who came from Swansea, by saying Newfoundland was another South Wales. Then the talk was of boys Ben had been at school with. 'Who was in your year?' Williams asked. Ben pointed to me. 'Ah yes,' said Williams, 'this lad here.' And, silent in the swirl of powerful talk, paralysingly aware of not knowing how to join in, it was what I felt I was: an attendant lad.

On the doorstep (it had suddenly become midnight), Williams said to Ben: 'Get Edward to bring you along next time.' And Ben said: 'He makes a good chaperone, doesn't he!'

And so we walked away from the house, Ben bristling with excitement. 'I wish Williams wouldn't try to find jobs for us,' he said. But he had plainly taken a high charge from the occasion. 'I suppose,' he said, 'one might marry. It gets rid of the desire for power, I suppose. We transfer all that to our children. That's why your father hates Williams, for adopting you in a . . . literary sense – caring for your writing, and so on. Williams made you his child, not your father's. It was a great loss of power.' But as we walked through the streets, he wasn't really with me. He was rapt, distractedly thrilled: like someone who'd been given some hours of intensive training in running a sprint, and had had to remind himself that there wouldn't for a long time be a sprint for him to take part in.

We said goodbye, and I watched him walk away through that wartime darkness that was unlike any other darkness I've ever known, being founded on the forbiddenness of light, and fear of it.

I was in the flat with the almost-view of Hampstead Heath. Ben said: 'I find I'm rather in the business of getting rid of everyone. I'd be glad to make the last few laps without anyone hanging on my arm. What's your view of all that?'

I stared at him. He was doing it again, half a century on: offering a piece of behaviour peculiarly his own as a topic for general debate.

I said: 'Well, I'll send Kate packing.'

And we laughed till Mr Chalk wept, and Mr Cheese had to propose that the only resort was to whisky.

7

'You'll be pleased to know,' said the eye surgeon, 'that your kind of cataract, which blots out the sight very fast, is usually found in the young.'

No, I wasn't pleased: if Fate was going in for flattery, it would have to do better than that. But I did have pleasure in finding myself in the hands of this surgeon, who was amusing and elegant: and had, I'd discovered, a remarkable reputation. It was for her skill at microsurgery: but it was also for the thought she gave to the plight of her patients. It was there to begin with in her appearance, which suggested great competence but also a lively, sharp but tender interest in people. She made life bearable for many of the old and inarticulate among her patients who, confronted with the language of eye surgery and the routines of clinic and hospital, found it easy to believe that their misfortunes were now beyond their understanding. 'She *listens* to you!' a woman had told me as we waited for attention: she being deaf and permanently startled, made clumsy and deeply nervous by old age.

To measure the condition of the eyes there was a machine that had probes that advanced towards the eyes until, delicately, they touched them. Keeping them open as this happened wasn't easy – the instinct to retire behind the defences being so great. I said I'd seen such a machine in Edward Bond's play, *Lear*: there it was used to blind Gloucester. Miss Angelou recoiled . . . She knew most of what was to be known about the eye, she said, and it was her daily work: but of something like *that* she couldn't bear to hear. I thought how clumsy I'd been to mention it, to someone whose concern with eyes was to preserve, not destroy them.

Well, she said, I had a choice. I could have a lens implant, which would solve the problem. Or I could leave things as they were. The reason for doing nothing would be that surgery wasn't infallible: if it went wrong, blindness would result. I said that I peculiarly needed my eyes, for workaday purposes of reading and writing. What would she recommend?

'I will write you into my diary,' she said.

8

The busy desultoriness of hospitals! I'd been asked to be there for pre-op tests at ten o'clock. Two hours later I'd not been called. Others had been taken away, and had reappeared, looking estranged, to wait to be taken away again. I hadn't expected anything else, and had no disposition to blame an institution that could not afford the luxury of precise appointments. But there was this inevitable sense of having been removed from the human rollcall. They would never get round to me. I pretended to read a novel, though I had no gift whatever for reading in circumstances like these. I couldn't read in an airport, waiting for a flight to be called. Keep me waiting, hold me in suspense, and I'd never read again, never again think an unagitated thought. At moments like this one I'd reflect that all my apparent cultivatedness depended absolutely on my not being kept hanging about. Seeing that so much of the world was everlastingly on tenterhooks, how anomalous my usual state of steady thoughtfulness was!

If Kate were here, without the least intrusiveness she'd be, by now, on useful terms with half a dozen. Oh, that willingness of mine never to address someone I didn't know! Without certain traditional arrangements by which people are inexorably introduced to one another – parents and children, for example – I might have gone through life smiling faintly to left and right. Kate said she'd been drawn to me fifty years before, passing me in Barton High Street and thinking how interestingly aloof I was. She wanted to speak but dared not. Oh, I'd say, with a fervour that never weakened, if only she had! It would have been like the relief of Mafeking!

Now I was so dismayed by being ignored by an entire institution that I spoke to a gentle-faced Indian woman who'd also sat there unsummoned. She'd been told to be there at 9.30, she said, and had been given the impression that she was the last. So I was the last after the last.

I thought how awful it would be to come to die in a hospital, especially one of this labyrinthine kind, a torment of corridors. You'd go your way to oblivion carrying sheaves of paper and notes about your condition from one absentmindedly benign office to another, everywhere meeting the battered kindness that was largely on offer.

It was tremendously hot. I felt my face reddening, explosiveness in my cheeks. I'd be here for ever, and would end up roasted.

Then suddenly I was called, and was at once found to have high blood pressure. I'd never had high blood pressure in my life, though I'd once been warned that I had low blood pressure to the point that, as I understood it, I might perish from internal frost. I thought: given the tension of being here, and the enormous heat of the place, it's not surprising I have high blood pressure.

Then I was in the presence of a preoccupied nurse who was attaching wires and pads to my chest. She had an apprentice with her, and said: 'You notice, the chest doesn't want shaving.' It was odd, having one's chest spoken of as if it had a separate existence. It was oddly like being cut dead by one's own body.

A machine assessed my left eye, and declared it to be deplorable. In a booth, preparing for an X-ray, I was amazed by the quantity of my clothes, and the sweating difficulty of storing them away in a plastic bag: and by the plain and perhaps intended impossibility of tying tapes behind my back to secure a rearward-opening gown, designed surely by some tease to challenge our shyness about showing our bottoms. Holding myself absurdly together I joined the Indian woman, who had triumphed over her gown, wearing it as if it were an austere sari. We glanced wryly at each other's plastic bags. The X-ray was so quick I hardly noticed it.

The trouble with hospitals, I thought as I made my way out, was that you found it hard to conceive that any great value could be set upon you. Why should it be? You were one of a whole world of casualties and collapses, major or minor, treading your path through a system that was intent on being as decent as it had the time and energy to be. You were aware of having a sort of tired value: but it could never be the value you had at home. Here, as I threaded the corridors in obedience to the surprisingly complex signposts, were so many people who'd been reduced to being formally the chest, the eye, the bladder, the heart, and who were aware of being, only a few miles away, not a limb or an organ, but a whole creature, and a centre of relatively passionate attention.

If you were really here to die, wouldn't you already be halfway to having your identity stripped from you, and to being nothing at all?

I was in a general state of apprehension. This made hardly any sense, since the greater part of me was – surely? – perfectly cool. Everyday operation, admirable surgeon. But in my nature there'd always been something that readily manufactured alarm. As I lay in the room I had to myself, being the only man in the Monday bunch, I thought that if my existence had been run by a government, one of the key posts would be that of Minister of Misgiving (a junior to the Secretary of State for Dread and Despair). Now he was largely worried that my blood pressure would still be too high and they'd call the operation off. I'd find that hard to bear. I was very tired of being one-eyed.

In the corridor there was a constant padding of feet, and sounds of things being wheeled. It was a long corridor, and everything took ages to approach and disappear. From another room came the sound of two women talking, with barely a pause: one always at length, the other uttering little beyond cries of astonishment. There'd be a long mumbling stretch and then a startled: 'Oh yeah!' Not the American but the Cockney 'Oh yeah' – a sort of dropped jaw of sound. I remembered women from my own Cockney background, aunts and others, who'd had this amazed, largely sceptical response to almost everything said to them. 'Oh yeah!' they'd cry, in a tone that suggested they'd been taken dramatically aback and driven close to disbelief. But then in my family it had seemed natural enough that disbelief should be expressed, and copiously. Even as a child I'd been able to detect enough lies in what was said – or patently doubtful statements – to decide that the truth wasn't the end aimed at. Clearly it was agreed that adult conversation should rest on an exchange of fabrications. 'Oh yeah,' an aunt would say, smiling, perhaps, but utterly and routinely unconvinced.

A smell of, I thought, mince advanced down the corridor; and I yearned for it, simply because I supposed myself unable to have it. No more eating, someone had said, before the operation in the morning. But now a young woman appeared to explain that midnight was the last moment when I might eat: meanwhile here was, certainly, mince. It would be followed – and it was – by a tiny custard sown with currants. In any other context this might have seemed a horrid meal. Here, and against the background of my belief that I was to be starved, it was a feast. I thought I might be undergoing severe disorientation, most of my sense of what was usual having vanished: an effect, perhaps, of the euphoria of being about to have the essence of my eye plucked out and restored. (The Minister of Misgiving leapt to his feet and began quoting *King Lear*.) However that was, I found myself waiting for the next development as if, rather than spending a prosaic evening in a corner of a battered hospital, I was taking part in an opera.

The corridor filled with the sound of visitors. Kate sat on my bed and valiantly made a tale out of the few hours since we'd last met. I noticed that from time to time she did a little, not quite surreptitious, tidying of my effects: in those few hours I had, in a phrase of hers that over the years had become laconic, spread myself about. She said the operation lasted only forty minutes. Oh, I said, startled: I'd thought it was five. That was the duration my mind had fixed on: in fact, I'd simply received the impression that it was to be magically brief. Kate said she had thought it would cheer me to know it was over so quickly, I couldn't remember ever having so hugely undermined a sympathiser.

Kate went, and the voices of visitors faded. I persuaded myself to leave my room, feeling I'd escaped from some years of imprisonment. I found the Indian woman I'd met during the pre-op tests. She occupied a room with the calm dignity of someone who had known worse exiles by far. It was odd, we agreed, like spending the evening in a queer kind of hotel, laced with strong elements of a gaol. Returned to my room, I was visited by a nurse who poured drops into my eyes, saying there'd be more to come. My eyes heaped with a strange moisture, I made myself leave the room again and walked the long corridors: from the one I was lodged in others flowed, long hollownesses full of dull echoes. My own footsteps appalled me. I thought Theseus's labyrinth might have been like this. The corridors spoke of desertion, of patient and visitor alike having retreated, of one movement implacably outward and another resignedly inward. Those who could withdraw had done so, filling their lungs with the air of the non-hospitalised world, as they left the car park roaring their engines more than was necessary. I returned to my room, remembering that when Kate was going I'd stepped into the corridor to wave her goodbye: and that made her return to say I'd irresistibly reminded her of a rabbit emerging from its warren, displaying a nervous readiness at any false move the world might make to flash back inside it. A nurse appeared: 'You know,' she said, smiling from the door, 'that you will have nothing to eat after 3 a.m.' Starvation was an infinitely postponable event.

Now a brisk young woman introduced herself as the anaesthetist. It was very much as one had read of prison scenes, the night before a hanging. No pre-med, she said, unless begged for: simply a jab in the hand in the theatre. Many people after a morning op were ready to eat their lunch. After-effects were not particularly painful – a gritty sensation summed it up. A nurse came to read my blood pressure. Despite what I feared might have been the fatal anxiety of my wishing it down, it *was* down.

From along the corridor came the voices of the anaesthetist and the exclamatory Cockney. 'Injection in your hand.' 'Oh yeah.' 'You sleep for half an hour.' 'Oh lovely!' 'Sleep well.' 'Oh yeah.'

The night staff was introduced. It was nine o'clock: the hospital had lapsed into silence. I thought of the possibility, which all these precautions seemed to propose, of death under anaesthetic. The Secretary of State for Dread and Despair was on his feet at once, making a statement to the House about the possibility (one that had never crossed my mind till this moment) that at home there might be something, some piece of treacherous paper, that I'd rather were not found if I was unexpectedly extinguished.

A nurse brought in a beaming black woman. 'This,' she said, 'is a left cataract for the morning.' The black woman nodded and smiled enormously at the left cataract: who at once and gratefully fell asleep.

'Would you like to get yourself washed take your watch off remove your teeth and anything artificial and put on your gown it ties at the back and these.' *These* were paper pants. The hospital was stirring immensely: everything possible was being wheeled down the corridor. Enough crockery was clattering past to provide a town with its breakfast. There were distant sounds that might have been gunshots. As I hunted for the strings that tied the gown, my back went. There was the sense of some heavy dislodgement at hip level, bones awkwardly getting themselves into false relations with other bones, the always amazing pain, the need to remain carefully twisted. Tension, I thought. Hadn't been aware of that! Had believed I was quite calm! Well, there'd been that traitor within who'd thrown his weight in the other direction and brought my body to a groaning standstill. I hobbled to the washbasin, having forgotten to shave. The door said: NOTHING BY MOUTH FROM 3 A.M. Shaving when your back wouldn't straighten was difficult. I hurried, the absence of punctuation from the nurse's instructions having given me a sense of dramatic urgency. I finished shaving. I waited. Nothing happened. I sat down, and continued waiting. The nurse reappeared and claimed my watch, bearing it off to safety. A very long wait followed. Feeling unmanageably absurd in my gaping gown and paper pants, I read fitfully: beginning to understand that things being done urgently didn't mean that the events for which they were a preparation would follow with similar urgency. Understandably enough, these preparations were ticked off a list according to some inelastic timetable: they were done in good time for fear that they might not be done at all. It meant that when you had a sharpened neurotic need to know the time, you had no watch to tell it by. And that you spent a rather long time dressed – or in certain awkward respects scarcely dressed at all – as a ghost.

Then outside the door, an eccentric carriage, was the trolley on which I was to be wheeled to the theatre. The absence of any real need for me to be taken there in that fashion, added to the absurdity of my dress, made it marvellously odd to board it. It was very high, and I made an attempt to mount with a single (as it turned out, not remotely possible) lift of the leg. My spine became hot with protest. One of the attendants pointed out that steps were provided. And so I stretched myself out high above the world and examined the ceiling as it unrolled. There were two attendants, man and woman, merrily young, both Irish: they exchanged what seemed to be jokes in a rapid brogue. They were incomprehensible cherubs (both had charming faces) accompanying a lofty skeletal bier. It was odd to come at the names of departments over doors, at their own level. It was as in the dreams of levitation I sometimes had, passing through the world at lintel-height whilst extended comfortably on the top of a tomb. Don't think of tombs, don't think of biers, I advised myself. Here was the sign OPERATING THEATRES, passing close to my chin. The jokes exchanged by my propellers evidently grew better and better: as they brought me to a halt in a narrow space that had the air of some ominous anteroom, they were in fits. They went, and were succeeded by a theatre attendant who set out to divert me. Strange things were happening in Russia, he said: and if it came to that, he had been on a week's package once to Moscow and Leningrad. One should get to know the world, surely! The Kremlin was a sight on sunny mornings! All of which caused me agitation, for I'd not been to Moscow or Leningrad, and could never understand why the very great desire to visit them did not produce the capacity to arrange to do so.

I felt a familiar melancholy coming on. I really should renew the suggestion that my son Tom come with me to Russia. I observed aloud that I needed a pee, and hoped I would not be incontinent during the operation. They'd not notice, said the attendant, their attention would be given entirely to my heartbeat. It was a detail I hadn't thought of, and the Minister of Misgiving (promoted within the past few seconds to Minister of Acute Misgiving) rose . . . But at once the anaesthetist appeared, and plunged a needle into the back of my hand. 'You'll be gone in twenty seconds,' he said. Well, he was wrong about that, I thought, ruminating at my ease on Moscow. Surely minutes had passed already and here I was, fully conscious: there was not the faintest waning of awareness. Immediately I found myself waking up, feeling terrible. A voice that was a mile away said I was in the recovery room, and that after I'd got used to the world again they'd wheel me back to my bed. In that total absence of an interval between my thoughts about Moscow and my present plight, I'd been given a patch for my eye, lashed into place with a bandage: my throat was full of rubbish. I was scandalously dry, and something had happened in the region of my chest, a congregation of rheums, that contradicted my need to breathe.

After a long period of feeling simply anguished I was wheeled back through the corridors, no Irish jesters in attendance, and sensed that the trolley (by what in my bemused state I took to be a feat of navigation of an epic kind) had been brought alongside my bed: it was then lowered, in some fashion, so that my shadowy friends were able to carry me (though it felt more like tipping) onto the bed. There I lay, feeling more dry than I'd imagined one could ever be. I was aware of my hands moving in front of me, plucking at the air, rising and falling, with a nervous aimlessness I remembered as being the character of my mother's hands when she was on the point of death. The Minister rose to his feet but was unable to sustain a standing position and fell behind the despatch box. I called for water, but was given a mouthwash, on some grounds about which I felt defeatedly cross. I lay, my hands fluttering ridiculously up and down, like those of a preacher suffering from serious loss of energy, mumbling to myself, and absurdly able to view the entire entertainment from some inner vantage point, coolly, as one who might be saying: 'Oh come on, this is all over-dramatic!' Well, it *was* over-dramatic, this gasping and helpless lifting and dropping of arms and hands (which I suppose by a sort of pumping helped the lungs with their labours). The body knew what it was up to, reflected the oddly, coldly embarrassed spectator inside me. If it needs to act like a ham actor, then let it do so.

There was grit in my eye. I could see tiny circular samples of the scene through holes in the patch. Kate came, finding me in the posture of neither wishing to do anything, nor wishing to do nothing. Her presence seemed to persuade my lungs that breathing was possible, and the inside observer brought himself to rejoin the rest of my scattered self. Kate went: I was surprisingly glad to eat a flabby bap, into which taramosalata and cucumber had been inserted: and, then, enormously, I slept. At once it was the extraordinary sort of morning that prevails in hospitals, and I was being asked to come downstairs and have my eye dressed. The fault of this kindly establishment continued to be that it accompanied that sort of summons with no hint of whether it was urgent or not. As always, I chose to think one ought to hurry, and went down with my dressing gown over the gown I'd worn for the operation, and the paper pants: only to discover that others were trim, fully dressed. My deshabille, all the same, seemed to be more suitable in a hospital that appeared to mistake us for tropical plants.

My patch removed, I was for a moment disappointed: there was freshness and brightness of colour, but, in the eye they'd operated on, a lack of focus. Miss Angelou's assistant said this was only the beginning: I'd have a course of drops, and then, of course, new glasses. A new lens could never be better than the one it replaced: and that eye was not my phenomenally precise right eye. And as I continued to look about me, I became amazed by the newly washed look of things, the depth and fullness of colour. I'd had no sense during my accelerating half-blindness of a dimming of colour, but here was colour as I'd not been aware of it for years! It was as if moment by moment colours ripened: red was astounding, but in no time would be more astounding still. I thought I must go at once to the National Gallery, before the astonishment of it faded.

And my portable fog! – that had gone. Minute by minute, focus revived: the edges of things having a sharpness you might cut yourself on. I sat, waiting for Miss Angelou, among the incredulous.

And here she was, cool, amused. She was pleased with what her eye-inspecting machine showed her. 'That seems . . . all right,' she said. 'Thank you for it,' I said. 'Thank *you* for coming in at such short notice,' she said. A hole had opened in her diary, and she'd invited me to fill it. 'I think there's a difference between our reasons for being grateful,' I said, not knowing at this brisk post-operational moment how to give the expression of my feelings sufficient force. Good God, it wasn't every day that half one's sight, and the confidence that comes

[67]

from full vision, are restored by the exercise of another person's exceptional skill. 'Well, thank you and . . . thank you and so forth,' I said, helplessly, and sketched a bow. 'Etcetera etcetera etcetera,' she replied, and curtseyed.

Now I met the Cockney voice: she was Mrs Johnson, whose 'Oh yeah' was clearly her response to anything that resembled or sounded like information: the guardedness of it covering not only her doubt as to the integrity of any informant, but her own great deafness. For the rest, she had a cry of 'Oh lovely!' delivered in a rich variety of tones: it served for enthusiasm as for the cagiest wish to be thought of as quite uncommitted. I knew *that* cry, too, from my childhood.

She asked me, forlornly, if I had any idea where the lavatory was. I'd noticed her peering at many unsuitable doors: a hospital going in terrifyingly for doors. Because of her deafness, it was not possible to give her directions: so I took her by her elbow (I'd known elbows like that, too) and steered her to her goal. Guessing that returning to where she'd started would be as difficult as her sighing search had been, I waited for her to emerge. 'How did I get here, dear?' she asked, and gave me out of the blue an enormous wink: and I knew then that she knew that I knew about her from having known my aunts.

I'd had, for so long, so little information from the left. It was now as if I and the world were twice as wide as we had been.

There were difficulties of convergence: my eyes seemed to belong to slightly different systems, and took time to agree to fix their attention on a particular point. The sense of balance between them, of brightness in one and fog in the other, seemed now reversed, though in my good eye there was as yet no palpable blur. And in merely moving about there seemed some element of peril, as if the very shine and depth of colour constituted a danger, or as if damage might come from walking through a scene so rich and vivacious.

But for days I was consumed by the happiness of simply having this wide view, of being rid of the fog that in the end had seemed to have weight and to make my eye exhaustedly heavy. Everywhere I looked the restorers had done their work. And I thought how extraordinary it was so late in life to have a whole sense so renewed and refreshed. It was a gain at a moment when the whole idea of gain had been abandoned.

9

And so we went to Östendorf, in the Tyrol, not with the intention of bringing my new eye to bear on colours worthy of it, but with that effect. There was a yellow church, and in the churchyard more pansies than I'd ever seen assembled in a single place; and through the air for much of the day there sidled and drifted and lazily twisted the multi-coloured nail-parings that were hang-gliders. And I couldn't believe that I'd ever before known red, or blue, or orange: and I fell in love with the church, and was infatuated with the churchyard.

We were staying in a hotel in the centre of the village: but it seemed more inn than hotel. It was *enormously* used for weddings; and at times became a scene of rioting, the rioters being tiny bridesmaids and pages, who ran in and out of the adult occasion, indulgently noticed and then forgotten: made a little mad by their costumes, and by the mixture of music, laughter and social and sexual excitement. Through a window as we ate we saw once a very small bridesmaid dancing, raptly, with a lamp-post. We learned to sleep in defiance of the nuptial uproar: but were always woken by the finale, some time after midnight – impossible to resent – a sudden immensely high-spirited and utterly delighted dance, played by half a dozen brass instruments. The players would be standing at the entrance to the hotel, but might as well have been in bed with us. There seemed, anyway, among the aims of such weddings, to be the wish to give everyone the impression of being about to be in bed with everyone else. There'd been tremendous dressing up, such suits, such a redundancy of skirts: and I'd rarely been so aware of a tendency to involve the imagination in thoughts of people not being dressed at all. I was back in Covent Garden, thinking how helplessly lustful we all were, and how intent we were on suggesting that we were not lustful at all. Most of the human race going through the sexual green channel, though you knew perfectly well what contraband they were carrying.

Kate reminded me that such thoughts had occurred to me in a cafe in Hythe. I'd asked her to imagine what many of those in the cafe were doing twelve hours earlier. Kate took a step I'd failed to take – she looked round the room. Most of those present were our contemporaries. 'Twelve hours ago,' she said, 'I think most of them were fast asleep.'

The church, too, might just as well have been in bed with us. Waking in the morning, and looking across our wooden verandah past our nearest neighbour, which was a prodigious chestnut, we felt we could touch the church. It seemed in that direction to be one of the true walls of the room. It had an onion-topped tower and a plain high-shouldered body, both sunnily yellow, with a deep roof of darkly grey shingles, though in the afternoon they'd become a much lighter gleaming grey. There were tiny dormers set into this roof, that in the later sunshine made improbably long shadows: each black chevron being of a length that it seemed impossible should have such a very small source. And here and there were small golden balls on spikes, that gathered to themselves any light there was. A few months later, in Moscow, I looked back on these as constituting a sort of shrunken Kremlin.

You walked round the verandah, our room being on a corner: and down there was the entrance to the churchyard. Every morning, early, it was the setting for a procession of watering cans. I thought I'd never known people so housewifely about death. Largely it was pansies that they watered: almost every grave being home to a brilliant mob of these. About each grave there was a great neatness, with its strict edges of pale stone and its ironwork, no design that we could see ever being exactly repeated. And always, in the morning, and again in the evening, so much brisk housework: such dead-heading, polishing and sweeping.

Being so close ourselves to dismissal from the scene, we thought how different it was at home: so many English churchyards being virtually unvisited. In any case, Kate and I intended to be reduced to ash, and to have that ash scattered. Oh Lord, such a distance: between this Austrian feeling for the grave as another room in the house, and our tendency to be simply neglectful, or to let the wind blow us away.

There were times when with this new eye I almost shrank from colour, from a world where everything seemed to have been repainted in the past half hour. We went up the mountain in a gondola, a handsome, efficient carriage that was hauled out of the station in the valley on its mile of cable with an odd desperate roughness, then settled down at once, and with laborious dignity, to a sequence of upward and downward swoops, until we reached a point halfway up the mountain, where the hang-gliders threw themselves off. At times there were scores of these garish haloes twisting in the great space between this level of the mountain and the floor of the valley, settled into some huge stability of air only to be subject to sudden invisible upward or sideways blasts, so spectacular you could hardly bear not to be able to see the powerful cause of such dramas. And they'd fall as if without hope of recovery only immensely to rise. About this beautiful sport there was such a silent gaiety! Even what could be heard belonged more to silence than to sound: there'd be, directly overhead, as a hang-glider turned an invisible corner, a curiously private rustle as of someone tightening a silk stocking.

Then we took the final gondola, and when we stepped out were confronted instantly with a massive flank of mountain, densely brown, with broad curving stripes of snow: a huge animal that had this moment chosen to squat there. I borrowed Kate's dark glasses, in need of a short retreat to dullness.

We walked. Kate wondered if we'd ever done anything half as good as walking had been. The happiness of being merely engaged in it. We followed the blue mark of the *Wanderweg*, much of the time steeply in forest, in a great brown gloom of trees. Once, with an eagle's view of the valley, we ate our lunch sitting on a drain, and decided it was the only romantic drain we'd ever known. As we wound back down again, it was always into a sea of dandelion clocks.

We agreed that, in this time when we couldn't avoid some feeling of dread, in respect of ourselves and of each other, it was important to avoid the infliction of suffocation by solicitude. Well, I worried about Kate, and she worried about me, and we had to worry without appearing to do so. You had to be honest about being rattled, and at the same time to avoid giving great demonstrations of that condition.

In another churchyard along the valley we found the grave of a priest who, thought of as a shepherd, was represented in an effigy in which he was stripped to his bones, and had, coiled round his neck and at his feet, sheep stripped to theirs. It was clearly part of that view of death that was celebrated everywhere here, in the wayside Christs: which seemed never quite to have become clichés, nearly every one having some troubling quality of agony, or plain misery. This handsome landscape, now full of people with a habit of pleasantness, that of those whose trade depended on it, was tethered to a notion of the horror of mortality. I supposed this might be why they were disinclined to allow the dead to fade away into neglected graves, or into the sort of pot poor Dennis now occupied. Coming back from his funeral, we'd been struck by a warning attached to his wheelie-bin: NO HOT ASHES. 'Better not put Dennis there,' I said, feeling at once the ignobility of making such a joke, the satisfaction of it, and the notion that, grumpily, Dennis would have enjoyed it.

But, I thought: even to most of those who punctiliously tended the graves of their dead, here, death couldn't seem so atrociously real as it did to anyone over seventy. That really was the dire watershed. It was easy to forget the amplitude of immortality one could be confident of until this late corner was turned.

On the last night I asked Kate how I could have grown so fond of a church. 'It is not because it is a church,' she said, comfortingly. 'It is because everything about it is likeable.' At that moment I observed that the clockface was splendid, and that the golden tips of its hands pointed to 8.05 p.m.

Jacob, one of the sons of the inn, was intense about his wish to be foolproof in English. I paid our bill to him. 'Give my best wishes,' he said, 'to your husband.'

IO

I caught Harry Frost scribbling in a notebook. It was something he'd heard from the other end of the pub, he said. There'd been a question raised about the use of telescopes, and one of the party had turned to another, saying he must know the answer because during the second world war he'd been in the Navy. 'Good God,' said the man. 'I was a stoker. You never used a telescope in the bloody boiler room.'

Harry said this remark had been followed by a strange silence: perhaps because there was something about it that was, grotesquely, devastating. The ex-stoker had seemed to be pointing to some immense possibility of false assumption and assertion that had silenced the whole party. *Of course* you never used telescopes in bloody boiler rooms! If you could make it necessary for someone to point to a truth as plain (if bizarre) as that, what chance had you of ever saying anything that would stand up? Harry said that after a time the man had laughed nervously, as if he'd meant to make his point in a telling fashion but, for God's sake, not in such a telling fashion as that.

I noticed that Harry had given his notebook a title, on a piece of paper gummed to the cover. It was: *!.* 'I've got another I call *!!*,' he said. 'And, I'm afraid, one called *?*.' In most things said by Harry there was a civilised hint of apology, and now he was ready to move on. Well, that was it, I said, not so ready: in your seventies you found your life was divided between amazement and inquiry. Many of my own notes under these headings followed nowadays from sudden memories of myself doing this or that: unbelievably silly this, improbably unsuitable that. At times I was glad of Kate's deafness: she couldn't hear those groans in the night: 'Oh no!' 'Oh God!' It was a matter, sometimes, of an embarrassment fifty years old. At best I'd been unbearably clumsy: at worst, unforgivably inept.

Lately I'd seen a film, much of it in close-up and slow motion, that made evident an astonishing fact that bees may be appalling aviators.

Arriving back at the hive, many collided with the hive itself. The sound, magnified, was that of creatures foolishly crashing into surfaces that, by the exercise of perfectly ordinary competence, they ought to have avoided. Bees collided with bees: and some, dashingly landing, ended up on their backs.

I thought it was hardly likely that bees regarded themselves as the farcically inefficient species this film showed them to be. Approaching the hive, they didn't hesitate, as surely you'd have expected of creatures who for millions of years had failed in what ought to have been a central skill: aware, at this moment of landing, that the odds were they'd end up with their legs in the air. Following from this insouciance of the bees, mightn't it be seen, given some quite small amount of close-up and slow motion, that human beings were blunderers of the same order, and equally unaware of it? At this end of life, I rather hoped that might be so. As an explanation of the sense of my existence I now had as a long sequence of gaffes, it would point a merciful finger at a design fault.

Harry said that trying to find a discreet way out of the Town Hall recently he had come face to face with a door that bore the announcement: THIS DOOR IS ALARMED. So perhaps it wasn't just septuagenarians who were exhibiting high levels of unease.

As he knew, I said, I was soon off with my son Tom on a week's visit to Moscow and St Petersburg. (The prod provided by the operating theatre attendant had been decisive.) Having been engaged in the unhinging business of booking the journey, and obtaining visas, I was alarmed enough, and would be glad of any reassuring observations Harry had to make.

He said he'd like to begin by buying me another pint of beer. I said I clearly shouldn't accept, because from one indulgence and another I was becoming larger than I should be. But then it had struck me lately that, if I had to choose, I would sooner explode than peter out.

Harry returned from the bar with the beer but also with a question. 'I'm sorry,' he said, 'but has it struck you that you might explode *and* peter out?'

Part Two

———

I

'I wish they wouldn't call it the terminal building,' said Tom.

You were allowed, we'd learned from a notice, to bring in only half a litre of spirits. I had a litre of whisky. So Tom would go through the green channel, and I would go through the red. My first encounter with official Russia would be in circumstances in which I had to explain my infringement of a regulation. I prepared for much ado about nothing, Moscow-style.

You passed in front of a snaking desk. The uniformed man behind it had an air of . . . *terminal* boredom. He was vacantly rapt: he didn't look at us, he didn't look at the papers dropped in front of him. A rubber stamp in his hand hovered, and appeared unlikely to do anything else. But then it came down on a document, seemingly unexamined: he shrugged, the owner of the document picked it up and moved away: another document was placed before him, and again it was impossible to believe he was giving it his attention. The rubber stamp hovered, fell: he shrugged. Never had anyone brought such weary indifference to the stamping of forms.

YOU ARE FORBIDDEN, it said over his shoulder, TO OFFER MONEY OR SOUVENIRS TO OFFICIALS OF THE PASSPORT SERVICE.

I wondered what souvenirs a visitor from Britain might be tempted to offer. Where you were being warned against attempts at corruption, souvenirs of whatever kind seemed feeble inducements. Perhaps I had never quite understood what a souvenir might be?

I was not asked why I was in the red channel. The utterly uninterested stamp hovered, fell. Moscow had admitted me.

Then we were in a bus and being driven through a twilight dotted with snow, that hovered like the rubber stamp. 'Here we are in Russia,' said Tom. 'Can you believe it?' Well, it *was* extraordinary to be there, and at a moment when what had been difficult to penetrate seemed to lie helplessly open. Getting through customs so easily had been like finding that some ogre's castle in a fairytale, in its nature intricately and sinisterly defended, could be entered with ease. Of course, it couldn't be like that at all. The hazards and prohibitions must simply have taken other forms.

But here we were.

With Tanya, our guide. She had blonde hair, in fashionable curly strings: and a delicately intelligent face, clearly subject to amusement. She was saying – throwing us at once into the middle of things – that a Metro ticket used to be 15 copecks: then it was 30 copecks: then it was 1 rouble: then it was 3 roubles: and now it was 6 roubles. And they said within two days it would be 10 roubles. The church we were passing was an *active* church. It was held to be lucky if a visitor was welcomed by snow.

The snow hovered and perhaps fell – though I saw small evidence of that – in front of the banal facades of buildings endlessly pale, endlessly square.

Along the wide streets, their surface broken, came what appeared to be the same Lada, again and again, battered, sour cream in colour. Tom had once owned a Lada, and had become the cheerful butt of jokes about these blunt cars that his pupils directed at him. 'Man went in a garage, sir. "Windscreen wiper for a Lada?" "Seems a fair swop," said the garage man.' It was odd, I thought: as it had to be, when what elsewhere is a joke turns out to be the regular sober way of things.

Tanya said that today – the 12th April, 1993 – was the thirty-fourth anniversary of Gagarin's being launched into space. And *there* was the Space Monument, celebrating the event. In the snow-dotted darkness, it was an immense titanium fly-whisk – in fact a rocket's smoke-trail, the rocket itself on the very tip of it. And here, opposite, was the Cosmos, built for the Olympic Games, and offering –

[78]

I forget how many beds. About three thousand. A curved cliff of a hotel, in which Tom and I had a room along a very high curving corridor.

2

After dinner we walked out of the hotel and stepped into Moscow.

The main dish at dinner had been, as it was almost invariably to be, a small cut of meat, difficult to identify or chew, accompanied by tiny, hectically coloured chips. To drink there were bottles of Pepsi, and rival bottles of local mineral water: the rivalry expressed by faint variations of a dingy label: such difference as there was between them being the difference between one quite loathsome chemical smell and another. Tanya had sat briefly with the twenty of us who formed this week's party. We were to think of ourselves as the Gruppa Anglia. If we were lost, we should say: 'I am of the party of the Anglias.' I asked if she was more, or less, hopeful about what was happening in Russia. She was, she said, a happy pessimist.

Now we walked from the curving Cosmos in the direction of a Metro station which, over there on the further side of a buzzing road, presented itself as, in every sense, a hub. It was round. It was surrounded by busy behaviour.

To get to it, we had to step into an underpass. In the experience of both of us, underpasses were blanks, full of dull echoes: at most, in these recent disgraced years at home, the setting for a murmuring beggar or two. This underpass was a theatre. It rang with sound. Dominant was an accordionist who made me think Petrushka might appear at any moment. There was in the air the saddest thrilling sensation of breathless dancing. One . . . we walked on . . . two . . . we walked on . . . three long tables clogged with books. It was as if Waterstone's had taken to tunnels. A majestically blind man, erect most nobly against a wall, extended a palm. A man, improbably dressed – but a stranger's eye could not account for this feeling of improbability – seemed to be offering an entire drama, the Bolshoi on a table. An old woman crouched and read, in a resonant *sotto voce*, what Tom guessed was a religious text. Her being there suggested that she desired an audience, yet there was every sign that she was indifferent to us. In her neighbourhood the underpass became an intensely private, yet intensely public, place of worship. And here was a silent man who was legless. He had artificial legs, that is: and to make the point he had rolled up his trousers to expose the most clumsy prostheses imaginable, a matter of crude metal struts, wires, some sort of pink plastic. The accordionist, having made it seem odd that we weren't dancing, played a passage designed, quite simply, to break the heart. We stepped out of the underpass on the other side.

The Metro station was richly local, as the characterless crescent of a hotel across the road was not. In front of it, a long line, mostly of women, and most of them old, making a passive offer in their hands, in open suitcases, on little tables, of . . . It was a packet of cigarettes, a bottle of Pepsi, a dress, a belt, some unidentifiable small personal possession. They looked as if they'd been there for ever: there was a droop to their bodies that had an appalling patience about it. To left and right of them, flowersellers. The entrance to the Metro drew people in, and darkly breathed them out into air through which the snow continued to fall, meagrely, idly.

And we felt deeply lost and bemused.

What could you hope to learn from walking about for an hour or so in some quarter of Moscow, soon after arrival on a first visit? The fact is that I carried away from that evening a vision as intense as if we'd walked from one end of Russia to the other.

A wideness of roads, somehow alien. I'd known wide roads, but here, pitted, profoundly muddy, were roads that seemed wide beyond reason. Crossing one you found yourself in the dangerous-seeming midst of what was not so much a road as a dark mysterious space. The roads ran round small parks. Among the trees, little shabby lawns of snow.

Over all there was a kind of grand decrepitude that left you wondering what the grandeur had been that had become so blighted.

There seemed to have been a general intention that things should be huge: hugeness was everything. No building had so much as a hint of the modest about it. But it was all banal, with nothing for the eye to seize upon: size for its own stunningly dull sake. There was an almost complete absence of colour, beyond what seemed a universal sallow cream.

And in the midst of these exaggerations – roads that aspired to be avenues in a city for giants, buildings that invited you to be daunted by their sheer featureless rectangular expanse – there were monumentalities that seemed quite crazily stupendous.

Uneasily we crossed a road in the lee of an enormous heroic worker with his enormous companion, their breasts (heaven knows how many feet above street level) swelling, their hands made into fists the size of small cars, their hair flowing, their eyes emptily gleaming. It was extraordinary to be walking in a city that had given birth to such bloated representations of what it is to be human, at a moment when the system that made mad sense of them had collapsed, and the vulnerable smallness of human beings had become the more apparent for having such a setting.

The ironies were obvious and awful. So obvious and awful that you wanted *not* to be ironical. Any easy sense of superiority on the part of a visitor to this scene would surely be unforgivable. A melancholy awe – even that might be presumptuous.

Well, here was a great triumphal arch, left in the lurch by the deflation of all triumph: it was topped with effigies of farmworkers, manically jubilant, he brandishing above his head a sheaf of corn of somehow ludicrous size. As an old farmworker I shrank from that madly exorbitant sheaf. Once you launched upon fake enthusiasm there was clearly no end to the exaggerations you were committed to. And here was a bus station. It was built for Brobdingnag, and now in the shabby darkness a few morose Lilliputians waited for buses.

Tom and I felt spectacularly small.

Beyond the window of our hotel room, sudden explosions, tremendous flarings. Oh, said Tom, they'd turned hostile again. But then the flarings became multi-coloured, spilled into gushes of golden fire. They were fireworks – not many of them, but a brave show for five minutes or so – in celebration of the first Sputnik, that extension of Soviet hugeness into the hugeness of space.

We'd bathed in vaguely warm and yellowy water when there was a knock at the door. The Thompson brothers had come to invite us to join them in some bar on the ground floor. They were members of our party, Sam and Alec, both students, neither having been abroad before, and amazed by almost everything. I was amazed by their amazement – not, I suppose, believing that, in a generation so sophisticatedly got at, being young could any longer mean being fresh and startled.

Over dinner, asked by Sam Thompson if I did this or that – danced, or played a sport – I said I'd given all that up in 1813. He laughed, before drawing his head back searchingly, plainly checking on the idea that I might have made a joke. It was part of Sam's readiness to be astonished: I came to notice, sympathetically, that from my jokes he backed a little, like a batsman giving himself room to deal with a dubious ball. It was partly, I suspected, because being white-haired I should have been graver. I was a living googly.

I thought as I lay in bed that our walk among those huge avenues with their broken surfaces and those seemingly meaningless open spaces had been a walk in the country of my customary dreams, the landscape for which had always been assembled by the designers who'd constructed modern Moscow. And then, asleep, I found myself where roadways were in the process of being made from immense rolls of muddy cloth, laid (of course) over ragged and bottomless ravines. If my dreams suggested anything at all, it was, pretty monotonously, that seventy-three years had not been enough for me to muster confidence in the earth's crust.

3

Tom and I were out early, standing by the space monument, watching people going to work. Only that didn't seem to describe it. Stretching away from the base of the monument was a great unfenced park, criss-crossed with paths: a bare brownness with snow laid fitfully on it: and along the paths, from all directions, people came, most of them strikingly alone. I didn't think of the people of Moscow as being any more ant-like than any other city-dwellers: yet there was this curious effect, strengthened by so many of them walking singly, as of ants, streaming. The scene was a large flat geometry with this unceasing flow of people marking out the lines of it. I didn't know anywhere in London where I could see people streaming in this fashion, at the same hour, across such flatness.

Tom laughed. He felt the same: but thought we were probably engaged in an ancient useless activity. We were trying to point to what made a scene, totally fresh to us, appear foreign. And we were feeding into it that sense of foreignness we had from the long history of East and West, of the worlds coldly at war with each other. We might be disorientated by the astonishment of being admitted to this other world. Tom said he had a friend who'd come from Northern Ireland to Manchester, and at the end of his first day there said he'd never known anything so foreign and difficult to make out.

It was the beginning of the attempt Tom and I felt we had to make not to exclaim, 'How Russian!' But as we made our way to the coach that was taking us to Red Square, we passed a band of musicians. Elaborately wrapped, so that they were not unlike the drawings of bands accompanying carol-singers in our Christmas comics, all scarves and mittens, they were playing a dance tune. Everywhere in Moscow, amid all that rapt trudging and bustling, these invitations to the dance!

On an easel in front of the band, a tin at its base, was an appeal: IF YOU PASS US BY, WHO WILL STOP?

Damn it, that had a quite foreign eloquence about it – a wistful wit! And was possibly very Russian . . .

Since the word 'red' in Russian also means 'beautiful', and Red Square is amazingly beautiful, the square would be perfectly named if only it were a square. It is not. But it won't do to replace the word with another in any sort of hurry. It is a spot you stunningly arrive in: being

[83]

astonished, in our case (on this morning of a winter refusing to give way to spring) by the discovery that the great cobbled surface narrows as it passes St Basil's Cathedral, and then tumbles down to the street below. All those brutally large carriers burdened with missiles aimed at the sky were bound, after they'd had their moment in the square, for something of a martial squeeze, as they made their way out of it.

You think that, inevitably, trying to match this space with the setting in all those newsreels: but the fact is that when taking your first steps into the square you feel a positive need not to come to any brisk conclusion about it. Of course, its being best-known to the outside world as a place crammed, it is startling when seen for what it is most of the time, a space almost empty. Over there in the great silver distance is the queue of people waiting to visit Lenin's tomb: and there are policemen: and there are common Muscovites going about their common errands. But this leaves a simple hugeness of square unoccupied. It's a silver-grey ocean in the midst of the city. And this idea of its being water isn't whimsical: the cobbles suggest a rippling movement, a liveliness as of small waves. There's this astonishingly active floor that is a sort of mirror to the sky: and there is the sky, a huge partner to the square. First impression, in so far as you can sort out the impressions as they come: of two great squares, the cobbled one and the sky. You're standing in an immense container of silver air.

But then, if this is the way you have come in, you are compelled to take note of St Basil's. To an unaccustomed eye this is an outrageous alliance of the nearly august and the absolutely and exhilaratingly absurd. Out of a red-brick body that's subject to every kind of deviation from the four-square (though it *is* essentially four-square) grow tremendous pots of unequal height, all having applied to them at this or that point clusters of eyebrow-like arcadings, and all ending in what Tanya called queue-pearlers. These pots and cupolas form a family, with little ones squeezed in between larger ones: and the cupolas themselves are coloured follies: here rippling bands of red and white, here flowing segments of white and green, here with the bands running angularly over the shoulders of an onion, red and green perhaps, pimpled as if the cupola were a lunatic version of a pineapple. There is no way of guessing at the number of varieties of geometrical figures of which the cathedral is composed. Its very point seems to be that it cannot be accounted for by architectural analysis. It's a great bunch of shapes standing at the furthest limit of the square. It is the hugest and most turbulent of cruets. You are torn between the desire simply on the one hand to stare into the square, not absolutely believing that there can be such a great silver-greyness of space, and on the other to stare up at St Basil's, thinking that those cupolas are out of fairytales, and are also bizarre sweets: are, upon a building that is stern up to its shoulders, great childishnesses. They are – it is – wonderful: and wholly and thrillingly beyond ordinary understanding.

But you've only begun. The second amazement is the Kremlin wall. It is of red brick, crenellated, and was completed three years after Columbus blundered upon the Americas. And the long strong redness of it takes your breath, when you look to it from the silver cobbles, and then away again from that perdurable brick.

And here your capacity to tick off the marvels in some sort of order disappears. You are aware of the great Spassky Gate, through which you'd seen those black Zils come and go in film, not understanding how black they must have seemed on the spot, where every colour is intense. And, rising above the Kremlin walls, other yellow ochre walls that you'd never known of, the walls as it turned out of some of the bedlam of palaces the Kremlin contained: and various flashes of gold. As a child I'd had a fort, standing on its own wooden hill: and the hill had a door underneath which you could open by way of a hook: and there, the most sensible secondary use of a fort ever, was storage room for the mixed tin armies I had, scarlet hussars from one sort of war and khaki soldiers from my father's war, and cowboys and Indians and farmers and milkmaids and railway porters whom I'd ruthlessly called to the colours. Standing in Red Square, I was aware of being in the unexpectedly, monstrously beautiful shadow of the apotheosis of all forts.

Unexpectedness. Well, there was Lenin's tomb. I'd thought this must be simply pompous. It turned out to be stunningly handsome. It's of dark red granite, the noblest red in this great patch of Moscow dedicated to redness. (I'd spent much of my youth thinking the Red Flag pointed to the future, and I now saw that it as arguably pointed

[85]

to the past.) The whole low structure (it looks low in relation to the great height of the Kremlin walls) has a mourning band of labradorite – a rich and velvety black. Lenin's name over the entrance is of inlaid porphyry. Of porphyry I'd never made much, having been struck during my childhood reading by the notion that it was, not entirely interestingly, a feature of the environment of the rich. Almost anything in a rich man's home, I thought when I was ten or so – and later – might be made of porphyry. Ormolu and lapis lazuli lagged some way behind. In the case of Lenin's tomb, the porphyry is the most glorious turquoise in colour, having a sheen suggesting at once stone and silk.

And the sentries come straight from that storage space in my own fort, c1927. It took them precisely and invariably two minutes forty-five seconds to make their way, the keys by which they were wound up almost visible, from their barracks to the door of the tomb.

Tanya, her crumpled curls blowing across her smile, said it was widely thought that Lenin wouldn't stay in his tomb much longer. 'They will give him a decent Christian burial,' she said.

It was one of the things uttered or seen during these days that had the quality of a sort of brusque surrealism. Who could ever have dreamed that a supreme atheist would be threatened with such indignity, couched in terms suggesting that amends were being made? And what an audience for such a remark – a slovenly crew of insignificant capitalists! So, at any rate, Tanya must have thought of us. One of the oddities of this experience was that couriers in command of groups of tourists were *spilling the beans* to awful outsiders: but that what was said wasn't, with Tanya certainly, addressed to us. It was a kind of furious self-communing. So she spoke of the supposed reform of the KGB. 'But they are the same people,' she cried. 'It has to change – it cannot remain but still – ' She lowered the microphone that in such a setting of courier and tourists was associated with blander sorts of commentary. Lifting it again, 'They switch on some information and tell us what to do,' she said. 'It is horrible.' The true audience for this was not a random group in a tourist bus. We were intruders upon a deeply agitated Russian soliloquy.

And over there, on the side of Red Square opposite to the Kremlin walls, another (to me) unexpectedness. This was the GUM department

store. It was a tremendously long Selfridges, crossed with Harrods: a
pre-revolutionary set of shopping arcades. About the time it was built,
my father (he and his brothers early slaves of the department store)
was engaged in his first paid occupation, polishing the brass outside
Waring & Gillows. Until this visit to Moscow, I had no idea that one
shore of that great sea of a square (in one direction a quarter of a mile
long) consisted of a shop. Standing on their rostrum above the tomb,
the massive-faced masters of the Soviet Union had looked across at
mere trade.

And then, breathlessly, to the Lenin Hills, having unsatisfactory
glimpses of things on the way. We found we were being whisked, for
example, past Pushkin and Tolstoy: and of Gogol had time only to
take in the fact that he was twenty-one feet high and that his head was
out of sight. I thought Gogol might have liked that, and have written
a story called 'The Head', about a man who, waking one morning to
find he didn't exist above his shoulders, set out on a hunt for the
missing part of himself, which he was confident had been taken while
he slept by his neighbour, a second-class official known throughout
Moscow for his dislike of his own ears.

And Tolstoy glowered in what might have been the largest stone
armchair in the world. His petrified fury seemed fitting for what he
must have felt, powerless to intervene as our century followed with
dreadful logic from his.

I'd thought of the Lenin Hills as hills of a positive sort, on the top
of each of which, perhaps, Lenin would have orated. Instead there was
this general, not particularly noticeable rise above the city, until you
were on a sort of extremely large terrace, with Moscow disarmingly in
evidence on both sides. I'd never before seen a city that offered, where
you might expect some towering cathedral, a straightforward set of
industrial chimneys. It was cold up here, and the light was bleakly
strong: and along the balustrade of this aerial terrace were trestle table
after trestle table, set up with babushkas, painted eggs and items of Red
Army uniform. You could be photographed shaking hands with a
lifesize cut-out Gorbachev or Yeltsin. And to the ranks of matrioshkas
(ranks if you set them out in a line, but there must be some other word
for what happened to them when these dolls were fitted one after

another into the largest of them) were added Gorbachevs, with grossly birthmarked brow, and Yeltsins, bursting with what was most alarming about him, now one stood in his exploding Moscow: his self-belief.

4

At breakfast a curiously sad man circulating among us, who might have been handing out random death warrants, had turned out to be offering tickets for that night's ballet at the Bolshoi. So that's where our day, Tom's and mine, would end. As to the afternoon, we longed simply to be adrift in Moscow. We'd need, as we worked it out, to reach a station on the Metro called Turgenevska. Named, we noted, after a writer. We tried to think of any London tube station that looked for its name to literature. But the London underground clung to geography. It meant you knew where you were, but ... How nice to be bound for St Paul's and to get out at John Donne.

Tom bought the tokens. I was experiencing what I found to be a late pleasure of fatherhood: that of being, in brisk everyday matters, one's child's child. It would have taken me three times as long to make out what had to be done. What you didn't realise when you were young was that you had the gift of quick adaptability. You moved fast – were, in a general way, lithe and rapid of thought, and so forth. So there we were with our tokens; and we inserted them into the barrier and were admitted, and became part of a swarm moving towards three tunnel openings. The crowded Cyrillics on the brow of each seemed to offer anything but Turgenevska. I spotted a uniformed woman by the turnstiles we'd entered by and hurried across to her. I indicated the three tunnels. I indicated bemusement. 'Turgenevska?' I asked.

And she took me by the hand and led me through the swarm to where Tom stood. She pointed to the middle tunnel. 'Turgenevska,' she said: and turned and went back to the turnstiles. I turned, too, wanting gratefully to wave if she was also turning. And she *was* turning, and took the initiative: blowing me a kiss, with a fine flourish of the hand that wafted it to me.

I thought: 'I must not be absurd: I must not think "How Russian!"'

But then I thought: 'I can however think that such a thing never happened to me in Leicester Square tube station.'

These escalators descend for ever. We felt the strangeness of people who'd come from a world of shallow escalators to a world where they flow steeply on and on, downwards (not one to be seen that was defective, unlike London where little else is offered). And this is where Tom and I failed utterly in our resolve not to find Russia simply Russian. Face after face came up towards us, wonderfully, incontrovertibly out of Tolstoy and Gorki and Gogol and Chekhov and Dostoevsky. There was no point in attempting to be sophisticated about this – that's what they were. And *here* was a woman with . . . oh, such a face, half-angel: and another with hair that was golden as the halo on an icon is golden: and several with splendid hats, trilby-shaped, burgundy red or jet black. The escalator flowed downwards, the faces flowed upwards: and as Tom and I stepped off among the chandeliers and mosaics below, we had one wish only: to go back up the escalator, amazed by the faces coming down, and then to come down, amazed by the faces coming up.

An hour later we were experiencing what was the more tormenting for being a simple need, of a kind you expected any city to offer to satisfy every few yards. We wanted to sit – on a chair, a bench: as the torment went on, we began to hallucinate about kinds of seating – and drink. A cup of tea, anything. It was nowhere possible. In a shop, if it was a shop, in a street full of the illusion of places of refreshment that turned out to be something else – though we weren't always sure what the something else was – we saw apparent rolls being queued for, and apparent paper mugs being filled: but when we stepped inside, the procedure of obtaining anything at all was so inscrutable, and the smell so odd, so generally rancid, that we left, hurriedly. Then we were in Red Square, with which, after less than a day, we felt ridiculously familiar, and were in the GUM department store. Not that that's what it really is any more. In this, as it seemed, Edwardian folly – all the arcades in Piccadilly packed under a single glass roof – unGUM-like names appeared: Estee Lauder, Benetton. Here, drifting under overhanging baskets of flowers, were clearly the Russians who were doing well out of collapse. This was part of the Russian world in which the only currency was dollars. We'd looked into GUM's bitter mirror image – the department store called NUM – where the only currency was roubles. Such a scarcity of everything: what was there, so drab: and a space crammed with women, the shelves behind the counter displaying a thin scatter of cosmetics. Another space offered about thirty identical basic women's hats, all blue.

In this offensively other world of GUM, we paced more and more feverishly down arcade after arcade, and more and more feverishly registered the fact that nowhere was there a place in which people were able simply to sit and simply to drink. But Tom had dredged out of our official visit to Red Square the memory of a notice: it had said SMIRNOFF BAR. He was certain that is what it had said. He was certain it was in GUM, and nowhere else.

But there was no Smirnoff Bar, anywhere.

With further dredging Tom concluded that he'd caught sight of the sign not whilst inside the building but whilst outside it. By now crazed with the desire to sit down, to perform some quite elementary act of drinking, we left the store and walked along the line of windows that faced Red Square. Nothing. From St Basil's to the end. Nothing. From the end back to St Basil's. Nothing. And then, at the third trawl, Tom cried out with weary excitement. There, in the depths of a window, tiny but distinct, was a notice. SMIRNOFF BAR, it cruelly hinted.

We noted where it was, in relation to the entire length of the building, hurried back inside, paced down the arcade that provided the windows onto the Square, and found nothing. Tom said perhaps it wasn't a whole bar occupying a whole shop-space. Perhaps it was to be found by passing through a shop into whatever was beyond. We went outside again. We made the same computation. We came inside and at the right moment (as we judged with an instinct that had become crazily sensitive) dived into a shop devoted to the sale of cosmetics (all the shelves here sparklingly and fragrantly crammed) and passed through a curtain.

And we were in the Smirnoff Bar.

There were three flimsily elegant tables, with chairs in the same style. There was a parody of a 1920ish bar. There were tiny cups of coffee.

We sat, and drank, guilty and grateful. We drank one terribly expensive coffee each, and then another terribly expensive coffee each. We sat on the edge of the grim square where the rockets and nuclear warheads had rolled on their carriers and the terrible squat rulers had stood on their red rostrum, and we spent dollars on coffee and on the privilege of sitting quietly and at leisure in the midst of a city strained, footsore, hungry, thirsty.

5

We had now that sort of grasp of this part of Moscow that is a feature of the madness that seizes any newcomer to a city. Well, of course, the most seasoned of Muscovites, you came out of Red Square by this relatively narrow street, and were at once at the Lenin Museum (not unlike St Pancras railway station, you vaguely thought: outside it the workless, the crippled, the demented, seemed to gather): and there you were on the edge of the great square with all the theatres in it. including the Bolshoi.

Suddenly a thin woman, with three small haggard children . . . Tom, weary of passing by, felt in his pocket for roubles, and gave them to her. At once one of the children, a girl, flew at his arm and clung to it, uttering the most awful cry, an unbroken weeping scream. There was a gabble of words somewhere in it, but it didn't seem like ordinary begging, that might be appeased: there was something about it that took it out of reach of any possibility of satisfaction. We walked on, she fiercely hanging on to Tom's arm, shrieking this dreadful shriek that was as if all the desperate pleas in the world had become jammed

at their shrillest pitch, impossible to turn off. It was a long way round
Theatre Square, the walk to the Bolshoi. We'd become dumb, walking
stiffly as if we did not have this shocking attachment. Then suddenly,
after perhaps ten minutes, she vanished.

Until the next morning we were unable even to speak of it.

We'd decided not to go back to the Cosmos for dinner – for one of
those pocket-diary-sized fragments of nameless meat, and those apoplectic chips. Now that we'd sat down and drunk our tiny fierce
coffees we felt on surprisingly good terms with our stomachs. It was
to be, we saw, a ballet based on a story by Chekhov. We sat in the
little park behind which rise the columns that support the facade of
the Bolshoi: and looked across at the massive mask of Karl Marx in
another little park opposite. Over the road, at a corner, was the
extraordinarily handsome former hotel, slender-columned, silver and
white, where one of the first parliaments after the ousting of the tsar
had assembled. It really was astonishing – in a single day to have seen
Red Square, looked down on Moscow, observed every character in
Russian fiction coming up towards us on escalators, passionately
stalked and captured the most elusive coffee bar in the world: with,
still to come, the Bolshoi.

We toiled up so many staircases we lost all sense of where we were,
showing our tickets at every bend and always being shrugged upwards:
and at last, having been not too unkindly commanded to leave our
coats at a counter, stepped through doors and found ourselves looking
down a precipice of red and gold. We had altogether the relation to
the stage that a fly on the ceiling of a very high room would have to
the fireplace. The theatre hummed, chattered, stared through opera
glasses, nudged its neighbours. It was like any other great theatre in
the world: but it was the Bolshoi . . .

This was the story Chekhov called 'An Anna on the Neck', about a
young woman whose father drinks away his family's hopes of happiness, and who vows to avenge herself on men. She marries, and sets
out to deceive a foolish, unattractive, sycophantic official. He longs
for a medal: she gets it for him by sleeping with his superior. It was
tender, and cruel, and had a dance for clerks that made dancers out of
their desks: with a wonderfully comic exhilaration for moments when

the chief clerk was absent, and a delicious cancellation of it when he returned. There was a *pas de deux* for lovers that was most gently elegiac. And there was a scene where the husband knew that, behind that grand door, his wife was being ferociously enjoyed by his master, but must (for the sake of his medal) feign intense satisfaction, and grotesquely indicate that he knew exactly the themes about which, over cups of tea, they were conversing. It seemed such good luck, on this first visit to the Bolshoi, to have encountered a ballet so . . .

So Russian, damn it.

There was a young woman next to me, between me and the stage, who elected to rest an elbow on the rail and nurse her chin with her hand, offering me a fidgeting triangle through which, by fidgetings of my own, I could keep an eye on the main action. I longed to ask her not to do this, but saw that my attempts to whisper my wish would be limited by my lack of Russian. Even if you were learning the language, what a teaser it might be to say: 'Please could you remove your elbow from the rail because, owing to the angle and our proximity, it is possible for me to have only an intermittent view of things.' If I tried to convey my message by pantomime, I might be seriously misunderstood. And simply removing her arm from the rail might be worse.

Outside the theatre we found the Thompson brothers. They had taken the opportunity offered by the combined efforts of Chekhov, the composer Gavrilov and the Bolshoi dancers to make the acquaintance not only of (as it seemed to me) a very large number of young Russian women, but also a substantial group from an English girls' school. I had forgotten that some have this impetuous skill of mass flirtation.

Back at the Cosmos, Tom and I did not so much fall asleep as find ourselves hurled into it. Tomorrow we were booked for what Tanya insisted on calling the Crumlin.

6

WE ARE FOR YOU – AND YOU? inquired the placard propped up in front of the little brass band as we left the hotel in a new drift of snow.

The Crumlin and two cathedrals, Tanya had promised. But first, as we walked through the Kremlin walls: those who wished would visit the Armoury. This was a museum of Tsarist history: court dress, coronation robes, state coaches . . . icon frames. Tanya spoke repeatedly of icon frames, as if in them lay the Armoury's chief and irresistible attraction.

'Oh, let's skip that,' said Tom. 'I see enough icon frames at home.'

I thought I had some curiosity about the awful splendours of the Russian throne, but found it easy to agree with Tom's impatience with them. Let us, while the others were gazing at Fabergé eggs, breathe in the Moscow air, wander a little in the Kremlin: *be there*.

'Strange world where you can't get into the Kremlin except with dollars,' said someone as they queued at the entrance to the Armoury. Tom and I, with the Thompson brothers, who were here on a pair of shoestrings at best and had been seriously troubled by the stress on icon frames, strolled gently uphill towards the heart of the Kremlin.

It was sharply cold. We made our slow, fairly bemused way along the fine pale wall of the Armoury. The pavement ran alongside a road, climbing up from the Borovitsky Tower. (Such bristling names! A wire-haired language!) On the other side of the road was the Kremlin wall. It seemed extraordinary, to be here in such a banal role, as unsupervised sightseers: there was a feeling as if it were the Tower of London on some deeply wintry morning during a tourists' strike, given that the Tower was still (as Tanya said of Moscow's reopened churches) active.

And here was one of those long black cars that in newsreels we'd seen entering by the Spassky Gate: in August 1991, leaving by it as the conspirators went in search of hiding places that didn't exist.

Queerly awful cars, slug-like: part of their awfulness lying in the impression they gave of being empty. Something sinister about cars or carriages that offered no sight of their occupants. Behind the Zil came a lesser car, and behind that an Army jeep.

And so we came to Cathedral Square: to the two cathedrals that Tanya had promised and several more besides. And in the air, all round us, groves of golden onions, Tanya's queue-pearlers. The air had been taken over by a golden mob. They were beautiful, extravagant, playfully varied, grave, not at all credible to an eye unaccustomed to the free display of gold. And they rose above buildings that were the most splendid religious hangars imaginable: with enormous verve making it clear that they enclosed immense holy inner spaces. There were painted doorways that forty feet above the ground had puckered golden eyebrows. Tucked away there were classical pavilions that would have been at home in a street in Florence, and little churches or sub-churches (just as St Basil's was nine churches in one, so there seemed no way of being certain that any apparent church here wasn't a dozen) that were packets of cylinders: they might be white, they might have eyeshades profoundly green. There were everywhere eyes, tall, narrow, short incisions in a soaring white wall: and everywhere whatever acted as a shade to eyes. The square looked out, looked in, was secret, stared, retreated, blankly peered behind golden blindfolds, and was, in the marvellous air of that marvellous morning, abrim with the golden onions that one couldn't stop looking at, in some kind of dazed appreciation that perhaps resolved itself into a foolish desire .... to count them. I found myself mesmerised by a particular group that stood together in a family huddle, topped with crosses that seemed to have the ambition to become golden spider's webs. I was stunned by the thought that this (to us) indecipherable notation of extravagant symbols should have survived and be present in 1993 as part of the backdrop to events that . . .

I was ready to think that these events of our time would have baffled the creators of Cathedral Square. But then it struck me that the madly wonderful language spoken by those cathedrals, those goldennesses, must have been the product of imaginations easily able to understand the nightmares of any age. Tyrants had gone in and out, plotters and oppressors in this or that form of the Zil, and the astonishing golden statements had remained: pretending (I thought) to be particular statements about a precise doctrinal view of things, but in fact, as they matched fantasy with weird elegance, making a durable comment on our madness.

I couldn't help thinking the square was some form of quite extraordinarily beautiful, perpetually applicable joke.

And from it we walked to the biggest cannon in the world, which was close to the biggest bell in the world, which was also the biggest broken bell in the world. I wondered that they'd not thought of driving the cannon through Red Square in those cavalcades of the cannon of our time, the sky-threatening rockets. This cannon (of 1586) declared its business by way of what might be the most ill-disposed and evil lion's head ever: its heavily puckered forehead suggesting the prodigious pain of having so much rage to express, its nostrils smaller cannon: its mouth, hugely agape, filled with curved spikes of teeth. The bell broke when it was in a fire: someone who didn't know what happened when you poured cold water on hot metal, poured cold water on it. For being so monumental, the great broken fragment and the hole it came from are wonders. In bas relief on the bell is the tsar of the time: you go close and see, from this immense curve, the very small foolishness of his nose, standing clear.

Trotsky said that all the barbarism of Moscow glared at him from the hole in that bell and the mouth of that cannon.

And now, in a corner, we noticed a shop offering arts and crafts: and knowing it would be a grand form of the familiar souvenir shop, went in. It appeared to be managed by Mikhail Gorbachev: the likeness was so great I thought we'd missed an item of news, this ultimate reduction of a president.

Here were superior matrioshkas, laid out in a superior fashion together with superior painted eggs and the rest. It was a sort of Fortnum and Mason of babushkeries. And there were two young women, most elegant, whose legs, my younger friends said later, were bewitching. I did not know this because I was preoccupied with a guilt I've always easily felt in some form or other in any shop: in this case, arising from the pursuit one of the young women made of us, edging with us round the display, a calculator at the ready, a pleasant finger hovering over the face of it. I felt it would have been uncivil to bring that elegant shadowing to naught: and, in a panic, purchased a ceramic lady, in the brightest colours, holding a pet dog in her arms. 'Of course, I shall never get it home,' I cried, hoping (I guess) that the young woman would gently bring her ominous calculations to an end, murmuring, 'Then of course we should not dream of holding you to your purchase.' I would have sworn I was the sort of person who would never, under the most agonising duress, buy a ceramic figure of a bonneted woman carrying a lapdog.

And now, when we got back to the Armoury, the rest of the party were out, ready with others to fill Cathedral Square (we were glad to have been there when it was empty), and, with Tanya, to enter the two cathedrals. And yes, that promise of astonishing immensities of inner space was held to! In the Cathedral of the Dormition it was a space full of fat columns: and on the towering walls, and every column, were painted scenes, figures, in colours that seemed to detach themselves and make the air itself coloured: where light fell there were spreads of peach and chalky red and blue. It was like standing in the midst of some hugely expanded children's book. I've never known a space to be so illustrated. Here, Napoleon's cavalry had stabled their horses. What a scene they must have made! The horses shifting and stamping, the floor deep in dung and straw, and everywhere you looked those glowing illustrations. The deliberate affront curiously adding to the magic of what was affronted! (Those illustrations were still able to glow because they were not detachable: Napoleon's soldiers burnt the icons as firewood.) As we left and I turned for a last look I realised that more than anything I'd been reminded of the transfers that when I was a boy we stuck on the backs of our hands, along our arms, on our knees. This was a great church that had had stuck over every square inch of it the biggest transfers ever.

When we went in the direction of the cannon and the bell, now as a party, I was puzzled by the occasional sharp sound of whistles: there was a note of warning about them. It was Tom, and the Thompsons, who pointed out that they came whenever I stepped into the roadway. You weren't allowed there. It was to be kept clear for Zils. And I thought how that was another measure of the gulf between old and young – the quickness with which they'd picked up this connection between the whistle and my stepping into the road. It was the young who noticed such things, having an alertness for local tricks and oddities.

I'd fallen into a sort of swooning sleep, all hope gone of making other use of the afternoon; and woke abruptly with a sensation as of someone who was where he shouldn't be in the presence of another person who ought also to have been elsewhere. I hung for a moment between the real and the surreal: then the moment of panic passed, and I was staring up at a very large, not quite convincingly apologetic woman, who was carrying a spanner.

'*Do not worry*,' she cried, '*I am electricity*.'

She had come to see to a faulty light switch.

I sank helplessly back into thick dark sleep. Tanya's description of tomorrow's expedition had involved a tempest of her most misleading vowels, and I had no idea where we were going. It was, I thought, beyond where they put the river Moskva in a tube, and was tangled with someone who had committed a suicide, as if it had been one of a sequence. I had become terribly aware that, at an age when a gaoler regularly appeared to make sure that sentences of sleep were served, giving a mere week to Moscow and St Petersburg was asking for it, rather.

7

Yeltsin suddenly appeared on the screen as Tom flicked from channel to channel on the TV in our hotel bedroom. He was talking to a young audience, and it was oddly plain that he was milking their appreciation – you saw, with listeners to whom political cajolery was new, how it was done, the pleasure on his face as his wiles, easily, worked. If a major mystery of 1993 was how anyone at all could maintain himself as master of the Russian scene, these few seconds of film offered a clue. He charmed, he teased, he was one of them who at the same time was dramatically not one of them, he was an uncle whose smile and frown were never out of sight of each other, he made his whole face fascinating – and then, a giveaway moment of detachment, he smirked with private satisfaction.

Tom knew where we were going. It was to Kolomenskoye, on one of Moscow's edges, once the tsar's summer retreat, where he and his family could get away from the clamorous Kremlin. We'd go there by bus, and once there Tanya would announce: 'We'll walk a bit on the ground.' Saying this, she'd make a worried confusion of her hair: which I thought had been carefully made into a fashionable confusion in the first place. She was always worried, though I guess it was the universal anxiety of the Muscovite at that moment: and her alarms would leak into her commentary on the passing scene, the historical background. So she'd suddenly mention that generals were buying whole dachas for 20,000 roubles – about £20. They called it privatising, she said: and I wondered what the Russian was for this late twentieth-century term for acts of theft. Or she'd throw in the fact that ten per cent of the inhabitants of Moscow lived in communal flats, and her belief that it would be their fate to die in such flats. She'd shrug.

At Kolomenskoye they'd restored the double-barrelled roofs on the entry gates – these being like upturned boats that had brewers' tubs sprouting from their sides – so that you were able to think you had some sense of how it might have been to enter this estate, any time from the early fourteenth century onwards, having left Moscow behind, and relieved in a holiday fashion to be in this enclosed, guarded world of farms and falconry. It was strange, what was left, a ghost of a place: though converted substantially enough since the 1930s into a museum of wooden architecture and folk craft. There was a wintry park as a sort of enormous pale front garden: the trees were slender, and if you wandered into them a little way you could look across and see in the air, through the fans of bare branches that the trees made, a crop of delicately blue onions. painted with golden stars and tipped with tall golden crosses. This was the Church of Our

Lady of Kazan: to strangers' eyes, another geometrical oddity of a church, being a powerful square carried on the shoulders of an arcade: with a narrower rectangle, from which those blue domes grew, mounted on the square. The roof was green. Under the Soviet regime this had remained an active church. Tanya led us up the broad stone staircase that took you inside – that again seeming odd, as if here was a church constructed largely out of features you'd expect in a secular building, perhaps a country house. The staircase was lined with beggars, a desperate guard of honour. To Tom and me, the church seemed more active than made it quite proper to be there, and we retreated; behind the beggars, as we stepped into the church, being open coffins, and weeping mourners.

If our puzzlement about the forms of which the church was constructed amounted to a question, we were almost at once in the museum, which had the answer. This was a museum that was quite remarkably enjoyable. One room was almost entirely devoted to ceramic lions, the work of artists who'd never seen a lion in their lives. You were impressed by the thought that the long processes of nature had got the lion marvellously right, but that, even given the perfectly adequate recipe these ceramicists had worked on – teeth, mane, claws, tail, snarl – it was easy to get it grotesquely wrong. There were tiled stoves, which must have made it appear that the interiors they stood in had found room for small orchards, miniature groves full of gorgeously implausible flowers, or indoor lakes complete with lilies. There were carved wooden overmantels from which painted mermaids, wonderfully plain of face, grinned down. There was a wedding sled for bride and groom: and a ceramic tile for which my second son, Tom's brother, Dan, had somehow posed, having been then (two hundred years ago) a saint with a halo that seemed to have seen some use as a dinner plate. And there was, in a glass case, a model of the four-storey wooden palace that had stood next to the Church of Our Lady of Kazan until Catherine the Great had ordered it to be torn down, at the same time commanding this model to be made. It was talked of once as the eighth wonder of the world, and had those fantastic elements that were the invention of carpenters as daring with wood, I guess, as anyone has ever been: barrel-shaped roofs, domes that must have creaked horribly in the wind, adventurous staircases under roofs like pyramids, great carved cockerels and double-headed eagles: all of these being ingredients, speaking of a woodworker's right-angles and his repertoire of joints, that after Catherine's impatient demolitions began to appear (causing surprise nearly three hundred years later to Tom and me) as stone in the Church of Our Lady of Kazan.

Or in the Church of the Ascension, which you come upon (though it gives the effect of coming upon you) as you step through an archway into what you suppose might be the stables, only to discover this powerful building, which you see at once is a carpenter's invention, ossified. There is an astonishing, complete absence of domes: instead, the church has a tent roof – a slim cone that to an English eye has the appearance of a failed spire – reared above a sort of ruff of monumental oystershells. At its base, as it were an orderly muddle of angled roofs over staircases: a child might regard it as a great teaser with the title: How Do You Actually Get into This Building?

The Grand Prince Basil III had this church built in 1532 to celebrate the birth of a son: who grew up to be Ivan the Terrible.

All this paleness, of shabby snow and stone (there's a near-whiteness about Ivan's church): and you look to your left, and there is a broad curve of Moscow's river: tower blocks beyond, but here, immediately, banks brown with scrub: a winter tree or two. How difficult it is to understand other people's landscapes! So much of Moscow seems to hesitate between town and country: of its nine hundred square kilometres, a third being parkland. This view of the pallid river, a narrow patch of a much older scene caught between the remnants of the one-time royal estate and the city it was once comforting miles from, moved me as one is moved at such moments by a sense of one of the melancholy consequences of passing time: that it presents us everywhere with a not quite manageable juxtaposition of now and then. Perhaps the vague pain this produces stems from our knowing that we are examples of the same condition: carrying around with us – in our memories – those disparate yesterdays, some amazingly remote, some so close that they threaten us with suffocation. We may feel this melancholy, it seems to me, intensely in some great unfamiliar spot. Well, it's a Wednesday morning, and you step through an arch and there's a massive memento of Ivan the Terrible, and a loop of the river Moskva, and the fog-smudged outer towers of Moscow! And you return to the entry gates, glancing as you go at a prison tower built in Bratsk in 1652, and a tower from which the people of Karelsk began to look out for their enemies in 1690, both of wood: a material here so beguilingly celebrated that you are beginning to have fantasies, of St Paul's or Canterbury or Westminster Abbey translated into, of course, largely, oak.

It is not your usual sort of Wednesday.

On our way back to the Cosmos for lunch we passed through a small forest of statues, and Tanya named as many as she could: suddenly saying, to herself as much as to us: 'There are not so many female statues in this country.' And as she always did at such moments she collected from us whatever grins were offered, responses to her own, which was wry.

8

We wanted to see the Metro at its most gorgeous: and Tanya had recommended Komsomolskaya, where we'd also find above ground the Square of the Three Stations. The Thompsons came with us. It was soon obvious that better than any handbook or map as guides through a complex system were two young men. By a process of which there was no outward show at all, the operation of an instinct that had not yet learned to doubt itself, they knew which tunnel to take, and figured out some fashion in which a language they could not read could be turned into the most straightforward informative plainness. This way! they called, under a mosaic of Lenin orating. There was a haze of gold in the mosaic, and the confidence of it was staggering as, seventy years after the idealised moment represented on the ceiling, Lenin's ruined heirs streamed into and out of some of the grandest tunnels ever created. The trains were wider than we were accustomed to, and we had that particular sensation of foreignness you have when you make use of other people's transport systems. We were ridiculously eager and interested, and were surrounded by exhausted persons who had made an everydayness out of this subterranean pomp. Tom and I noticed how many women wore, magnificently if with fatigue, reds, purples, strong lilacs, mauves.

Tanya had hinted that Komsomolskaya would plunge us into the busiest, buzzingest kind of Moscow, and here it was, with three famous railway stations: the Kazansky, begun in 1913 but not completed until 1926, part-palace, part-ambiguous church, with turrets, a tent roof, and a most glorious clock: the Yaroslavl, as to its main features (including a broad embracing entrance) as modern as anything was likely to have been in 1904, but displaying, as to detail, that spirit that makes you think St Basil's might as well be named after Baba Yagar, the witch in Russian fairytales: and Leningradskaya, a station generally thought unworthy of the destination of its trains, and from which that evening we were to leave for what had hesitantly become St Petersburg. And here, in general, was another addition to that problem of knowing, when you found yourself on so foreign a scene, what you were looking at. There were these stations, a confusion of mostly attractive architectural parodies: and over there was the Leningradskaya Hotel, one of the twenty-eight-storeyed monsters Stalin was blamed for, always referred to as wedding cakes, though that allusion is too jolly: they are solid unfriendliness up to their shoulders, above which they wear forbidding cap and bells – apparent salt cellars tipped with gold, a lantern, a thin thorn of a tent roof that appears to be flying a balloon. There was a handsome classical building, white and pale gold, that might have been an offcut from one of the palaces in the Kremlin: and a tremendous flow of people. Gatherings were for a market, of a conventional sort: and for one or two alternatives, clearly not conventional at all, each centred on a lorry that was like a fleeting hypermarket paying the square an electrically nervous visit, with a clientele passionately queuing. Everywhere, a sense of trudging, heads down, trudging, trudging: a sudden startling absence of movement proving to be another line of women silently offering for sale a bottle of Pepsi, a pair of meagre chickens, a shoe-horn, a worn handbag.

We walked back to the hotel, a journey taking us past many such lines, as well as the multitude of booths, tiny shops, that now lined the streets. And then there was a scene, or details of a scene, that I seemed weirdly to recognise.

A torn landscape, such as you might find in a suburb under construction: yet there were elements in it that had clearly been there for centuries. Particularly, a church, on the brow of a slight hill: nesting on it, a flock of domes, deeply blue, gold-starred. Down from the church the ground tumbled away, widely, with much gashed clay, towards the main road we were following. We walked across this damaged ground and found, at its lowest point, two neglected houses of a distinguished kind in the midst of an area cut off from the rest by a stockade composed of an extraordinary miscellany of planks.

I felt I knew this mixture of the old, long-established and shabby, and the raw. And when it came to the stockade, I knew that well: had known it, those planks of which none matched its neighbour, in Barton in my childhood, when the twentieth century was untidily busy, tearing up much of a nineteenth-century scene.

The Barton version of this stockade marked off the territory owned, though I guess it might have been erratically and untrustworthily rented, by Mr Mincher.

I doubt if there is such a person left in England now. He was a rag-and-bone merchant who, behind such stockades, in various parts of the town, had several stores of the amazing rubbish he collected. I can't believe there was anything, offered or to be quietly appropriated, that he ever refused. As a child I recognised him as someone as indifferent as you could be to one of my father's precepts: that you should never pick up anything anywhere, because you didn't know where it had been. On principle Mr Mincher didn't know where most of the things he accumulated had been. I felt he treasured them for that. He and his huge wife and their unaccountable children occupied, fleetingly, a house at the top of the road I lived in. It was a modest early nineteenth-century house that today has been infinitely tidied, and last sold for a quarter of a million pounds: but then it was a grubby home for the Minchers, whose wares spilled into the front garden. I'd make my way again and again through this garden, which had become a bizarre forest of wringers and hat boxes and chamber-pots and mattresses and bundles of magazines tied with string and vague garments and ruptured items of furniture, into the house itself: to a room where, to be hunted for among faded rugs and, always, a top-hat or two, were books: any of them mine for a penny, sometimes no more than a ha'penny. For I was oddly a favourite of Mrs Mincher's, who I think found this juvenile book-hunter interestingly amusing. I understood from her that she could see little sense in reading herself, but she conveyed the idea that the skill and habit of it must make a gentleman of me. She meant, though she didn't know it, that in quite another world, when this handsome hovel had been prettified, I might be in a position to live in it myself. She always seemed to be clad in garments as subject to variety of ownership as those on display in the garden. I couldn't imagine her ever undressing. Her clothes appeared to be a permanent part of her.

He was on her scale, had a pony and trap and a gasping sort of car, generally believed to be held together with string. (That cry of our childhood – 'It's held together by string!' Seventy years later, I think this might apply to the entire world.) Like Mrs Mincher, he had a grimy crust of clothing: and I can smell to this day the heavy stink of him. They had these large unverifiable sons and daughters and cousins and aunts and uncles and dependent friends. It was a family that might have been just such a totter's harvest as their garden – and house – and trapfuls of exhausted objects were. I knew they had a desperate reputation. They were murmured against among the neighbours. The trade in domestic refuse was held to be a cover for darker dealings. In that world of the 1920s a child could feel the Minchers and their associates were a set of necessary rascals, part of the pattern of things: existing precisely so that they might be deplored. I had a nervous love of them, I suppose because they were so interestingly scandalous, and represented an absolute rebellion against all the decent irksomenesses of life – dressing with uncomfortable correctness, washing intermi-nably, guarding against dropped aitches. And I loved them as a source of books – weird stuff mostly, novels worse than forgotten, pious tracts, volumes of verse by poets whose very names, being indefinably unsuitable, should have warned them that they had no future.

And then came a major scandal. They'd been to a fair twenty miles from Barton, in Mr Mincher's big fragile car: and coming back, he'd driven them into a deep stream, and, too drunk even to think of pushing themselves out of it, they had lapsed into sleep there: and the water-level rose, or the car collapsed under them, and three of Mr Mincher's passengers were drowned. And Mr Mincher was charged with manslaughter, and went to prison, and the family vanished. I never saw vast Mrs Mincher again.

I wondered as we made our way across to the Cosmos how in Moscow, even given that stockade, I'd found myself back (in terms of a quickly dizzying sense of a connection) with the Minchers. But then, being a child in Barton had been much like being, so briefly, a visitor to Moscow. A child is a thinly instructed stranger in a world that barely knows how to explain itself to itself, let alone to this tyro.

Tom and I both felt we were in love with the city, partly for the little we'd seen and sensed of it, partly for the huge amount of it we'd not seen at all. We were curious about St Petersburg, but resentful of having to go there. We thought that, after the coarseness and muddle of ugliness and beauty that seemed to be Moscow and drew us to it, St Petersburg might be rather refined. It might, relatively speaking, be a city with its nose in the air.

Here in Moscow we'd been made angry and horrified by the desperation that every street corner, in the long lines of men and women with their hands held out, made mutely plain. We'd hated what we'd sensed as the arrival on the scene of triumphant hucksters, from within and without. There'd been this wicked game that powerful men had been playing, and these people we moved among, all these trudging people, were among those whose masters had lost the game: and they were paying the price, for us all.

Well, we'd fallen for Moscow, then. We'd fallen for the red and purple hats of the women, and whatever it is that makes it possible for you to turn a corner and find yourself, for God's sake, in Kresto-yozdvizhersky Lane.

9

I hadn't at all the measure of vodka – knew it was powerful but still couldn't help believing that little harm could come from a spirit so transparent and colourless. You had to shake the bottle to know it was there! So I had a glass or two – or perhaps it was three or four. The rattling evening took shape around me, but quite soon became misshapen, a consequence surely of its occurring in these narrow clattering conditions. Tom was away in a compartment that roared a lot, and I was perhaps conversing with Sam Thompson – there was certainly about our association an air as of conversation – and Alec Thompson was standing at the door of the compartment, passing glasses to me to fill from the vodka bottle (or bottles – some uncertainty there). He was passing them into the corridor – I had a sense as of a chain of glasses of vodka travelling from end to end of this mutteringly jolting train. Almost at once I was lying down in some manner that excluded the idea of ever rising again, and the world had rattled itself to pieces perhaps impossible to reassemble. Tom was back with us, and with him someone I had no hope of naming though of course I knew him intimately. They were dictating Sam's diary to him, and their laughter lurched and was running on clumsy wheels through a foreign darkness. I had that extraordinary sense I never failed to have, being on a train running through the night – as if the unlikelihood of it, felt on my first journey of the kind, had never faded. The night blared dolefully.

Then, and at once, it was enormously much later. What had been cheerful noises had been abruptly converted into absolute silence – except that you could hear the night scurrying and tittering past. And everyone was asleep. Perhaps I was asleep too, but that left this fellow who was feeling along an extraordinarily elastic corridor to the ... Yes, the lavatory. And here it was, and it didn't work, and hadn't worked for hours. There were immense congestions of waste! The smell burnt the nose! Then, in the space between one shudder of the train and the next, it had become frailly, rawly morning, and someone who was perhaps me but hadn't settled down into any reliable identity was standing in the corridor watching a thinly white world go past. There were scrubbinesses of silver birch, and among them what seemed to be up-ended bedsteads: but these in fact marked graves. There were, in those ragged copses, fragmentary cemeteries. Tom was standing beside me and was severe. It turned out to be curiously agreeable, to be scolded by one's son. Too much vodka, he seemed to be saying, but was frail himself, I thought: and I did not believe there was much sobriety about the queerly inconsecutive glimpses I'd had of him in the night. In my sleep, he said, I'd called out 'Poor old man!', and he'd worried that I might be ill. I was thinking perhaps, I said, of the man I'd seen in that underpass in Moscow, with his artificial leg revealed: but as I said this it struck me that 'Poor old man!' might well have been an account my bifurcated consciousness was giving of itself.

And here were the first signs of the great city of St Petersburg, and they were ugly. And this was the station. We had arrived. Feeling horrifyingly frail we were met on the platform by our new guide, another Tanya, who led us to the waiting bus.

Once we were in the cold air on this edge of the city, a thin ice of air, we were swooped upon by youths. They were large, batlike in their sudden appearance and in their flitting among us and enfolding us, offering – could it be? – t-shirts. We were surely a foolishly chosen clientele for t-shirts? And then, batlike, they'd gone. That quick fluster of wings coming had become a quick fluster of wings going. In the shaken silence that followed, someone said there'd been attempts to undo our shoulder bags. One had been fully opened, but an American in the party had noticed and made fists at the youth whose hands were on the zip. I checked my own bag and it was unzipped and my camera had gone.

It wasn't the loss of the camera that made me suddenly heavy-hearted, though I was fond of it, but the unsuitability of arriving for the first time in St Petersburg and having the moment filled with such an abrupt theft.

It was very early and there was little traffic. The train journey had removed most of my sense of being anywhere in particular, and the swarming thieves had made things less real still. And now there was this marvel of St Petersburg to be taken in between this and breakfast. I'd known about these long buildings, and I knew about the Neva and wasn't surprised that whole meadow-sized rafts of ice were afloat in it: but I'd not guessed at the colours (I'd vaguely taken it that the buildings were grey), or at the way everything monumentally crouched close to the line the river made. It was like driving through one of those pictures that invite you to put your eye at the level of some squash of lines, only to find that they stand up and make an image of the usual depth. We were moving through a hand-tinted geometry in which all the action was confined to this ravishing belt across the middle of things, and the rest was an enormous frozen sky: and I had lost my camera, and thought of losing my camera, and counted the pictures I'd lost with it on a nearly completed film.

And here we were at the Pribaltiskaya, which sounded like a dancer but meant 'Seaside' (or the hotel on the edge of the Baltic, perhaps): and from the window of our room Tom and I looked down at the sea, which turned out to be the Gulf of Finland, Helsinki being a couple of hundred miles up there on the left; and the fringe of the sea was pure craggy ice, and we needed to replace a large range of sleep that had also been stolen from us by some process of batlike swarming and unzipping.

So we slept.

10

They'd said St Petersburg had only fifty sunny days in the year. It turned out that we were there for three of them. They'd also said that when the year's first sun came, men and women in bathing suits would stand against the walls of the Peter and Paul Fortress, turn themselves to the sun and, with ice in the river before them and the icy pallor of stone behind them, would bask, and not stop basking for whole mornings, whole afternoons. And this we saw too. Those walls slope away from the river, so the sunbathers seemed not so much to stand on the rim of stone above the water as to lie back, tilted, perfectly arranged for adoring that distant warmth, or the illusion of it.

It was at first difficult to know where one was, or to have any strong sense of being where the notion of occupying this space rather than that was important. Absurd, of course: this city had a geography like any other. Yet, even where the skyline was pricked with golden spires, and there were many palaces (an extraordinary number of them, Tanya II seemed to be saying, given by Catherine the Great as baroque handshakes to her lovers), and tremendous churches, you had a feeling as of making your way across the surface of some delicately beautiful plate: you were never much above the level of the gilded rim. Or, once you became aware that the city rested on a network of canals, it was such a spider's web as might have been constructed by Fabergé, working on an immense scale. And this sense of the horizontality of everything was not at all contradicted by the central column in the massive space behind the Winter Palace – a column that anywhere else would have seemed to tower, but here was merely a great pin impaling and holding down the general flatness. (No column anywhere can have been disapproved of at higher literary levels, Pushkin making a mock of it in a poem, and Vladimir Nabokov, who started life more or less round the corner, saying it *obsessed* rather than adorned the great space it stood in.) The space itself was like Red Square, in seeming a thrilling wantonness of cobbles. Over there were the gates inset in the handsome walls of the palace over which, in Eisenstein's untrustworthy, thrilling film, *October*, the revolutionary mob went pouring.

Tanya II had permitted us to be there. She was solid, peremptory, and had in her eye the gleam of someone who would like to have you at her disposal, perhaps ultimately to be eaten. She strove to be suitably indulgent, but could not manage it. 'You will take a picture.' 'We will have fifteen minutes here.' At best she'd say: 'You want to take a picture, don't you?' The tone withered any inclination one might have had to take a picture. Once she said: 'You can take a picture if you like.' It was the language but hardly the spirit of permission. 'We will combine two pleasures' was a favourite phrase of hers as we descended from the bus: and it was impossible not to feel that one of these pleasures must involve a dungeon, Tanya in the long black boots she wore everywhere, and a whip. In fact the subsidiary pleasure usually sprang from the dreary arrangement she had with souvenir shops, into a visit to one of which any grand journey of ours was likely to narrow. You'd have the Hermitage in prospect but would suddenly be back among the matrioshkas, the painted eggs, the shawls. Tanya would be talking to the proprietor, perhaps making arrangements to thrash him at the weekend.

There was the question of my stolen camera. I'd need for the insurance to be effective to have some document declaring that the theft had taken place. Tanya thought I might get one from the security men at the hotel. So after breakfast on our second morning she rounded me up and strode with me through reception to an office at the rear. Here, as on some pointedly minimal stage set, were two men, artfully arranged. One, young, with angry dark eyes, sat behind a desk, on which lay only a chilly folder or two. The other, a little older, sat on a chair sideways on to the desk: his head was bowed, his hands clasped: he did not look up: he had an extensive moustache. It was a pattern of interrogation: one to stare, the other to listen, his gaze withheld. Eyes, ears. Tanya, with a scornful gesture in my direction, began her tale, her tone furious. The man behind the desk answered her even more furiously. I knew at once that there would be no document. The menacing atmosphere of refusal, the gestures of disgust and general flagellatory pantomime, seemed wasted on so trivial a matter: they would have served for some great political summit. His distaste for Tanya's proposal was retorted to by her in tones more disdainful still. The battle continued, shrugs, eyeballs rolled, though it was perfectly clear that our cause was already lost. The other man still did not look up, but heaved his shoulders, ground his hands together: expressed with his slumping spine the hopelessness – perhaps the near-unlawfulness – of our petition.

They were against providing a document, Tanya told me at last, because it might cause the insurance company to ask why the hotel did not look after its guests better. I saw that, I said: and after all, they hadn't been witnesses, it hadn't even happened in the hotel. Tanya alarmingly translated this into what sounded like a tirade. It would end in arrest or worse, I thought. And indeed the younger man turned his full stare on me, dark wrath undiluted. So I thought: but then his face collapsed into a smile of the most extraordinary charm. 'It is' – he ventured into English – 'just a little Russian problem!' The other man allowed himself to be slightly less slumped, rubbed his hands, nodded in agreement. 'We'll leave it at that,' I said, and turned to go before Tanya could translate this into some blistering bark. The two men were already returning to their original poses, and it was impossible to imagine they ever occupied other positions: that one came out from behind the desk, or that the other stood up.

Tanya's blood, which I suspected of being in a constant state of arousal, was now roused indeed. We would go the following after- noon, she said, to the railway police, and see what happened there. I was horrified. I knew that whatever happened there would take a long time. Even if it meant no insurance money, I wasn't willing to lose what might be a whole afternoon, and our last, in St Petersburg. Tom and I had determined to avoid all other arrangements, whatever grand visits to whatever grand places, in order at leisure to walk up the Nevsky Prospekt. I told Tanya to forget it. I'd think of some other way of acquiring evidence of the theft. Others in the party would sign a statement for me. She smiled the smile of someone who despises its object, and sighed: summing me up with unamiable amusement, I thought, for my suitability for, say, flaying. And then, simply enor- mously, she shrugged.

II

And here we were at the Kirov, now anxious to call itself by its older name: the Marinsky. It was Prokofiev's *Romeo and Juliet*: with a Romeo whose love, alas, was plainly for himself. He was dancing in quite another ballet, called *Romeo and Romeo*. But there was a wonderful, tiny Mercutio a frailness in black, whose dying dance, the machinery of that deft mischief running totteringly down, was deeply moving. The trouble was that when the curtain fell on Act One, there was at once an immense ceremony of acclaim, as if it had been the final curtain. Bouquets were enormously on offer: Romeo sketched out a delight in himself that left Juliet nowhere. And then, between Acts One and Two, there was not so much an interval as a protracted vacancy. We left our charming little fauteuil (so charming that I could think of it only in terms of this word that I'd never expected to have cause to use) and circulated along the promenade that followed the ring the auditorium made. Here the Russian fury in respect of smoking made itself felt. Whoever was not smoking was plainly about to light the next cigarette from the last. A vast fuminess accumulated. Visibility lessened. I thought how little headway, in these circumstances, a claim to bronchial asthma could hope for. And seeing delicate women, many carrying roses, from whose lips huge frontal systems emerged, whole choking storms of smoke, I found myself wondering that the dancers themselves had refrained from this national habit.

Time ticked smokily on. One's memory of this being a performance of *Romeo and Juliet* became vague. They began again: but it was as if it were another evening, another ballet: and after Act Two came more bouquets, another long interval, much more smoke.

I felt terrible, being at the Kirov only half-gratefully.

And when we left, the coach was waiting, full of the other half of us who'd been to the circus. That, presumably with a different outlook as to intervals, had ended more than an hour before. But there had been no going back to the hotel with those who were full of memories of clowns and acrobats, and coming back for us, full of memories of bouquets and smoke.

There wasn't enough petrol to make even such a short journey twice.

12

The Thompson brothers, having had several glowing love affairs in Moscow, had fallen in love afresh in St Petersburg. I was astonished by the speed with which their hearts were engaged, the genuineness of each engagement, and the willing promptness with which their signals were received by young women available for wooing only for the length of time we were in, for example, one of those souvenir shops into which we were ruthlessly unloaded by Tanya II. Wherever we went, we seemed to run into Sam and Alec, hand-in-hand with their always beautiful captives. I'd been brought up on a notion of love affairs as being monstrously difficult to set up, and almost impossible to end: it was as if I had known them as a form of laborious longhand, and now, it seemed, their quality was that of a charming and very rapid shorthand. It was clearly no problem, for Sam and Alec, composed as they seemed to be of pure energy, to combine being rushed round two unfamiliar cities (remaining perfectly attentive to both) with a large number of amorous achievements.

A diarist, I had a diarist as a son. It was because of this energy that came from being younger, I thought, that Tom was able, even in these overtaxed circumstances, to keep his record as a continuous narrative, while I was reduced to desperate note-making. We sat in our hotel room, engaged in an activity that was natural enough to us, but to some might seem extraordinarily odd. Why, we wondered, did we have this need that, when we tried to explain it to ourselves, seemed to amount to a great requirement that when life waved to us we ought to wave back. Or to a feeling that it would be infamous, having for example been provided with St Petersburg, not to make some return by way of comment, description, pure record. Yes, yes, you were saying: it has happened, it has not gone unnoticed.

Oh, the very sharp fear that you might be guilty of a failure to notice!

Behind us as we wrote, our backs to the window, there was an astonishing sunset over the Gulf: the sun enormous, making a wide, blindingly burnished golden ribbon across the ice. On the edge, blackened by the light, stood people, staring. There seemed to be scarcely a movement among them. Here, the sun was never taken for granted.

Earlier, we'd walked down there, on a grey promenade. The city took itself to the very rim of the Gulf, so that there was a startlingly direct transition from concrete to the stale, upheaved end-of-winter crust of ice that stretched as far as the eye could see. Some way out, in a golden spotlight, was a squat man, a dark brown apparent hunchback, fishing through some crevice. He made his way towards us: on his feet, scarcely larger than he'd been when seated. With him he brought the bucket he'd been sitting on, and offered it to Tom with his line, on which hung a tiny fish. It was for a photograph: which I took with Tom's camera. Elsewhere one might have backed away from such an invitation, mumbling, smiling, hurrying off: aware of being foolish – a tourist making a claim not to be a tourist. But here, the offer being made by a man who had generally the air of a walrus, was anxious that we should know his forename (Mishka), and didn't so much volunteer to take a picture of us both as insist on doing it, brushing aside a whole range of modest objections that we had not made, and stage-managing us as he did so (Tom was not to entertain foolish ideas of doing anything but sit, and I must accept that the only pose for me was to stand with a hand on his shoulder), to say No would have been horribly humourless. When he announced that we owed him a dollar it sounded not so much the statement of a standard exaction as a request for a memento. He sketched out with gestures the idea that we'd be more satisfied with the consequences of this encounter than we could ever guess, took the dollar with a busy grin, and trudged back to his distant crack in the ice.

13

I was by now in a kind of delirium as to gold leaf. Here in St Petersburg the best golden wonders were spikes. Most thrilling of them all (and they thrilled through a combination of ostentation and often fragile grace) was the gleaming thorn that rose above the Fortress of Peter and Paul, being the spire of the cathedral that stood in the middle of it.

To the fortress we were herded by Tanya II: though the nature of the group made her efforts as a scornful shepherdess fairly ineffective. We hadn't the gift for being shepherded. For example, the American family whose children had been brought to Russia to be warned off socialism for ever were natural drifters. They kept, in the end, together, but there was a vagueness about it. The parents appeared to feel genial despair about the possibility that Wesley and her brothers could ever be brought to heel on any issue at all (except, one supposed, this one of their political outlook). One of the boys, Grant, went as far in the direction of serious reproof as any of them when he'd say to his younger brother, who was at that stage when a small boy is mere imp: 'Oh Peter, you are *gross!*' They would all pleasantly agree with this judgement. Yes, certainly Peter was gross. In this city (and especially in this fortress) that had been the scene of so many unspeakable severities and repressions, it seemed odd to have among us this example of a thoroughly languid and resigned style of domestic management.

On a green in the fortress was a seated statue of Peter the Great, the most unlikely representation of an all-powerful monarch: un-uni-formed, skeletal, he looked like a scholar who'd become skin and bones from his scholarship. The statue was famously friendly to children: who were encouraged to sit in its lap, which had become shiny from their doing so. The American children took their turns on the lap, for photographs: except that the imp was not at home with the idea of taking turns, and squirmed himself into everyone else's photo. His mother murmured: 'Peter the Great and Peter-the-not-so-good!' Tanya II made impatient noises, the result it seemed of bastinadoing the roof of her mouth with her tongue. To her, we were all small American children. 'Oh, Peter, you are so *gross!*' cried Grant, from inside a war of elbows – two of them of bronze, the tsar's. A voice was to be made out, crisply furtive, one that had accompanied us everywhere: 'Another of those American civil wars,' it was murmuring, 'with which you have become familiar.' It was Mike Philadelphia confiding in his camcorder.

There were two American Mikes in the party. One, for his resemblance to a character in a television serial we had watched together thirty years earlier, was known to Tom and me as Mike Hiram Holliday. He was a quiet man who seemed to find life disconcerting, and liked it that way. Mike Philadelphia, of course, came from Philadelphia: though there was a sense in which he seemed not to have left it, for he spent much of his time addressing, to the microphone attached to his camcorder, voice-over comments that I could have sworn were directed at particular persons in an audience perhaps already assembled in that city. It was as if we had added to us another, phantom group.

Arrived at the fort, you were greeted by a small band, dressed in Ruritanian uniform. They had a national anthem ready for each busload: in our case, Americans notwithstanding, it was 'God Save the Queen'. 'You want to take a photograph?' Tanya asked discouragingly; but we already had. All, that is, except Reg and Mavis, who were gentle people, opposed even to such comic militarism as this. Both had been teachers: he having the sweet and admirably absurd quality of a man who saw the whole world as a classroom, filled with children who were, on the whole, causes of grave anxiety: though one had, in a sort of obstinate professional way, a hope of eventual, if remote, improvement. 'He successfully murdered the tsarina in this very place,' Tanya would say (making it necessary to attempt to imagine an unsuccessful murder): and Reg's face would cloud, as if here was another playground misdemeanour the staff had failed to prevent. He was given to wondering what might have happened if all the bad but none of the good people had failed to be present at monstrous historical turning points. Mavis shared his views but after a long marriage was still capable of being amazed by some of Reg's propositions. He would suddenly wonder how things would have turned out if that train that brought Lenin in 1917 to the Finland Station here in St Petersburg had suffered a commonplace mechanical failure. Mavis would laugh with affectionate helplessness. 'It's a big if, Reg,' she'd say, taking his arm into protective custody, as if his Utopian speculations might have endangered him physically. Reg and Mavis were further causes why we were not the group Tanya II clearly dreamed of, arranged perhaps in twos, voluntarily breaking into a trot when the situation (you had so long and no longer for getting round the Fortress of Peter and Paul) called for it.

We were in time, all the same, for the firing of the noonday gun: which, through all the convulsions of things, had rarely failed to happen. It was an oddly companionable event. We arrived as part of an expectant crowd on the Naryshkin Bastion, to find ourselves alongside the gun itself. A figure out of *War and Peace*, a military walrus, who took care to seem unaware of us, stood ready to fire it. We kept an eye on our watches. The icefloes in the river below had that quality icefloes have, of seeming to be illustrations of very precise, but unusual, geometrical figures. The Americans took amused and unconvincing steps in the direction of preventing the imp from firing the gun prematurely. Under us, invisible, leaning back against the walls of the fortress, were certainly the tilted sunbathers. A few yards to our right (in the Trubetskoi Bastion) were the cells in which Lenin's brother, Alexander Ulyanov, had awaited execution for his part in the assassination of Alexander III, and Maxim Gorki had almost died of tuberculosis, having been imprisoned for writing a political leaflet: being saved by the representations of fellow writers, headed by Anatole France. We chattered. Tanya II clearly wished there was a generally agreed punishment for chattering. Then it was the hour, and we should have been perfectly prepared. But no one, I guess, is prepared for the noonday gun. It shook us out of our senses as if we'd had no idea it would ever be fired.

'And so it's noon in Leningrad,' muttered Mike Philadelphia, to an audience that can't have needed the information, and might well have been too deafened to hear it.

14

'Leningrad', Mike Philadelphia had said: and 'Leningrad' Tom and I mostly found ourselves thinking, and saying.

Whatever was to be made of the years since 1917, it seemed too facile, too careless – too indifferent to all that complex suffering – to leap back over them, from Leningrad to St Petersburg, as if they had never happened. If 'Leningrad' must go, it was difficult to think of a respectable reason for letting 'St Petersburg' take over too easily, in the mind or on the tongue. In the domestic sense it was a matter for the citizens, and our thoughts were impertinent: but outsiders could hardly avoid having some private sensitivity in the matter. There were obvious respects in which 'Leningrad' remained the city's name, difficult to dismiss. Under that name the nine hundred day siege by the Nazis had been endured, when every golden spike was given a dulling and protective cover, and bullet or shell, for all their easy harvest, killed fewer than hunger. I remembered interviewing Galina Vishnevskaya, the soprano, Rostropovich's wife, who, the couple having harboured Solzhenitsyn and spoken for him, was made a nobody by the Soviet authorities, her name removed from all her recordings. She'd talked of being a fourteen-year-old child in an apartment in Leningrad, alone except for her dead grandmother. At night, from the street outside, came clinking sounds. 'Clinking' was a light, slight word, and one thought of glass – bottles, light metal. But these clinking sounds were made by bodies, being thrown into carts. They clinked because they had become solid ice.

And in the Nevsky Prospekt you could still read the notice that said you were marginally safer from snipers on that side of the street than you were on the other. This was not far from the shop where I'd tried to buy a record of the symphony Shostakovich wrote in the midst of the siege, and that he called the Leningrad. The shop had sold out, and instead I took away with me a performance of the Third Quartet, written two years after the blockade was broken. The terse oddity of the sleevenote seemed right for Shostakovich. 'Central movements,' it said, 'are the most difficult in content. They are full of painful feelings connected with the recent past. Tense third movement is like a call to the fight with evil. Intrusion of the imperious recitative means the beginning of the next movement, wonderful passacaglia, dedicated, as Shostakovich always does, to the sphere of lofty philosophical images. The idea of imperishableness of human ideals runs through the rimming movements of the Quartet.'

The opening sounds are to me those of a most melancholy and ironical ghost, dancing, the sourest steps, along the Nevsky Prospekt.

It sounds like Leningrad. It doesn't sound at all like St Petersburg. And I think it's the sound of the city as we saw it in 1993.

Not, of course, that the St Petersburg side of things failed to have its effect on us. We were lunching on a boat moored in the river, opposite the Winter Palace. An extraordinary number of black-headed gulls gave the icefloes the appearance of overcrowded rafts. Philippa, a quiet-mannered ex-teacher, given to gusts of apologetic nervousness, said (her surprise anticipating ours) that she'd found herself, in her sleep the night before, transmogrified into Catherine the Great. 'I seemed to be perfectly at home,' she said. 'I gave two men – two head teachers I know – three, or it might have been four, palaces each. But then Tanya arrived and said they mustn't have them.'

A little later, in the Hermitage, Tanya was understood by us all to say: 'No tourists upstairs.' Since everything to be seen here was upstairs, this seemed as brutal as snatching palaces from under the noses of headmasters. But it turned out that she was urging us to pee while we could. It was toilets there were none of, upstairs. I had an awful thought of what she might make of my dilatoriness in these matters, not improbably in the form of public censure. The Russian for 'loitering in the toilets' might sound even worse than the English. I stayed put.

To spend any time at all in the Hermitage is marvellous, but to have been there for two hours is a kind of nonsense. Wesley was best at it, treating the geometry of the superb floors as a succession of spacious frames for hopscotch. (They were once to be trodden on only if you were wearing the soft overshoes issued to every visitor: but there was no money now for those, neither roubles nor dollars.) She danced up the stairs where everything is gold, and through the room where everything is malachite, and through the room where the clock was stopped at the moment when Kerensky and his government were arrested (in that very room) by the Bolsheviks: and she danced past the da Vincis, and the Rembrandts – which almost certainly I'd never see again (. . . a sad-faced woman, such love he had for women) – and past one of the few things that were going ridiculously to be remembered out of all this, a painting of dogs being hanged, by order of the Parliament of Animals, for helping Man the Hunter. And so we came to the Impressionists and lost all awareness of Wesley and her dancing. There were pictures here to stop the heart. There were Cezannes I'd not seen even in reproduction. There was the work (Tom and I made a useless note) of Auguste Chabaud, 1882–1952. There was a sense of the utter absurdity of being so fleetingly in the midst of such richness. Suddenly I could not bear (or quite understand) Kate's absence. Then there was Wesley again, dancing our withdrawal.

As we walked away, along the river, past the antique cruiser from which the gun was fired that was the signal for the Revolution, I cried, as I'd cried (in Tom's view, but also by now in my own) too often: 'Where's my bag?' It was, as in such circumstances it usually was, on my shoulder.

'Dad, don't do this to me,' said Tom.

What did I mean, making anything of Philippa being nervous? Lord, I was remarkably nervous myself. I'd always worried about losing things. It was because, I thought, I had this over-extended imagination, which made it imperative that I should keep a tally of what might go wrong, and be ready to find that I had failed in some detail of the vigilance required. During journeys, when the inability to lay your hands on passport or money or any of a dozen documents might lead to complex forms of misery, my uneasiness was always likely to pounce. I'd be gloriously relaxed, as now after the visit to the Hermitage, and then, in a split second, my outlook would blacken: I would feel in pockets, undo zips. 'Where is my – ?' As often as not it was where I'd forgotten I'd transferred it, for even greater safety. Tom would groan.

Extraordinary, I thought, to be in the company of my fatherly son. He was taller than I was, walked more swiftly, was quicker to understand the geography of a new city. He was wiser when it came to crossing roads. 'Come back!' he'd snap. He was not thrown by the tangled instructions given by our Tanyas. His role and mine had become curiously and pleasantly confused. Nearly forty years ago it had been I who'd had to slow down for him; I was the one who was against dashing into roads, who knew where we were and what the man had said. A major concern, then: that Tom came to no harm. Now it was Tom seeing sooner than I did that what I was about to do was senseless. 'Dad – !' I'd missed by virtue of his hand on my shoulder being complicatedly crushed by a thundering cross-section of Russian traffic: though, more often, the danger was of my being laid low by some ruthless advance of elderly ladies. Of course, like many fathers he was over-anxious. But capable fathers need to be.

It was, I'd always thought, a bizarre relationship, that of parent and child. In my seventies I understood that just such a shift of role between me and my father, in *his* seventies, was among the causes of his furious dislike of me. In some respects I'd become, as he must have thought of it, insolently more competent than he was. And I wished, not for the first time, that he could have enjoyed the comedy in that: and not been left by his desperate childhood and youth in the slums of West London and the trenches of the Western Front with a view of other people that saw them, almost without exception, as persons intent on making themselves powerful by making him powerless.

Tom and I were much alike: tended to make similar jokes (sometimes the same joke), kept diaries, were teachers. But there was one vast difference between us (apart from the other vast differences that exist between any two human beings), which this journey was making clear to me. It followed from his being Kate's son. From the start of his acquaintance with almost anyone, he had great and natural ease and curiosity. In a group, without being in any respect overbearing, he became a means by which they hung together. He was a brightener. He knew how to speak to strangers: feeling at once for some element of common language. The response he made to what people said to him was a full one. And none of this was thought out, intended: it was how he was. I would come to breakfast flinching from the need to build upon the slender knowledge I had of Mike Philadelphia, or Reg and Mavis. I ached for privacy: I longed (whilst not being sorry I was here) to be home again.

This wasn't, in the end, interesting because it was me and Tom (though of course that did interest me): rather, as so often with such differences, because it seemed to point to the, as it were, cookbook quality of human character. So there was the recipe from which I was made: I was my mother's son – she having an inclination to be in love with everybody – and I was my father's son – he finding that life was as simple as he needed it to be if he started from the premise that everyone was an enemy. Result, for me, that while I was subject to being helplessly swamped by undifferentiated floods of love, in my mother's style, I was also aloof, cagily private, in my father's. And among the ingredients from which Tom was made were elements of both these styles; but he was also a derivative of Kate, with her (often, to me, astonishing) openness. Only uncommon restraints could have prevented her from addressing, anywhere in the world, a stranger who was momentarily her neighbour.

It was now, walking away from the Hermitage, these thoughts in my head, that I found myself alongside Sam Thompson. He'd been amazed by those wonders housed in the Winter Palace. I, too, had been amazed: but I felt that I was in the presence of an order of astonishment from which I'd long been shut out. Walking beside Sam, I simply remembered being young: with that kind of remembering that's not of the mind – a matter of describing to yourself what you once knew – but that suddenly fills you with the original sensation. In this case, the sensation of amazement, as it once was: being, in relation to such feelings as you have later in life – which much of the time seem strong enough: you're not aware of any loss of the power to be astounded – an *amazing* amazement. I'd been able once to feel just as

Sam was feeling as we turned together onto a bridge crossing the Neva. That had been when the enormous age of the world had seemed only an aspect of its absolute novelty.

I was filled again, fleetingly, with the awe by which I'd once been possessed, caused by the apparent fact that, for my modest adventures, a setting had been provided by the creation of an entire and astonishing city. It was 1938, the year of my first love; and for our encounters they'd laid on Trafalgar Square, the Mall, Buckingham Palace (which we contemned), Hyde Park, a dazzling avenue of laburnum trees, and (at that time residents of Hyde Park) a flock of sheep: who, when we lay on the grass to make such ineptly tentative love as I was capable of, would glance up from their chewing with a discouraging (but wholly justified) absence of interest. Now I saw that for Sam and his succession of innocent loves, Moscow and St Petersburg themselves would have seemed to have been hurriedly flung up, along with their centuries of history – an ancient package put together this morning: and including, as a particularly hair-raising feature of the backcloth that was St Petersburg, that huge repository of marvels, the Hermitage.

'I want life,' said Sam now, choosing his own words for all this complexity, 'to remain simple.'

15

There were the mornings, when we were taken about, under Tanya's stern eye, in our small clattering bus. On the smoothest of roads it would have clattered, and here there was no smoothness at all. Everywhere were potholes on their way to becoming pot chasms. When the bus stopped and decanted us ('You would like to get out?' – disdainfully), another, usually wonderful, confused impression would be added to our understanding of St Petersburg which must of course contain huge elements of misunderstanding. It was Easter, and here we were in what Tanya declared to be a *functioning* church, where it seemed that whole meals were being brought in to be blessed. The atmosphere was that generated by very large numbers of people who were trying to get too much in against the clock, many of them subject on an immense scale to the risks of collision taken by waiters at the height of a busy dinner: I'd never imagined such a rapt earnestness of dish-carrying, such attempts to hang on to plates and tureens whilst using the hands to make reverent gestures. The priests, carrying out their offices at a score of stations throughout the church, looked even more anxious, more pressed for time. They blessed, helter-skelter. There was the heavy sound of chanting. To Tom and me it seemed that our presence, as ludicrously unsuitable voyeurs in a space that barely had room for its legitimate users, was more than could be borne. They were all much too busy to notice us: but after the experience of Russian churches we'd had in the last few days, we were easily able to imagine that we were subject to the angry gaze, somewhere above us, of a saint with narrow golden face and castigator eyes: a kind of impotent holy bouncer. So we slipped out.

Or we were outside the Smolny Institute. Smolny was a name I knew from literature: one of those sounds-in-the-head that evoked Russia, being mysteriously sullen, smoky, smouldering. Now Tanya said, casually, that it meant 'tar'. This was the site of an old tarworks. What I must now think of as the Tar Institute (near neighbour to the exquisite Tar Convent) had been a school for young ladies: and for a few weeks in 1917 Lenin had occupied one of the rooms. The legend over the door of that room was CLASS MISTRESS. It was useless, oddly enjoyable information: part of that collage which, at moments, it seems history really is – there being times when, if you are susceptible to the comedy of accidental detail, you have difficulty in taking history seriously.

Then we were outside a church topped with a mob of onions any one of which might have been given away as a prize at Barton Fair. Back home, one of Ben's brothers had been a genius with a fairground rifle, picking off tin soldiers marching drunkenly behind a tin battlement. The prizes he'd won filled an unstable corner cabinet in their living room. They were all wonderfully horrible: vases, jugs, teapots, abominably shaped, hideously coloured. And here were holy globes surely from the same factory. Our eyes must be wrong – they couldn't

[125]

be as garish as they seemed. But how to cross such a ravine between taste and taste?

16

Somewhere along the way, she couldn't remember whether from book or film, Kate had picked up a passion for the idea of a wild night ride in a troika. The spirited horses, predominantly a matter of nostrils breathing out smoke: the stars turning the sky into an immense chandelier: the hiss of the runners on the crisp snow! The exhilaration! One would be in furs, and one's eyes would shine! She was clear about her decision if it came to outspeeding a pack of wolves: the chance of a troika-ride might not come again, and it was I who would be tossed out, unhesitatingly if not altogether without apology.

And here I was in the land of the troika, and I must find a representation of one to take home to her. It would not be the best thing, but would certainly be the next best thing. And at once troikas appeared, on enamelled boxes. All conveyed the extreme of excitement that Kate had in mind. Across the black night of the box-lid, sometimes among very faintly luminous trees, the three horses flew, their slender, usually orange or pale apricot legs stretched to the limit fore and aft, suggesting the very idea of speed: though it was common for the middle horse to have its front legs flying high – had it not been turning its head backwards to share the excitement of the riders, its knees would have been threatening its chin. Tails rippled, manes were golden scrolls, flying. The runners were golden, too, fine wires, the sled a seashell that leaned in the direction in which, all gold and red and oyster brown, they were shearing their way through the night. The charioteer, who held high the merest looping notion of golden reins, leaned that way too. He was all beard, huge-eyed, wearing a tiny red fur-rimmed hat: the whip in his left hand was another hair-fine golden flourish close to the stars. His companion alone leaned back against the direction of flight: a solid man, his hat a tall one but also red and with a white rim of fur. He alone represented anything like detached appreciation of this troika ride – he was where Kate would be, after I'd been thrown out. Otherwise the box-lid was all wild and thrilling urgency, all the better for being unaccountable. Again, what was suggested was the very idea of urgency. On Kate's dressing table it would be three inches by one of gleaming manic action.

17

Tom had brought to Russia with him an immense sausage. It had been given to him by a friend, to be delivered to one or other of two friends of his: the first living in Moscow, the second in St Petersburg. The Moscow address had turned out to be too deep in the suburbs for us to reach: but we knew the street the other lived in was a turning off the Nevsky Prospekt. However, here *was* the Nevsky Prospekt, and it was four kilometres long. We had no detailed map of the city. It was hopeless, asking for help ('Ulitsa Gertsena?') from this thin young man with cascading hair, for it was immediately evident that he was drunk. You could see that he very much wanted to square up to our inquiry, his face attempting to make sense of the bits and pieces of a charming smile. But if we'd been looking for someone who didn't know where anything was, anywhere, this was our man. We spread our hands gratefully and made ready to move on. 'Ulitsa Gertsena!' he exclaimed: laughed, and was puzzled by his own laughter. Then a finger made circles and ended up pointing directly across the road. 'Ulitsa Gertsena!' he cried: and bowed, deeply, perilously.

Directly across the road, we found, was Ulitsa Gertsena.

The address we had was, mystifyingly, Ulitsa Gertsena 59 A8. But as we set off down it we saw that at regular intervals a marker appeared, inserted into the brickwork at the level of a ground floor lintel: it was white, shaped like a cut of cheese, and bore a number. At this end, on the right-hand side (where it turned out the odd numbers always were), the number was 1. A long way ahead would be 59.

Every number marked the entrance to a courtyard. Having found 59 we'd need to look inside the courtyard for another door marked A8.

This was to be the severest test of my ability to keep up. If you draw upon a limited amount of energy, making your way towards the number 59 down a street which starts at 1 and takes a minute to move you on to 3 brings about a faintness of spirit to add to faintness of flesh. I felt terrible, Tom having burden enough with the sausage. But he seized my arm, vigorously considerate, and numbers flew past. I concentrated on not being left too far behind by my own feet.

Number 59 marked a pair of battered wooden doors, standing open. And within was the courtyard, with further double doors around it, all clearly having been long in use. Over there was A8. Tom rapped on it with his knuckles. We thought of Raskolnikoff, in *Crime and Punishment*, coming into such a courtyard, to such a door, *exactly* such a courtyard and door, and making his fatal way up the stairs to visit the old woman. Now we waited, a long wait: until at last there were small sounds of feet descending stairs. Then the door, hesitantly, opened. A young woman stood there, desperately pale, in a dressing-gown. Tom explained his errand.

She said, in English: 'I fear I am ill. I shall not be able to invite you in. I am so sorry about this. But there it is. I am ill.'

We offered mumbled sympathy, regret. She must not worry. We perfectly understood. We had not thought of being invited in. Was there, Tom asked, anything her friends in England could do for her?

She said: 'What I need is medicines. There are no medicines. It is what many of us need, and cannot have.' She was clutching the great parcel that contained the sausage. 'I tell you that,' she said, 'not for your pity, but as a fact of our life.'

We smiled, she returned her pale smile, and it was altogether difficult to bear: being friends of a friend, and having prepared ourselves for a mixture of surprise and amused delight, and finding ourselves so useless.

18

The first street I ever knew was called Long Street: in the early 1920s I played in it, taking its simple name to be a token of the way names in general were given to the bits of the world. Standing outside our house and looking north through the railway bridge (put there so you could shout under it for the sake of the echoes), you couldn't see the end of the street. It rose in the direction of the unlikely world towards which my father made his way every morning, and from which he had the cunning (qualifying him to be my father) to return every evening. I loved the elementary principle to which, as I took it, this patently long street owed its title. Not much later the local council, no doubt thinking it was improving on a naivety, renamed it after a councillor. Plain durable Long Street became trumpery Longmore Avenue.

Although the Russians tend to translate 'Prospekt' as 'Avenue' (a perfectly good word for a fine wide street, but trivialised by its aimless use in thousands of small towns, and its coupling with the names of thousands of unmemorable councillors), I'd thought of the Nevsky Prospekt as the Long Street of St Petersburg. The official guidebook describes it as the string to the bow that the river makes. It came to exist because iron and sailcloth and ropes and oak and oakum had to be brought in carts from Novgorod to the Admiralty in the newly-invented city; and the carts could get there only by going, in a roundabout way, along narrow paths. So it was decided to cut, through what was then woodland, a 'great perspective road' with the Admiralty as its destination. After fifty years of calling it the Nevsky Perspective Road (because it followed the flow of the Neva) they were ready for something shorter. So it became the Nevsky Prospekt.

In 1993 it was, as much as anything else, a four kilometre-long art gallery and bookshop. That's to say, every other citizen seemed to have set up a stall smothered with books: and every space on the pavement that was not filled with such stalls was filled instead with

screens to which paintings and prints were pinned. I remember the
following scene – an Army officer, dapperly military, with a young
stiffness and sternness about him, having bought a large art book, had
opened his obligatory briefcase to stow the book away in it. I'd been
thinking that the Nevsky Prospekt might unsatisfactorily be described
as a fusion of Piccadilly, the Strand, Oxford Street and a straightened-
out Regent Street, and that it was not easy to imagine any of those
streets making such an unrelenting offer of literature and art. I now
thought that if they had done so, it would be no easier to imagine a
guards officer pausing to purchase a book devoted to the work of the
Constructivists.

It was here that, stinking rich with dollars, we became also stinking
rich with roubles. In some shops it was roubles only that you could
use. We were in a tremendous store called the House of Books, which
might well have been called the House of Books, Prints, Small
Paintings, Maps, Astonishing Posters and Painted Spoons. There were
floors heaped on floors, and little marvels everywhere. So Tom bought
a woodcut profile of a stretch of St Petersburg, an horizon of palaces
prickling with gold, delicately coloured, for something like 75p. For
little more, I bought another woodcut, signed like Tom's by the artist:
a book plate for the Dostoevsky Museum. Against a similar horizon,
the tall figure of the writer: his hand outstretched and on the open
palm an anguished woman standing. Then I bought, for perhaps £2, a
most handsome book of paintings and sketches of Pushkin's St
Petersburg, which made it clear how irresistible had always been the
temptation to see the city in terms of exquisite, but also sometimes
turbulent, even matter-of-fact horizons: with, here and there, given
that the foundations of St Petersburg were not much more than water,
scenes of flood: poets, horses, prints, painted spoons and army officers
and their three-cornered hats being swept away in the general direction
of Helsinki.

I found I wanted to take home – bought in this House of Books, in
his own city – a volume of Pushkin. But, they strangely said, they had
none in stock. So Tom and I both chose a little paperbound volume of
the poet Mandelstam, with a biography and photographs. In this
jostling, elbowing tenement devoted to books the method of paying

for purchases was clumsy: the assistant noted the amount on a torn-off scrap of paper, which you took across to the cashier sitting in her sawn-off sentrybox. For the two volumes of Mandelstam we paid the equivalent of 3p.

Thereafter we wandered down this astonishing street that, much of the time, where other great thoroughfares in other cities have side streets, has canals: and so, bridges, each with its particular ironwork (amazing horses, for example, quarrelling with their riders). Down *there* had lived Tchaikovsky: and down *there* had lived Gogol: and down *there* (it happened to be Ulitsa Gertsena, where on our return from our melancholy mission with the sausage we'd been startled by a plaque) had lived the Nabokovs, in a palazzo with a facade in the Florentine style that Vladimir Nabokov's father had refused to illuminate in celebration of royal birthdays. And here was a great cathedral, rechristened (but perhaps dechristened) by the Soviets as the Museum of Religion and Atheism: a tremendous arc of stone fronted with gardens and a companion arc of benches: on one of which, whenever we passed, sat the Thompsons, with young women of the city, all of them amorously stunned.

It was almost time to go home. In two or three days I'd be sitting in the Friar's Holt with Harry Frost, feeling absurd. That is, I'd be trying to express deep feelings about what was surely a shallow experience. Out of a whole lifetime, a week in Russia! What could I have to say about it? What could I know about it? I had better say nothing, in the Holt or anywhere else! But then it struck me, as Tom and I arm-in-arm passed a palace that was almost certainly a department store and then a department store that was almost certainly a palace, that the condition of not being on a scene long enough to know anything much – of responding deeply and towards the end desperately to a setting minimally understood – was exactly the condition of being alive. If I managed to live another seven years I'd have clocked up a meagre eighty years on earth: and measured against that fact, having spent a week in Russia was perhaps not the massive disqualification it appeared for having anything to say about Russia.

19

On the bus to the airport, Tanya said that round about here, if you kept your eyes open, you'd see a surviving Lenin. He was outside a local council office – ah, there he was! – *see*! And there, indeed, he was, in a pose not unlike Pushkin's in an exhilaratingly romantic statue that stands in a garden close to the Russian Museum: one of those literary statues that lean on the notion that a poet can always be identified by the wide sweeps he makes with his arms, with special reference to the fluttering eloquence of his fingers. Lenin's hands were soaring in illustration of some terrible assertion; and the wind had hold of him, made his coat-tails fly, the whole of him fly. He was known, said Tanya, as the dancing Lenin! And then you saw that the wind was the wind of music, and that, whatever the sculptor intended, it was some perfectly unpolitical gaiety that had seized him. Stern of beard, that narrow triangle of face tilted upwards, Lenin waltzed. I thought as he disappeared from view of the difference between public statuary in Russia and at home. I couldn't think of a statue in London that was anything but stockstill, watching for the birdie; whereas in Russia even Lenin had energy in the tails of his formal jacket – even Lenin danced!

At the airport our attempt to check in was received with amazement. No such persons were to be found in the passenger-list of the plane we alleged we were to travel by. Tanya had vanished. We were suddenly a little group of unescorted people who didn't exist and were making foolish claims to instant transport. There would be other planes, it seemed to be suggested, and somehow, at some time or other, we might possibly expect – perhaps in ones and twos, over days and weeks – to be taken back to London. Exhaustion made us stoical. We were not as appalled as we should have been that Philippa, the ex-teacher, was not with us. We wandered among the few shops there were in this corner of the airport, easily avoiding the purchase of matryoshkas. Mike Philadelphia filmed the check-in desk, encouraging laughter in the audience back home that he'd had every hope of presenting himself to, perhaps as early as the day after tomorrow.

Philippa re-appeared. She had thought, she said, that it must be proper to offer Tanya a farewell drink. She'd imagined we might all be involved in this: but what happened was that Tanya took her off at once to the nearest bar, which wasn't at all near. There Philippa asked Tanya what she would drink. Tanya said she drank nothing but champagne. It turned out that champagne could be bought only in bottles. Philippa herself was allergic to champagne. The bottle was emptied, strangely fast, Philippa thought, and Tanya, pointing her towards the rest of the party, vanished. 'It seemed the polite thing to do,' said Philippa, with the helpless decency in which one could read her whole history as a teacher.

At this point the airline beckoned us over to say it had reviewed the situation, and that, if the impression had been given that there was room for none of us on the plane, we should put it aside, replacing it with the impression that there was room for us all.

We'd not understood the ease of our arrival in Russia. As we shrugged off our despair and collected our boarding passes, we found we had no wish at all to ask questions about the difficulty of our departure.

Part Three

I

Harry Frost, who had just been to the Maritime Museum and was desperately trying not to be sucked into the history of seventeenth-century naval warfare, listened courteously to my talk of Russia: but I could see he was anxious not to be moved by it to any new enthusiasm.

He'd just seen, he said, a notice on an Underground platform, one of those notices that glide along under the details of expected arrivals, which began: 'Due to a person under a train . . .' Was he made angry, Harry wondered, by that graceless grunt – 'due to': or by the use of the word 'person', which always suggested a distaste for the human being involved: or perhaps by the callous-sounding abridgement of the account of the tragedy? He'd also had the painfully unsuitable thought that 'a person under a train' might be the subject of one of Edward Lear's drawings: discovering Lear having tempted him – but he hadn't the time, he said, always astonished by the limited character of this dimension – to take up water colours.

I told him how I'd become aware, gazing at all that Russian gold-in-the-air, that my good eye was turning, beyond doubt, by a stealthy advance of fog, into my bad eye. I also seemed to be giving more time to peeing than this valuable function quite deserved. Dashing recently to appease my bladder (which had suffered a change of character, unable to make its commonplace announcement of need without hysteria), I'd thought: a pee in time saves nine. It seemed soothing to have a proverb or two of this sort to mutter. A pee in the hand is worth two in the bush.

Harry's high blood pressure was lower, but not low enough. 'The trap closes' was his phrase for the things that were happening to us. But he had no time for all that, he said: there simply wasn't room in his life for these misfunctions and the fuss they gave rise to.

Well . . . time, I said. It seemed to me more and more that a major human problem was simply that of keeping abreast. In this last period the impossibility of responding with even minimal adequacy to the whirlwind of stimuli with which you were presented became specially difficult to endure. Human beings, you came to see, were creatures programmed to reply to what was addressed to them, who discovered that what was addressed to them was ridiculously, tormentingly too profuse for their powers of response to cope with it.

And for the ageing, the transformation of the world they'd known into a world increasingly unfamiliar was a private nightmare. It was like standing on stage, prepared and dressed to take part in a certain play, and slowly realising that the stage machinery, whirling round, was now concerned with the setting for a play of an unrecognisably different kind. For God's sake, what were you doing in *these* costumes, having learned *these* lines! The notion of its being a theatre was much to the point, for Kate and me. Nowadays we'd read an entire programme and not recognise the name of a single actor. It was like being shifted, probably overnight, to a planet that was deceitfully similar but in fact utterly different.

But then this was a stretch of history – likely to be followed by others even more intent on innovation – when the young could be virtually out of sight of their elders, even when these were not all that less young. I remembered an encounter I'd recently had when I'd gone looking for Mabel Street School, the first school I'd ever been to.

That had been (when I arrived there, in 1925) a tremendous crate of an old Board School in East Barton: and as I was savaged in its playground, Ben, six months younger, was queuing up to be savaged there himself. Thirty or so years ago it had been transformed. The horrid loftiness that had so frightened me as a five-year-old, finding myself in a building where the ceilings were out of sight, had been reduced, and a low rambling school had been made out of that cruelly tall one. Now, on this latest visit, I discovered that education had thrown in the towel altogether. Where the school had been was a number of small, chastely-curtained blocks of maisonettes (as the dainty term was). And on the fairly precise spot where, seventy years earlier, I had struggled to absorb the discovery that many human beings liked to throw other human beings to the ground and then make a crowing heap of themselves above their victims, a block had been created that, on its bland facade, bore, several times, a notice that struck me as one of the bleakest I'd ever seen, anywhere. In or out of context, it suggested the end of all delight. NO BALL GAMES IN MABEL COURT, it said. There was no way of knowing if it was an admonition, or a boast.

As I turned away I saw coming towards me two adolescent children, brother and sister, in the company of their mother. They had the old-fashioned faces of children out of a story by Edith Nesbit. But he was in a battleship-grey roll-necked jersey, that hung close to his knees: the arms being so long causing his hands to be lost. The apparent general intention of rejecting the natural punctuation of the body (knees, elbow, hips) was further declared by his shorts, which had the nature of a pair of parallel black tents, and seemed to begin (the length of the jersey making it impossible to be sure) well below the waist, coming to a depressed end halfway down the calves. The total effect was one of depression: his clothes hung with a voluminous despondency, and he was despondent inside them. The very material seemed unhappy, as if it felt itself to be mocked.

His sister (and the certainty with which she could be identified as his sister was part of their old-fashionedness) was wearing a white shirt that hung like a brief curtain from the points of her apprentice breasts, and three-quarter-length tights striped in green, orange, pink, purple and yellow. She seemed to be standing on a pair of sticks of seaside rock. Dressed like a clown, she appeared glum and discomfited.

Their mother was glummer: her dress straightforward, banal, sensible. And I thought how the whirligig of fashion for the young, ruthlessly kept spinning by the helpless market they offered, gave many no chance of relating what they wore to what they were. These two had been forcibly dressed by the exploiters of the double teenage fear of looking like their elders, and failing to look like their peers.

[139]

But their faces, and some stiffness about them, as well as something in the way they were formally and obediently in the company of their mother, belonged to a far older family style, one enormously familiar to me when I was a child. My sister and I had accompanied our mother in just this fashion: though, of course, our appearance being determined by her and my father, we'd seemed all of a piece. Our remaining suitable associates for our parents had been something my father had insisted upon as a measure of our general acceptability. It had been my gross failure in that field that he'd pointed to when I grew my first beard. 'Good God,' he'd cried. 'How do you expect your mother to go out with you if you look like that!'

A mere beard! . . . I seemed to see my mother, now, as she'd have been nearly seventy years ago, taking me through that infinitely distant East Barton to Mabel Road School on my first day and then, astoundingly, leaving me there: I seemed to see, that is, her ghost: and then thought that, given the speed of all these transformations, the swells of novelty that every year swept us bewilderingly further from our past (and, in any case, in no time at all piled newly-minted past upon newly-minted past), I must think of her as a ghost of a ghost of a ghost . . .

Harry told me, apologetically, of his recently-identified hernia: and, apologetically, I told him of the phone-call I'd had from Dr Rowe.

2

'Sorry,' Dr Rowe had said. 'That prostate test. The profile is a bit up. We'd better get the consultant to have a look. Now, don't have sleepless nights.'

I promised not to have sleepless nights and put the phone down and had several. It was difficult not to. I hadn't asked what the profile was and what was meant by its being up, partly because I suspected I wouldn't understand the reply, but mostly because I had no great desire for precise information. The consultant, as it happened, was attached to a hospital, established in the mid-nineteenth century to cope with Stone and other Urinary Diseases, that until recently had had its home in Covent Garden. I was ridiculously cheered by this chance, even though the hospital was now part of a larger one a mile away. It was possible to think that the consultant, Mr Jumper, was the latest in a line of engineers, their field being our (incidentally) amorous machinery, on whose services the Great Square of Venus had had a constant need to call.

Three months passed: Harry Frost had a date for his hernia operation, but I had none for my consultation. It was curious, I thought, that alarm at this lapse of time (if the profile might be up for the worst of reasons, shouldn't urgency come into it somewhere?), was modified by disbelief that it was occurring. Somehow, three limping months must be consistent with a (possibly) life-saving sprint.

Then the summons came. I was to see Mr Jumper on Wednesday of next week.

On Tuesday a voice on the phone asked if I could come and have my lens implant next day. There'd been a cancellation. My right eye now being utter fog, it would have seemed wildly unnatural to say No. I said Yes, and then rang Mr Jumper's department. Well, they said, of course they understood, but it might be some time before a new appointment with Mr Jumper could be fixed. I rang Dr Rowe, who sounded as close to dismay as he ever did. The letter to Mr Jumper, written three months earlier, in asking for me to be seen had used the word 'soon'. He'd frankly be unhappy if there was further delay. In his view, I should arrange a private consultation.

Which – with reluctance, for I hated the whole idea of jumping the queue – I did: setting off first to have my second eye miraculously improved.

I knew it was there, having rather often lately been challenged to read these charts. But with my right eye I could not have sworn to the giant A at the top of the pyramid of letters. 'Very bad,' said Miss Angelou's assistant: and I was unaccountably pleased.

My room-mate was an elderly Indian, who'd been born in Nairobi and educated in India, and had worked as a clerk here and there in East Africa before coming to Britain to be with his children. His

English was good but slow, his words seeming to be composed of letters as large as that invisible A on the chart. Addressed in any faintly unusual turn of phrase he was politely puzzled. Such an honest, unexciting man, I thought: and told him (with slowness matching his and the careful exclusion of all comic touches, which seemed particularly to throw him) what he was to expect.

He frowned over the evening's menu, and went to ring a son. Within an hour the son, and a daughter-in-law, and three grandchildren, all brilliantly clad, arrived with a meal. They spoke in what my roommate later told me was Gujarati: and I did not know him. His slow speech became a swift stream, with a lilt of emphases. He was – one didn't have to know Gujarati to be sure of it – sardonic, wittily allusive, lyrical: tender with them all, but picking up whatever they said on the wing, making away with it, offering it back (still on the wing) with variations. His voice was forever in flight, a bird of a voice: which sometimes found a perch and began a solo that made me smile, laugh or gasp, though I had no idea what was being said.

And then they went, and he fell to earth and spoke English again.

The technology was different, in details: a needle in the back of the hand – 'This may hurt a bit.' 'No worse than blackberrying,' I said, and was at once in the recovery room, in that condition that resembles a belligerent sort of drunkenness. Kate, invisible, spoke words from the ceiling. Return to ordinariness was quicker than before.

And my new lens was a marvel. Several lines below the great A was a row of very tiny letters, and I read half of them. 'Very good,' said Miss Angelou's assistant, and my pleasure was unaccountably deep.

And one morning a week later Kate and I made our way to the titanic flat in which Mr Jumper exercised his role as a private consultant, all ease and space and whispering promptitude compared with the setting in which he exercised his role as a public consultant. We waited in a desert of a drawing room, with more sofas in it than I'd ever seen assembled in a single space. A young woman with noiselessly twinkling legs escorted me to a boudoir in which I pissed into a bowl that politely measured the quantity and pace of my performance. Thence, through a door from which all the brutal quality of being a door had been removed by the curtains that hung in front of it, to meet with Mr Jumper, in a drawing room that made the room in which Kate and I had waited seem the merest parlour. I had never been in the presence of so much carpet. Mr Jumper directed me to what, having seen an *Antiques Roadshow* or two, I thought was a table that it might be sensible not to use in this fashion, and murmuringly directed me to stretch myself on it whilst he inserted a gloved finger into my bottom. Well, he said, now let us go and sit at the table in the middle of the room. We made our way there, and he said he'd found no sign of malignity. But the prostate was very much enlarged. Some (he seemed to suggest) laboriously bloody surgery might be involved. Would I be private or public? Or, to put it in another way, was I immensely rich? I was not even meagrely rich, I said. It would be public. Well, he said, then we would meet again on the day of the operation. I asked if I should give the young woman a cheque before we left. Oh no, no, *no*, he said: his account would reach me in due course. I collected Kate and we stepped back into the real world.

3

'We've got to give ourselves half a second.' 'A nip and a tuck should do that.' Each began to spin a great reel of tape, feeling for sound as a surgeon might feel inside a stomach. Triumphantly, they spun the excess half second into being and, with a slicing stroke of a razor blade, out of it. Having sliced, he nipped, she tucked, and it was done . . . Something like that.

One of the best things I've ever known, I thought: being in a BBC studio, putting a programme together. There is, perhaps, the writer, who's going to narrate it: and the producer; and the technicians. These last are people who know how to hold sound suspended, how to make it hover or dash, how to slide a sound under another sound, how exactly to match a passage of words with a passage of music: how, given an inflexible conjunction of voices and effects, to make that conjunction flexible. Today, in Manchester, putting together one of a run of programmes, we had the luck of having the local technical stars as you might have any set of wizards. They knew what was wanted before you knew it yourself: they knew ways out of impasses, they could turn suddenly discovered disasters in the script into satisfactions: they could set half a dozen turntables spinning and (after an amused mishap or two) have them all reaching a climax together. The two of them, in terms of tape, understood each other perfectly. I said, when it was over, that it had been a long sequence of *pas de deux*, and that all that hadn't happened was that he hadn't, as a climax, lifted her above his head. It would have been matter-of-factly suitable, if he had.

Of course, now all that was on the brink of being destroyed. The internal market was established, and nothing could be done without its being costed. It was as if it was held that, before accountancy became the very breath of everything, people had been perfectly indifferent to the expense of what they did. Now they were obliged to think of cost before they thought of anything else, because of the forms that had to be filled in, the sums that had to be calculated: the applications that had to be made: the decisions that were essentially and worriedly arithmetical. If a gramophone record was needed, from the BBC's own library, an invoice had to be made out, the expense of the transaction had to be assessed. There were tales of producers who found it quicker and cheaper and less of an interference with their business of making programmes to go out and buy their own copy of a record. It was altogether as if the studio had begun to fill up with phantom managers and accountants. And indeed, on the way to it you passed more and more new rooms devoted to management.

It was all part, I was convinced, of what had really begun in 1979. Always, famously and obviously, there'd been, over there, those who saw the making and management of money as the only rational human drive: and, over here, those who were primarily driven by other intents. These two busy sorts of people had never got on particularly well, but they'd not in any large or methodically destructive way trespassed upon each other's territory. At best, they had a sensible, sometimes comically rueful language in which to allude to their dependence on each other. Now that had changed. Now one of these tribes, having been given enormous power over the other, had set out to undermine whatever it instinctively knew were attitudes that lay at the heart of what the other did. A producer had told me how, summoned to a 'management exercise', she'd been asked who, in her department, she'd fire. She'd said, astonished, that that wasn't how she looked at her colleagues, as the fireable or the unfireable. 'But you must learn to fire people,' she was told.

It wasn't an onslaught upon the inefficient by the efficient. It amounted to a claim that, on this complex scene, there was only one kind of efficiency.

And there was the newest technology. I knew that, in my seventies, I could slip easily into being a Luddite: but in these busy studios, exercising their old magic, there were Luddites half my age. As an example of what brought this about, there was the gadgetry that could make everyone except the producer unnecessary. The wizards whose work was pure ballet were no longer required. What you had was this screen, and the mouse to be directed round it: and the producer would sit in solitude, creating the programme with twitches of her fingers. The bubbling warmth of co-operative programme-making would be superseded by this silent solo. Oh well, they'd say: seeing that it led to the same result, hard luck on the wizards! But it couldn't lead to the same result: because that old warm way of doing things brought a number of experienced minds to bear on a programme, and made for creative high spirits that became part of its quality.

A day or two after my return from Manchester, in Saturday afternoon Barton, I ran into George Straker, who (with an effect of unease on both sides) had been a classmate of mine at the grammar school. He'd held that managers ought to take over the world, long before they did. Nowadays he spoke to me, as a transparent non-manager, in the tones of the severer sort of probation officer addressing a minor criminal. First he'd ask about my writing (the subtext being that he was keeping an eye on my activities in this shady field), and then would probe a little deeper, with some reference to the BBC. This was to remind me that he was, and would continue to be, aware that I had associations with that organisation. He'd express firmly his fear that those brought in to set a sloppy institution to rights – to hollow out its creative substance and replace it with a stuffing of almost total management – were too likely to be softened by the insidious forces of the old order. Saying this, he'd fix me with a cold eye: clearly believing that at this very moment in time (a ghastly usage always on his lips) I was part of a team involved in transforming the steel that had made the Director General the man for his post into jelly.

Now he asked me what I was doing in the way of programmes (a question which he somehow made clear was asked not so he might hear them, but so they might be avoided), and I told him about Manchester and my fear as to what might be lost if the wizards were dispensed with. I knew, of course, that anything I said along these lines would chill the never-warm George below freezing point, but I wasn't going to spend any part of my Saturday steering a course among his prejudices. The only pleasure in an encounter with him nowadays lay, anyway, in selectively appalling him. So I said I loved the wizards' language: all that business of wondering if they had any room to cut on, and of deciding they had to give themselves half a second.

'I would suggest,' said George, 'that you tell your *friends*' (making a shuddering euphemism of the word) 'that they have no time to give themselves at all. From what you say, I conclude that their time is up.'

'Well, then,' I said: 'I think you might like to hear about my recent interview with Anthony Burgess and Gore Vidal, both of them together': knowing that, these being writers of the most unmanagerial kind, he would hate it.

4

I was presenting an arts programme in the World Service, and the producer had suggested we might cover a new collection of short stories by Burgess, and a novel by Vidal. He went away, brooded mischievously, and came back with the suggestion that we might interview both at once. Gore Vidal would be staying at a hotel in Mayfair, and Burgess too would be in London. Was I willing to take the risk, as he seemed to think it, of talking to the two together? I saw there was some element of an invitation to interview a pair of rival prima donnas, but I could imagine nothing but the amusement of it. Vidal had once written an account of Burgess and his work under the title, 'Why I am Eight Years Younger than Anthony Burgess'. It was (though not perfectly) respectful. I thought the interview might turn out to be a matter of not utterly watertight expressions of mutual admiration.

Burgess I'd known, in a bumping-into sort of way, for years: ever since in the mid-fifties we'd met at a party in Barton where everyone was at the beginning of things. He himself had barely set out on that course that was to make of him a sort of literary industrial complex, and that followed from his being told that he had only a year to live: after which books, and strangely barked pronouncements on intricate matters, poured out of him. The modesty of that first encounter remained the tone of all our later meetings. It was something I liked about him: a sometimes elaborately expressed insistence on remembering that distant evening, and on acting as if it were the sort of bond I had with those I'd been at Barley Road School with. But then in a sense we *had* been at the same school, were both products and survivors of coarsely riotous playgrounds, could communicate if need be in nudges. Though, of course, Burgess would have converted even nudges into great seminars of elbows.

I'd last met him on the publication of one of his novels, when he'd come to the BBC at Bush House to be interviewed for a book programme I was presenting. The day before, a review of the novel had appeared in *The Observer*, on a page on which Burgess himself had long been the star. It was a studiedly impudent review, mocking Burgess's baroque verbal pedantry and swagger, and his being inclined to mention that he was married to an Italian countess. Burgess turned out to have been horribly distressed by this review. What should he do? he asked. Should he write a letter to the paper, replying to the reviewer's audacities? Should he perhaps refuse ever to review for *The Observer* again? I was astonished, as a junior tradesman, to be consulted by such a grand senior, and in such terms. Surely he knew, if anyone did, that the only reply to such an attack was to make no reply at all. Left to itself, it would soon be forgotten: to turn it into a duel might make it memorable. Well, said Burgess, who *was* the reviewer, anyway? I had to say to this one-time poor boy from Manchester that the reviewer was a one-time poor boy from Manchester.

After the interview we talked, inevitably, about finding that we'd been frogmarched from our thirties, where we'd been when we first met, to our seventies. We talked, in fact, of bladders. In his house in Rome, Burgess said, he'd just had a lavatory installed inside the front door. That was as far as, on most occasions when he was returning from an outing, he could hope to get without disgrace.

I came to the occasion of the double interview meaning to ask Vidal what he thought of Burgess's book, and Burgess what he thought of Vidal's: and then to switch to a duet . . . an allusively vivid discussion, as it surely would be, of contemporary fiction. I explained this to my producer, who I didn't then know as I came to know him. I was unaware that his first instinct was always a pessimistic one. So now, at the mere sketching-out of my plan, pessimism flooded over him. He made the face of someone who thought I might be endangering the BBC's charter. He'd have preferred something much more controlled, he said. He'd hoped I'd have worked out perhaps a dozen strict questions. I said I liked a freer form of interview, which had some sense of where it might go but was open to surprise, and didn't deny itself the pleasure that sometimes emerged when talk ran away with itself. The producer's face darkened further. He had arranged that we had individual microphones in our lapels. These were fine, he said, until you came to sofas. He thought it only too likely that a hotel sitting room in Mayfair would offer sofas, and nothing but sofas: and deep, soft, sybaritic sofas, at that. And now my eschewal of a stern plan threatened to add to the danger that we'd loll physically the danger that we'd also loll conversationally.

We found Burgess in reception and made our way together to Gore Vidal's room. Or rooms, as they turned out to be. The door was opened by the novelist himself. He threw up his arms in one of his gestures of sculpturesque irony and cried: 'Welcome to the *Poverty Suite!*' It was not clear to me, who have limited experience of the dimensions of suites in one order of hotel and another, whether this was a cry of dismay as to the cramped nature of his accommodation, or one of shame at its extensiveness. But it was immediately evident that my producer had been right about sofas. There might have been as many in the rooms where I'd consulted Mr Jumper, but those were short-stay sofas. These in Gore Vidal's sitting room existed on the narrow frontier between comfort and fatal submersion. We sank into them, Anthony Burgess ready to do his drowned best to boom, as I thought (though in fact he settled for muttering), Gore Vidal to be wittily cruel, my producer to frown.

Of Vidal's book, Burgess spoke parenthetically, with an effect as of someone diving into dense eddies of second and third thoughts, a rumbling discursiveness – it never tidied itself into what might be seen as an opinion – and of Burgess's, Vidal spoke with highly-charged, unspecific amusement, not a single sentence offering itself for use in an advertisement. When it came to modern fiction, Burgess was of a mind to say (and did say) that one would admire this or that, if that or this didn't force one to turn to the question of how admiration (given a background of some thousands of years of literature) might be defined. Vidal, since he was sitting in London, felt bound to say that the British capital had become the source of an extraordinary crop of *little* novels. They were *very, very lit-* (he threw his head back and opened his mouth amazingly wide, with an immense display of teeth) *-tle* novels. They were produced by *ladies* (he made his eyes wide and balefully sorrowful), and he had to mention Miss Brookner, Miss *Broooooook-ner* (the name derisively cooed), though the truly awful name that had to be spoken was that of Margaret Drabble . . . Of this name he made a piece of hilarious bubble-gum, stretching it out (DRAAAABBBBBLE) and then stretching it out again (DRAAAAAAAAAABBBBBBLE), as if Margaret Drabble's actually having that name had made it inevitable that she'd write the novels he deplored: which were based on the belief that her little world ('her very LIIIIITTTTLE world') was of interest beyond its own shrunken bounds. I thought of how, in *Rowan and Martin's Laugh-In*, Lily Tomlin would say 'Gore Vidal?' when she was feigning to ring him about his failure to pay his telephone bill: 'Is that *Mr Gore Vidal* to whom I am speaking?', with a snort that made an improbable name seem even less probable. You can, I thought, do almost anything you like with almost any name: but, since none of us has a name likely to be perfectly unmockable, it was a field in which one did well to step lightly. I thought also of the world, much smaller than Margaret Drabble's, that I wrote about myself, and how I believed this was one of those respects in which size didn't matter. You could discern whatever you had the luck to discern of life from observation of human activity on any scale whatever.

When it was over (my ankles black and blue from little kicks my producer had directed at them, he gloomily of the view that the BBC would not recover from this), Anthony Burgess said with gallant and uncomplaining sadness that he wished I'd asked him about the title of his book. It involved a musical term. Burgess had always dreamt that he might add, to his massive repute as a writer, massive repute as a composer: and he never travelled without an electronic keyboard that could be slipped into a pocket, ready for the trying out of any musical idea that came. He could, he sighed, have illustrated his answer on this keyboard. I said, moving my ankles out of fire, that I'd be delighted, of course, to ask that question.

And Gore Vidal, who for some moments had been displaying a patrician sort of impatience, clearly wanting us out of the Poverty Suite, crossed the room and flung open a window, admitting the huge sound of the traffic in Piccadilly, together with the scarcely less huge sound of the traffic in its tributaries.

It was the last time I saw Anthony Burgess: forty years almost since we'd leaned our elbows on our host's grand piano in Barton and talked of teaching, and of how one might write about teaching.

When I met the producer, the next day, I told him of the bad night I'd spent, recalling – or struggling not to recall – foolish questions I'd asked, points made by one or the other that I'd not picked up. As for the producer, it was as if he had never in his life kicked an interviewer's ankles. He now had twenty-four edited minutes, he said: and perhaps he had gone soft on it, but he found it had a strange charm. He'd decided to give the whole half hour programme to it. 'I've twigged you,' I said. 'You always begin pessimistic and then become more cheerful.' 'Ah, but then *I*'ve twigged *you*,' he said. 'You always begin cheerful and then become pessimistic.' And it was true, and either made our working relationship an ideal one, or a disaster. Neither of us was ever able to decide which.

Though I offered George Straker only the outline of this story, I could see it had been enough to spoil his Saturday: and would have meant the end of the BBC, had he been in a position to bring it about.

5

I was recording the narration for a programme in a tiny studio in Broadcasting House when I became aware of a pain in the belly that within minutes had turned the whole world into nastiness. There was nothing to be said at all for being alive. In so far as I *was* alive, it was deep inside this belly-ache. Life was a boundless belly, and it boundlessly ached.

And when the ache ceased, many hours later, and as heavy day followed heavy day, I found that an activity I'd taken for granted for more than seventy years (since under my father's tutelage I'd become a more and more nonchalant master of the po) had ceased. The factory had closed: the workers had gone home. There wasn't even a nightwatchman or a guard-dog. I began to suspect that the very site had been levelled.

Dr Rowe suggested I seek the services of the district nurse. The district nurse came. She was a charming young woman, who took me through the necessary steps with such delicacy that, without too much offence, we might have incorporated what we did into a genteel afternoon tea party. The relief was enormous: but the sequel disappointing. Yes, it could be done, by a sort of ceremonious dynamiting, and at the expense of the district nurse's valuable time. But ordinary activity, now beginning to seem quite extraordinary activity, was in no mood to resume.

One of Dr Rowe's partners said it looked very much as if the trouble was in the colon. Well, she said, not to beat about the bush, it could be cancer of the colon. This, however, if caught in time, was an *eminently* curable form of cancer. She made it sound as though there was a case for being grateful for having it. There was a man at our local hospital, she said, who was a wizard at this sort of thing. She would put me down for a consultation with him.

And so I joined another of those queues of which a feature is that you have no idea where you stand in them. However long a visible queue is, it gives some hint of the degree of patience required. For all I knew, this queue might have stretched twice round the world. I tried not to remember what the doctor had said about catching an otherwise amenable cancer in time.

Now and then the district nurse came with her major sorts of explosive. Now and then I set off minor detonations of my own, with the help of materials provided by Dr Rowe. I waited.

Kate apologised for being unable to resist saying: 'Your colon has become a full stop.'

I began to worry because the colon was my favourite piece of punctuation. For some reason, I liked it as a hinge, sometimes a sequence of hinges, for whatever I had to say. I vaguely believed I'd picked up the practice from Bernard Shaw. There'd been a bad moment some years before when a literary journal had attempted to replace the colons, in a review of mine, with commas. This triggered a dread I suspect all writers harbour, that one day they'll be presented with something they're alleged to have written and will realise that all is over. The knack has gone. Here, in the morning post, was a proof of my review, and it was . . . Oh my God, I thought. The words, that were surely not mine, hung limply. I rushed for my carbon copy. No, a great many of the words, and much of the syntax, were not mine. An editor, for whom colons were clearly a cause of very great rage, had gone through the piece, ripping them all out. This is like going through a house and removing, wherever it's found, some item that the architect has favoured as a kind of general pin to hold the house together. What is left is a heap of bricks, wood and piping. The editor had reduced my piece to a heap of words, and as he began to attempt to reassemble it with the help of commas (which inevitably involved serious changes in everything I'd written) he began also to be aware of his hatred of the words I'd used. In a very free way, reconstructing this review which now had only a remote connection with the one I'd written, he tossed my words aside, and replaced them with words of his own choice. It was this travesty that ruined my breakfast that morning.

I wrote to the editor of the journal saying that if it was printed with my name under it I would make it known as widely as I could that the review was fraudulent. He wrote to say that I could have it restored to its original form if I wished, but he thought his copy editors knew what would be at home in the pages of the journal. I was furious at this notion that writers must be levelled to a general style, for the comfort of the journal that had invited them to write for it. I asked him what he'd have done about D.H.Lawrence, whose manner as a reviewer was exclamatory, often picturesquely abusive, and not intent on making itself at home anywhere. I hated altogether the sort of editing that amounts to rewriting. The invitation to review is presumably rooted in the belief that you can write. Even more to the point, how something is said is a vital part of what is said. The task of an editor is not that of paraphraser. And so on. Kate said having a subversive colon of one kind was enough, without working myself into a fresh fury about attitudes to colons of the other sort.

And then I was summoned to the hospital. I told my story, of which I'd become enormously tired, to an assistant of the wizard. He carried out an examination I was growing familiar with ('You should hear what little old ladies say,' he remarked in mid-probe), and reported favourably on the first twenty centimetres of the colon. The obvious next step, he said – the only way of finding out what was happening to the rest of it – was a barium enema. I'd be given a date for that.

I waited.

Notification of the date came: followed, the day after, with notification, at last, of the date for the prostate operation. I should present myself for that two days before I was due to present myself for the other. Once again I had come to the head of two of my queues at virtually the same moment. I rang the surgery. What should I do? Get the prostate done, said the doctor on duty. He was horrified at the idea that a hospital bed might be spurned. I rang the wizard's office, and the appointment for the barium enema was postponed.

And so one morning I presented myself at the hospital: not the one where my colon was under review, but another in the heart of London. I was received by a young orderly, who gave me a wristband with my name on it (and, inevitably, my date of birth), and showed me to my bed: which was in a bay occupied by half a dozen men, some of whom greeted him with cries of defiance. It seemed that he was part of a general joke, in which he featured as a hospital orderly out of some Gothic farce, and they as his sullen victims. There was a pretence of vital tubing being ripped out of vital organs: and then he'd gone, and boredom took over. To reach a hospital bed you must queue, and endure the tedium of the queue: and when you are in it you are still queuing, and still deeply bored, your private affairs on seething hold. You are queuing for the moment of escape.

I was visited by three or four clipboards, each of which apologised for asking questions that had been asked, or would be asked, by the others. To one I mentioned the problem of the colon, and how it was to be dealt with in three weeks' time by way of a barium enema: and she became thoughtful, and said she would pass this news on to the consultant's registrar. He arrived to give me an account of what awaited me. The size of the average prostate operated on was represented by the figure 30: the very largest were 100 plus: mine was 70. Because of the size of mine, there was no certainty that it could be dealt with entirely by way of keyhole surgery. It might be necessary to fall back on something more old-fashioned. And he had to tell me that – since a sphincter must be severed – a probable effect of the operation was that I would find myself reduced to retrograde ejaculation. This meant that at traditional moments of excitement, when one had become accustomed to being a fountain, one would not be a fountain. There was no reason, he delicately suggested, why the excitement should disappear: but I might have to forgo the familiar evidence of it.

I thought how, sixty years earlier, when preventing this evidence from making itself obtrusive was a major anxiety, retrograde ejaculation would have been a tremendous boon. But for that sort of lightening of one's burden it now came (the whole vocabulary was riddled with pitfalls) far too late.

It struck me also that 'retrograde ejaculation' was a curiously ugly way of saying 'injaculation'. If one was able to ejaculate, then one must be able also to injaculate. In other contexts, it would be to frame in one's mind, but not utter, a strong comment. ' "How dare you speak to me like that!" he injaculated.'

The registrar added that I should not henceforth be able to father a child. I said it seemed possible to describe old age as an escalation of inconveniences, but this was not one of the worst.

Well, he said: that brought him to this question of the barium enema. He was uneasy about that being postponed any further. Almost certainly three weeks from now would be too early for it: not wholly healed. I wouldn't be able to cope with any violences there might be. A carcinoma could well be involved, and if one were discovered there should be no delay in dealing with it. Could he go away and think about this for five minutes? He returned without a decision, and said he must talk to colleagues. Well, here was my lunch, so I'd have something to do while I waited. He gave me a worried smile, and I felt how odd it was to have become, from one moment to the next, a dilemma.

No, he said, returning: no. They really felt they mustn't operate. Rotten business, coming in and being sent home again. But there was general regret that I'd delayed the enema, and it was hoped I might be able to have the original date restored. If, returning from the holiday I'd told him we were taking in six weeks' time, I got in touch and said all was well, then he'd try to put my name back in the surgeon's diary at a date as early as possible.

'You're going already?' asked a man two beds along. 'I was only invited for the lunch,' I said. The orderly took back my wristband, someone shouting as he did so that here was one man at least who'd got away without having his blood sucked in the middle of the night.

No, said the wizard's office. The original date for the enema was now fully booked. They'd let me have a new one when they could.

As if to match one's thoughts, which were of *growths* (a word always by adults spoken in hushed italics when I was a child – 'She has a *growth*!'), problems sprouted from one's problems. So to be in the only fit state for an enema, utter emptiness was necessary: and I had not yet hit upon an infallible means of achieving that emptiness. Even the district nurse could not always produce it. And the hospital was insistent that what should be used was Epsom Salts. I tried Epsom Salts, to find that this was where their legendary efficacy met its . . .

'Waterloo' was among the words and phrases Kate and I were trying to cut out of our vocabulary. 'I pooh-pooh all that,' said Kate, referring to a statement by a minister who'd done as much as anyone to make the tormenting of teachers a branch of government: and then apologised – not to this wretched politician, of course, but to me. There was no way, having this disorder, of not becoming impatient with the verbal gaucheries it was allowed to give rise to. So the doctors themselves talked of defecation, of motions. The surgeon's registrar had even talked of 'poo'. They were all such genteelisms! I could not begin to imagine what it was like to defecate: though I thought it could hardly be done without the aid of probably very large amounts of machinery. It simply didn't describe one of the commonest and most useful of human activities. It was like talking of osculation instead of kissing. Damn it, your only honest word was 'shit'.

I found myself weaving my way round the topic with cowardly gestures of the hands.

6

It's a curious thing, to be reduced to nervously waiting for one of the simplest of acts to become possible. Thank goodness, I'd think, that life was such a remorseless entertainment. You stepped out into the day, dogged by some dismal problem, and inevitably found yourself a spectator of one drama, however slight, after another. When I was a teacher I'd sometimes ask my boys to write for five minutes about the five minutes before they'd entered the classroom. The notion of any

class to whom I was addressing this request for the first time, that
nothing had happened, of course nothing had happened, how daft
could you be (simply being a teacher giving you a good start, but even
so) ... this notion could be undermined: sometimes by a question.
'Something in the way you and Perks came into the room – ?' 'He
made me mad. I had to hit him.' 'Nothing happened?' 'You want me
to write about hitting Perksie?' A shrug of the shoulders was all the
reply I needed to give.

About this time I was travelling uncomfortably through London by
Underground, and found myself sitting opposite a West Indian, a lean
man in a leather cap, with a big, uneasy dog at his feet. As people
pushed past, the dog seemed to be maddened by their scent, and would
half-rise, sniffing hugely and baring its teeth. 'You don't have to
worry,' said its owner to a woman who plainly thought that was
exactly what she had to do. He tightened the leash to force the dog
down again. The man had a large ease about him, and an air of being
anxious to offer reassurance and relax people – even when, as with the
dog, he was providing the cause of their tension. He beamed round
generally: a creature from some amazingly different world from that
of the London Underground. Here was bristling privacy, here were
numerous varieties of unease: and in the midst of it was this man
looking round companionably, hopefully offering smiles, his appetite
being for talk, and for being in the middle of talk. Next to him sat a
small elderly man, more tense than most: a widower, almost certainly,
everything about him speaking of sad solitude as everything about the
West Indian spoke of merry gregariousness. Suddenly, addressing him,
the West Indian cried: 'So many people don't live at all, you know. Do
you know that? So many people don't live at all!' The dog rose at the
sound of his voice, but he squeezed it back to the floor. 'You know,
they don't live at all, you know! You know what I mean?' The small
sad man made himself smaller. 'They go out to work at eight, you see,
and they come home at six, that's it, isn't it, and they don't live! They
don't spend their time with their loved ones! You know? Well, I do
nothing but look after my dog, and I'm *living*.' The sad man smiled
minimally. '*You're* living! I think *you're* living!' The man shrugged,
the smallest shrug imaginable. The West Indian in his turn grew larger,

easier: as if he had blundered upon a soulmate. 'You having a holiday? You giving yourself a holiday this year?' he asked. Yes, murmured the man, plainly not wanting to reply but not knowing how not to. Yes, he was. 'Where you going?' He was going to Majorca. 'Who you going with?' He was going by himself. 'Ah!' cried the West Indian. 'Don't you worry! Don't you worry about that! You'll find someone! You know what?' The dog seemed to think it was the object of this question, and had to be forced back on its growling haunches. 'You go to a disco!' cried the West Indian. 'Wear something bright!' The sad man seemed deeply appalled. It was impossible to believe that, at his jolliest, he had ever worn anything bright. The West Indian smiled to himself, nodded, looked smiling round the carriage: throwing the discussion open, in an atmosphere of startled closure. 'That's the thing to do!' he cried. 'Wear something bright!'

Then the train stopped and the sad man rose and made his way to the door. The dog rose, too, and growled horribly: and the West Indian smiled, a smile that didn't belong at all to a tunnel under London.

'I love you all the way,' he cried.

7

And I was given a date for the enema. The date approached: I drew upon my now huge repertoire of aperients. Nothing worked. On a Sunday I paid an emergency call at the surgery. Here, said the doctor on duty, were prescriptions for two nostrums, a milder (which was mild only by comparison), for the immediate problem: and another which was 'very nasty' for the final clearance. 'If you're suffering from anything after you take that,' she said, smilingly brutal, 'it won't be constipation.' We had to drive out of town to find a chemist open who could make up the stronger prescription. 'You are having an examination?' he asked. 'Yes, I am.' 'Because it is very potent.' I said I feared it needed to be.

The milder preparation was too mild. It did no more than scribble its noughts and crosses of pain across my guts at a greater pace than its predecessors. On the eve of the enema, I took the other, and went to bed. I didn't sleep. It was as if a team armed with machetes, who'd been training for the event, had set to work, accompanied by another making use of a medley of saws. It was astonishing what variations on this order of pain there could be. I was in the agonising grip of a laxative that held itself to be infallible but had failed, and was furious about it.

In the morning Kate rang the surgery: and in due course Dr Rowe himself appeared. It was a matter for the hospital, he said, and went off to the phone. I was a seventy-four-year-old, he told the doctor at the other end of the line (as reported by Kate), but was a working writer, twice as bright as himself and his colleague put together. Why, Kate and I wondered later, this extravagant account of his groaning patient? And then saw it must be because there had to be special pleading to get a sudden bed for someone of my age. I thought, guiltily, that the case still wasn't made for admitting me. No one could get in without keeping someone else out.

Dr Rowe returned to sit on my bed. It might be a carcinoma, he said (to my relief, not drawing a diagram): but cancer always travelled in the line of least resistance, and in the case of the colon, this lured it into a cul-de-sac, from which it was not able to spread. I was amazed to think of a gullible, or naive, cancer. The hospital would prepare me for the enema, and that, one way or the other, would solve the mystery. I would have to insert myself into the system by way of ACCIDENT AND EMERGENCY: being, of course, the latter, hoping not to develop into the former.

Being in Accident and Emergency, in a large reception area, was like being part of the scene of a multiple pile-up, involving hospital trolleys. We lay there at every sort of angle, amid a litter of relatives and friends, whilst doctors, nurses, persons with clipboards, weaved their way amongst us, sorting us out. I was wheeled off for an X-ray of my abdomen, and then back again. A bed being promised though not yet, Kate went, and I lay and stared at the ceiling. It was a moment very curiously of being left to oneself, having been withdrawn from the

customary traffic of things. It seemed to me there'd been moments like
this in childhood, when I'd been aware of being Teddy Blishen (a
tenuous and, at such moments, tremulous identity), staring at a ceiling,
having for one reason or another been found unsuitable for active,
mainline existence. I supposed – a thought that was saved from being
cheerless by the sheer interest of it – that there'd be many occasions of
the kind as I became more and more in need of repair, and valiant
invisible supporters of life, such as my colon, developed wearinesses.
Oh, that resemblance of experiences in childhood to those of old age!
– I was constantly running into it. You'd been tentative and shaky
from novelty, and now you were becoming tentative and shaky from
staleness. There was a neatness about it.

Then I was in Nightingale Ward, and was attached to a drip-feed
bottle by way of a tube embedded in a vein in the back of my hand,
and a large man lying on the bed opposite, who'd removed his jacket
but not his shoes and was still otherwise clothed, his braces being
amazingly scarlet, was telling me of his experiences as a bus conductor.
He'd been stabbed by passengers several times, he said, and then was
threatened with prosecution for carrying a ball of some kind in his
money bag to thwack an assailant with. He asked me to say if this was
fair or not. As it happened, I thought it was not: but I wouldn't
anyway have said it was, for he had the appearance of someone who,
refused support, could easily have induced himself to injure a working
writer, even (or especially) one twice as bright as a brace of doctors.
He said he was due to have his prostate operation next day. He was
only fifty-two, and this also seemed to him unfair. I readily agreed that
it was unfair.

In a corner of the ward a patient, very old, was talking to his wife
in spectacular whispers. Coming myself from the dying/moribund
world of marriage, I had no doubt it was his wife: only old marital
associates were ever whisperingly intimate in quite that way. As they
talked, she adjusted the collar of his pyjamas. It was what Kate was
always doing to me – acts of absentminded housewifery. Earlier still it
was what my mother did in what became a doomed lifelong struggle
with my crumpledness. I'd spelt out the danger of it to Kate. We'd be
approaching the heavenly gates, hand in hand, and as we reached

them, at the very moment before our admission to non-stop bliss, she would tidy my collar: and I would utter a single disqualificatory word and spin downwards out of her reach for ever.

I'd be dealt with next day, they said, by way of very special enemas. Meanwhile I must eat and drink nothing. I must lie in this kindly space, defined by a meagre geometry of lines made by the overhead railways for the bed-curtains, the tall standards to which drip-feed bottles were attached, the loops and droops of tubing. There was the constant distraction of the presence and predicaments of others: the stark routine: and the absence of privacy. One old man, bearded, deathly pale and sad, had dealt with this last by making for himself a separate world of silence. The rest of us might not have been there. At times he'd get out of bed, take his dressing-gown from under his pillow where, folded, it acted as a prop for his head, put it on, go to the bathroom (taking his silence with him), return and fold the dressing-gown with much care and replace it under his pillow, and then fall again into sad, pallid sleep.

It was a cold night. 'Did you see the polar bear walk through here – about three o'clock last night?' called Fred, from the bed opposite. 'Missed him,' said Reg, on the other side of him. 'But saw the penguins.' Fred had not helped himself by dispensing with a pyjama jacket, though his deeply tanned torso suggested that the two weeks he'd just spent in Ibiza had warmed him for life. He'd been preparing himself, he said, for that prostate operation that he thought he'd come to so unfairly young, and that was to take place today. Reg was also to be operated on, with three others.

We had breakfast. 'Congratulate the chef on the corn flakes!' called Fred, through his built-in megaphone.

Once more I was among my Cockney uncles. Every remark Fred offered was a fist aimed half-playfully at your midriff. I knew the comedy of that – Uncle Tom soliciting my opinion (I being seven or eight perhaps) and hinting by his jocular posture that the wrong response might lead to physical damage. Reg had my Uncle Dick's role – that of gentle confirmer. Fred, who'd graduated from buses to taxis, talked noisily, as the pre-op routine got under way, about death on the roads: caused, he said, by the mad desire to get somewhere a few minutes earlier than you might otherwise have done. 'Silly buggers! You know that, Reg? The world's full of silly buggers!' He told several horror stories, hideously unsuitable for the ears of those about to be subject to surgery: and Reg said: 'So, the moral of all that is: drive carefully.' 'That's *right*!' cried Fred, sounding amazed and grateful. 'You're *right*, Reg! Reg, that's *right*!'

Geoff, my immediate neighbour, merrily miserable in a style I recognised, told me of the effect of tablets he'd had to take to combat high blood pressure. They had brought his sex life to an end. He'd not minded too much ('You know what I mean?'), but it hadn't pleased his wife. She said in her sixties she was too young for that. He represented both their positions by making a face alternately furious in her style, and guilty, in his own. Apart from this problem, he said (the high blood pressure compounded by his wife's woebegoneness), he had three others, all fairly serious: and he spelt out his notion of how the doctors would deal with them. 'Then I'll be all right,' he said. 'And then I'll be run over by a bus.'

'I told you. I'm off the buses,' said Fred. 'I'll be run over by a taxi, then,' said Geoff.

Fred (a moment after he'd looked through a window and said: 'I see the Dynorods van has come!') was the first to have the curtains drawn round him and to be prepared for the theatre. He emerged in a white gown. 'Looks like I'm doing your operation,' he said to Reg. The immensely tall trolley called for him, and he climbed on to it: holding, I noticed, his little white mob cap in his hand, clearly not willing to put it on till he was out of sight. Someone called: 'Don't let him drive – he's only licensed for taxis!' He vanished, waving.

I was given the first of my dramatic enemas, by a nurse who'd not lost her sense of the comedy of these procedures. 'Try to hold on as long as you can,' she said. A commode was brought alongside for my use. It was a suddenly sunny day, and through gaps in the curtains drawn round my bed warm bars of light fell across me as I lay there, trying to hold on. I felt the quite beautiful oddity of it, for these stripes of sunshine increased the resemblance of the tent I was in to a medieval pavilion. I was in Church Farm Hospital, and I was inside a visual joke, and at the same time I was a figure in another joke, an intestinal one that might have been set up by the boys I'd clattered through Union Street with nearly seventy years earlier; and I was, it struck me, enjoying the huge embarrassment of it. And then (as I glanced impatiently at my watch – the nurse had said it would be best if I could hang on for twenty minutes) I remembered a radio occasion, long ago. It had been a programme concerned with new paperbacks, and I was there to be talked to by the panel about a book in which I'd described my experiences as a conscientious objector in the Second World War. And Irene Handl was one of the panel: that actress, tiny and square, who was a deeply convincing stage Cockney, but was also a novelist writing of the bizarre aristocrats among whom she'd been brought up. She said she'd liked the book, and especially the accounts of agricultural weathers and of the queer beauty of days spent in ditches or on cornstacks. And another panellist, the novelist Paul Theroux, said yes, but he had been aware of a kind of embarrassment in the tone of the book. And I said I was glad that was what he'd detected, since I did find that life was embarrassing: and then realised that what I'd said out of instinctive defensiveness was true. For me, life is an experience of having been rushed without apology onto as alarming a stage as could be imagined, and never being at all sure what role one's intended to play in the non-stop drama being presented on it. I'm often astonished by the success with which men and women outface the plain fact that what they are doing, sometimes their whole existence, is (not necessarily through any evident fault of their own), an embarrassment.

When the broadcast was over, I remembered (on the brink of being able to hold on no longer), Irene Handl had raised herself on tiptoe and kissed me on the lips: and had then lowered herself, stepped back and said: 'And did *that* embarrass you?'

I was emptied, but not so emptied that I could eat a mince that tasted furtively green. Fred was spared this by not being returned till after lunch. He'd been waited for by a woman whose hair was a golden heap: her arms had been taken over by bangles, her lips were as scarlet as his braces. She wore high-heeled shoes, and her legs were

stunningly assertive about being legs. Brisk, glittering, she supervised
the slow return to life of a Fred reduced to murmurs: about wanting a
pillow raised, and at once lowered, and a mouthwash provided, and
instantly withdrawn. Her patience was perfect, and we took it that,
for all her unmarital colourfulness, she must be Mrs Fred. But
questioned when she'd gone, Fred was shocked. No, no, bugger that,
she was simply one of his ladies. He had several. They all had a key to
his flat. You felt she'd happened to be the gleaming creature on duty
that day. 'Nothing heavy,' said Fred, shuddering in the midst of his
post-operational gadgetry: the drip-feed, the superior carrier bag on
the floor beside him in which, by way of tubing, blood and pee
accumulated. 'I couldn't tie myself down.'

The last to return was the old man whose wife I'd observed
absentmindedly adjusting the collar of his pyjamas. He was so awfully
the last that we feared for him, and for his wife, waiting beside his
empty bed: but then the slow traffic of information reached us – the
lift in which patients were taken down and brought back again had
failed. It took three hours to repair. He appeared at last, desperately
pale, an oxygen mask over his mouth, and she took him back into her
care. 'Glad to see you,' called Fred. 'And so's your wife. She was very
worried. Said she thought you might have had your passport with you.'

I was made a topic of discussion by a white-coated panel. The
problem that had brought me there, said one, was that my system had
defied that fabulously forceful laxative. Now I was in a perfect state
for a barium enema, said another, and the logic of things suggested I
should have one instantly. But the reality of things, said another, led
to the conclusion that the enema couldn't be hoped for until I'd
rejoined the queue and come to the top again. Inevitably, if I showed
that I could take food without pain or discomfort, I must go home –
tomorrow – and wait to be resummoned. Meanwhile, I'd be given a
regimen designed to ensure that what had been persuaded so dramatically to respond would not be allowed to fall again into the sulks.

At specified moments, a large, black, merry attendant brought tea.
But for Fred and Reg tea was best when it could be had at whim.
'Everyone tells us,' they'd say, 'that you're the best tea-maker in the
hospital.' The attendant shook with the laughter of one who wasn't

going to be fooled by flattery so gross and obvious. Within minutes, tea appeared.

As did the nurse in charge of us for the night. He was a young Indian, a delicately slim gliding man, who introduced himself as V.K., and addressed us as 'gentlemen'. His air was a curious mixture of concern and calm: he seemed ready for disaster, and anxious to make it clear that he could cope with it. Someone made a rash move and tore the tubing of the drip-feed out of the vein in the back of his hand. Blood flowed so copiously that V.K. couldn't go for help, or for the materials needed to staunch it, but sat on the man's bed, a finger stemming the worst of the flow: in a voice obviously designed to be penetrating without causing panic, calling for help into the open space that led into the next ward. When the little crisis was over, he moved about the ward as if prepared to reassure anyone who'd been disturbed by it. There was a sweet and oddly sad readiness of service about him.

And I lay there with a surprising thought in my head; that this was a strangely beguiling place. The devotion of everyone I'd seen to the easing of pains and miseries, making itself evident in the midst of a frantic tangle of small tasks, was remarkable and moving. Hospitals, I thought, were like schools – their existence rested, whatever happened in fact, on a belief in the duty owed by humans to humans that contrasted amazingly (and painfully) with the quite other philosophy that ruled the world outside their walls. Look on this picture and on that! Here, a world of care: there, a world of indifference.

In the night, having been woken by my bladder, I'd find myself gliding, barefoot, past V.K. We'd bow, slightly: and, slightly, smile.

He gave us over to another in the morning with the words: 'I hope you have a good day, gentlemen.' 'A nice sort of chap,' said Reg. 'Doesn't fuss.' 'Just sort of glides along,' said Fred.

Back home, I found I'd been made tremendously aware of the little cupboard of the guts. Having had it violently unpacked, I found myself putting things back into it with apologetic caution.

Dr Rowe said alas, no, it wouldn't make sense for us to have our imminent holiday in Greece. It wouldn't do to miss another date with the barium enema: and, in any case, until they knew what my colon was up to, I should stay within reach of reliable medical aid. As, one had to admit, medical aid might not be on that little island. It was largely an olive grove, and the roads, such as they were, were black with centuries of the spilled olive juice. They said it was where Antony and Cleopatra spent their last night together. We'd booked the lower floor of an apartment by the water: another thing they said was that you needed hardly to get out of bed – you could lie there and watch the world go by: if you didn't mind that the world had been reduced to a fishing boat or two, and a calm amount of sunlit blue water.

We resigned ourselves to the experience of *not* having this holiday.

8

About this time my Aunt Minnie died, who was the last of my father's family, and only sister to my little mob of uncles. To my surprise, she'd asked to be buried in the Cornish village that had been my grandmother's birthplace. Her tormented feet (in her last years she'd been taken over by arthritis, which had turned hands and feet into burning knobs and claws and had commandeered her joints for its own cruel purposes) were to be pointing to the sea.

At this end of things, when there was such a dreary danger that your thoughts would settle into final staleness, I found it cheering when someone I'd lazily believed I knew everything about (or could safely guess at whatever I didn't know) did something completely unexpected. I'd never have imagined that Minnie, who'd spent most of her life elsewhere, was so drawn to Cornwall. I had no idea where that request about the way she lay in the grave came from. (I supposed it was meant to ensure that when she rose on doomsday she'd immediately set eyes on the sea. I'd thought she was an entirely prosaic person, and had never known she had such feelings about the sea.)

In my earliest memory of her she was eighteen, a clumsy girl with a thick tongue and a great clatter of a laugh. To my horror, in the appalling absence of my mother, she was undressing me for bed. She was a large, noisy monster with a tormentor's delight in uncovering what I'd assumed to be the unbreachable privacy of my flesh. I knew in my thin child's only too blatant bones that she was taking my clothes off for the hell of it. This wasn't being undressed to go to bed as for four thoroughly satisfactory years I'd known it. It was being undressed to make some point about my being, in a respect I couldn't grasp but knew I'd be outraged if I did, ridiculously miniature. I had a child's understanding that here was a near-adult being naughty, and its instinct about the drift of the naughtiness. Minnie clattered with laughter, and it sounded rude and unkind. Seventy years later I find it easy to remember that laughter, and to guess at its chief causes as she stripped this risible shrimp of a nephew. She'd grown up with six elder brothers, all of them rougher teases than she ever was. How slyly (and rudely and unkindly) they'd have joked with, and about, this fleshy, giggling girl who'd arrived among them, the last-born. For her I must have been a god-sent example of a male younger than herself who'd been brought up soft and naive, lacking the jocularly brutal education six brothers could provide. If she'd been turned into a tormentor, I'd been turned into someone horribly easy to torment.

That had been at my grandmother's house in New Barton. I was being undressed by Aunt Minnie because that afternoon my mother had carried my brother, whose first birthday it was, across the triangle of grass in front of our council house in East Barton and across Long Street to Ferguson Road, where she disappeared. I was standing in our front room beside a neighbour, watching her go. It is a memory so intense that in some fashion I am still that small boy, watching. Ferguson Road was forbidden to me, and I thought in a general way that this was because it was the home of assorted villains, natural and supernatural: but I now think it was because those who lived in Ferguson Road were a shade less respectable than we were. In fact you had to go that way if you wanted to reach the railway station. That's where my mother needed to get so that, with her child in her arms, she could take the train to King's Cross, where my father met her. They took my brother then, by bus, to the children's hospital in Great Ormond Street, where he died that night.

In time, my mother told me, my grandmother sent a bill for my night's lodging.

I remembered my grandmother's little rented house as if it, too, clattered with laughter, not much of it very kind. When I knew it, it was an occasional gathering-place for my uncles, all of them married, most still living in East Barton: deeply quarrelsome men, whose delight lay in tormenting one another. I derived from the experience the powerful sense, never to be quite dislodged, that it was what a family existed for: to make one another the butts of a sort of ill-natured farce. They were readily angry, and the causes of their anger lay in such matters as, for example, that of their houses being rented. At least two of them, my father and Uncle George, were to become house-owners (and to be mocked for it): but even they, my childhood memories tell me, were made hot under the collar by thoughts of rent. They talked, anyway, about bloody landlords, who had bloody agents: and the bloody rent was always likely to be raised. They had bloody employers, too, given to taking bloody liberties. My grandmother's house in those days vibrated with this word, which I hardly thought of as the same as the word I was forbidden to use. It was, as uttered by my father and his brothers, a word expressive of their tremendous and generally derisive masculine energy. It was a clenched fist thrust under the nose of much of the world they moved in. There weren't many things that weren't bloody. Certainly each brother at some time or another became, to the others, a bloody brother. 'That bloody brother of mine.' It could, the words being my father's, be George, Jack, Harry, Will, Arthur . . . When their rages became methodical, they wrote to each other on toilet paper. In the end, as they entered middle age, they fought free of each other. Towards the end of his life my father told me, speaking with the special frostiness of utterance he reserved for statements of basic principle: 'We find it best to keep relatives at a distance.' When Auntie Minnie, to his sternest horror, once knocked at the door of his retirement home on the south coast, he said: 'I suppose she's come to cadge for clothes.' It was what, out of true need, they had all done when they were young. For the poor, cadging was a straightforward sensible activity. You missed no opportunity of putting yourself in the way of being patronised, given that the results were likely to be practical ones.

It struck me, as I thought of Aunt Minnie stretched out under Cornish soil, her toes turned towards the breakers, that one of the reasons why my father had found me detestable was that, once in the grammar school, I indulged myself in looking round. I sat back on a little heap of mild ideas and thought about what I might do in life: at one point resting on the view (based largely on my reading of novels) that I might do nothing at all. 'I'm not going to be turned into a wage slave,' I cried once, in our cramped living room. I see now that, given the desperate character of my father's attempt (and that of his brothers) to secure for themselves some modest comfort in life, such idle amateurism on my part must have inflamed him beyond bearing. He and my mother had never, at any moment, been able to lie back and reflect on what they'd do next. For them there had never been any elastic. They had been driven, for the entire vigorous part of their lives, from one forced position to another. It was quite other people who leaned on their walking sticks and, perhaps smiling, thought their way through various choices as to the way forward. And I wondered now, quite unhappily, at the suddenness with which, out of their world, so hideously lacking in give, scope, the possibility or even the notion of second thoughts, had come my world, insolently different. I had thought often enough about the distance first-generation grammar school children might have travelled from their roots: but until this moment of the news of Aunt Minnie's death, I had not fully felt the measure of it.

My father and my uncles had been, as much as anything, captives: and they had spawned creatures some of whom must have seemed to them insufferable dilettantes.

It was, anyway, a sudden burden of intense disbelief that I became aware of when I had that news of Minnie's going. Of that passionate tangle of hostilities, grudges endlessly harboured, revenges persistently taken, no trace now remained. Nothing, nothing at all. All those cornered creatures, given to cornering one another, had gone.

And God damn it, when we did go, wasn't the clear-out absolute!

There was a heap of gowns, variously blue, and I noted my hesitation, and the reasons for the choice I made: that this, I thought, was the prettiest blue, and (there was a mirror in the cubicle) that I looked nice in it. And as I sat waiting with Kate to be admitted to the presence of the radiographer, a passing nurse called out: 'Hey, that suits you!' 'I know,' I said. 'It's why I chose it.' 'Well,' she said to Kate. 'You know what to buy him for Christmas.' And I thought without shame (which had played havoc with my first seven decades but had increasingly found itself twiddling its thumbs during my eighth) that they'd have had little trouble, in this workaday corridor, in putting Narcissus at ease.

After my many unseemly misadventures – and though I'd been made ready by the district nurse, whose visits continued to have an unlikely delicate charm – I was sceptical about being in a fit state for the barium enema. But the radiographer, a stern Indian, turned out to have no doubt of it, and at once began the procedure of which the account given by the hospital, sensibly made simple, read like a phrase book. 'A small soft tube is inserted into your back passage. Some white liquid is run into your bowel. This is followed by some air. The doctor will take some pictures.' (With, it was difficult not to think, the camera handed to him by the postillion.)

There should have been another sentence: 'Leave your arms at home.' You lay on the hard surface of the X-ray table, and above you, often coming crushingly down upon you, was the huge camera: and you were given a dizzying sequence of instructions. 'On your left side,' and instantly: 'On your right side,' and instantly: 'On your back,' and instantly: 'On your front.' This could be done, though not easily, if you hadn't these bulky irrelevant tendrils, that had had little if any practice in being tucked in, got out of the way. With them, it turned out to be just possible: but you couldn't see how. The whole purpose of the exercise might have been to demonstrate how ill-made a human being is for rapid rotation in a confined space. At times you were in plain danger of wrecking wrists. Soon I was worrying about the need (which seemed to be encouraged by a doctor who'd emerge from a room in which I supposed he was watching the film) to go on and on (and on) with it. Surely the matter could have been settled one way or another with a half – a quarter – an eighth of all these cruel spinnings? Perhaps the radiographer and the doctor were simply fascinated by the ruin inside me? They began to leave me, bruised and wishing my arms away, for longer consultations. Once the radiographer appeared to say: 'You have a very long colon': and, fumbling for a response, I could come up only with a sensation of guilt, as if I'd been perfectly well aware that only colons of a certain length were allowed, and had nevertheless smuggled in one that infringed this clear rule.

But at last, after an hour, feeling beaten up, I was allowed to extract myself from the blue gown, and go.

What, I asked Dr Rowe, was I to do about medication while I waited for the consultant's verdict? He asked when they'd said I'd have that. Three weeks after the enema, I said. Oh, he said, that wouldn't do. The practice was opposed to such delays. He'd ring the hospital now, this moment, and insist on knowing what had been discovered. And he did so. Had a patient with him, he said, who'd had a barium enema a week ago, and was naturally anxious to know the result. He listened, tapping with his pencil, and I tried to come to absolutely no conclusion as to the meaning of the rhythm it made. And then: 'Oh – wonderful!'

There was no malignancy. What I had was a redundant colon – which had made photography difficult. He took a piece of paper, and I braced myself, but cheerfully, for the diagram. This colon, he said, had seriously lost shape, and had developed awkward pockets: and he drew what appeared to be an insane snake that, already having arthritic coils, had dined on a number of bizarre victims, succeeding in digesting none of them. Well, it was a colon, longer than there was any reason for it to be, that had seen better days. There would have to be some wooing of this crumpled colon. We'd need to experiment with medication. Meanwhile, he'd lend me a pamphlet on constipation, the best he knew, indeed a little masterpiece.

A just verdict, I discovered. Though, since some personal involvement in the problem was probably needed to carry a reader beyond a plain-spoken first sentence, I'd not recommend it on *Couldn't Put it Down.*

'Hallo,' said the wizard. Odd, rather. Not much he could offer by way of explanation. There was simply this long bowel, with its redundant loops. Yes, I would clearly have to persuade it. If there was anything he could ever do . . .

I'd been thinking of a phrase I'd picked up when I was sixteen or so from Aldous Huxley: *saccus stercoris*. It was what a Roman writer had said a human being was – a bag of shit. With intestines still fresh from the factory, with muscles oiled and eyes bright and legs that took in their stride any need I had to . . . stride, I went round c1936 saying (spurred by the pleasure I was given by such gloom wrapped in Latin) that man was a *saccus stercoris*. Now at the other end of things I drew the phrase up from my memory and thought: Yes. yes. But when it was life rather than literature that enforced this idea upon you it turned out to be far less awful than, romantically unromantic, you had once imagined. Of course the machinery was messy; but mess was not its intention. And intention was terribly important. I found I had a great need to make it clear to my colon that I felt no revulsion from it.

This whole matter of our feeling about our flesh . . . I remembered an exhibition of paintings by Stanley Spencer Kate and I had been to. Now, *there* was a man whose passion for human flesh was immense: an intent student of nakedness, who looked at bodies with a butcher's eyes. There he was, and his woman, and there in his painting of them both was that blueness under the skin, that redness on its surface, that sense of the skin itself as a membrane that could barely keep the tripes hidden . . . there was that vision of the human hide as stained with ugly red and uglier blue, and of its overstretched transparency, that you associated with butcher's slabs and hooks. Spencer's cock, as he painted it, was a sorry tube, halfway to leather; and her breasts were shapes in disgrace; and to make his grim point grimmer, along the bottom edge of the picture he'd painted a joint of meat. And yet behind the painting were adoration and fascination and enormous sexual appetite. His appalled eye was a thrilled eye. His sense of the body as a sordid packet hadn't made him opt for horrified chastity, but had drawn him, instead, compelled him, made him as amorous as if his eyes had been any romantic's. I didn't really care for Spencer's conclusion that we were mere meat. He had, surely, forced upon the image of himself and his lady that resemblance to butcher's products. But now, as my own slowly-failing carcase made itself known to me – lately, my eyes, my bowels, a major gland – I saw that one needed a view of it that could cover the worst conditions to which it was subject. It *was* withering meat – but to think of it only in those terms wouldn't do. Well: it could be said very plainly. Kate too was withering meat: but much more importantly, she was Kate. I remembered my mother in her last years, pallid flesh stretched tight over bones: but of course that had not been what she was. She had been a gallant creature, Lizzie Pye . . .

9

It was full summer. I would come down in the morning and there the garden was. I'd try to define it as if this word 'garden' wasn't available. It was a dense green container for sunlight, with swaying dabs of red, white, colours too complex to name but many playing with a basic idea you might call orange: roses, begonias, petunias, clematis. This decor the year had been preparing behind its series of drop curtains, winter and spring and summer at its more tentative, involved a million leaves, not one a twin of any other. The plan was to fill the air from end to end with a great mob of gently stirring coloured devices. In a pot on a wall, four pansies, yellow with moons of blue, had turned into forty, which folded themselves into elegantly crumpled hoods and were replaced, day after day, week after week: forty after forty after forty after forty . . .

Harry Frost said it was all very fine, and he really meant it was very fine, but now when the world made itself sumptuous like this, brimmed over so beautifully, you worried about whether you'd last through six months of bare stripped stage until it happened again. Since he lived in a flat, his personal contribution took the form of windowboxes, but he could see you didn't have to have a garden in order to dream up gardens: and he was taking great care not to read Gertrude Jekyll, for example. Were there any other writers on gardens, from his point of view dangerously well worth reading, whom I could warn him against?

Incidentally, he said, he'd noticed that our local hotel, which had been plain-spoken for as long as we could remember, had come under new management and had evidently turned its face against plain speech. Anyway, it was now offering FUNCTION SUITES WITH BEVER-AGE FACILITIES.

Kate and I worried about perhaps never going to Greece again. Well, there was (to find an image for the difficulty) this dependence on the district nurse. And many of the most deliciously warm places on earth seemed unlikely to provide efficient comfort in the case of (another image) a colon suddenly throwing in the towel. Or the equally sudden disappearance of your everyday certainty as to which way up you were and where the horizon was: this (disturbances of balance) being Kate's problem.

We thought of our need of Mediterranean warmth in terms of that journey D.H.Lawrence made, in 1912, from Nottingham to Lake Garda: coming there from Germany with Frieda Weekley, who'd left her husband and children for him. He'd written about that in *Twilight in Italy*: a book we'd taken with us when we'd holidayed in Malcesine, on the lake, almost exactly opposite the lemon-house, on the other shore, where he'd worked on *Sons and Lovers*.

'You read D.H. Lawrence, do you!' That was what our headmaster, Percy Chew, had cried once, in a horribly public fashion, during an attempt to discover why my sixth-form essays were not what you'd expect, the school having offered me every opportunity to convert into a gentleman. 'You would!' He'd laughed in the direction of several thousand invisible genteel sages, all nodding, all absolutely of his opinion. 'You would! You would!'

It was a sort of hammering of the other person into the ground, his making triplets of every remark.

[174]

And I did. I did. I did. Lawrence was nothing so lukewarm as a hero of mine: he was a superhero, for adding to his breathtaking ability to write, the most thrilling awkwardness of disposition. I felt myself, at seventeen or eighteen, a phantom hanger-on of his. But all the biographical excitement apart, I read him for the joy he had to offer, of being made half a dozen times more alive than you were when you weren't reading him. There was no one else who wrote like that, the writing seeming to be what was written about. It was a flower he had seen, and you saw and smelt the flower and were perfectly present at that moment: out of his words and the sensuous truth and breath of them came this immediacy, and stunning freshness.

In *Twilight in Italy*, what he set down in this fashion, so that it exists there on the page, was, as much as anything, the astonishing heat, and the astonishing light. He'd come from the English Midlands to this world of 'busy sunshine', the like of which he'd not known, this world of 'glowing light' that may fracture into 'a glitter, a spangle, a clutch of spangles, a great unbearable sun-track flashing across the milky lake'. He found words that carry in them the enraptured amazement of a northerner who is suddenly where light and heat are not untrustworthy visitors, but are as intrinsic to the scene as the rocks, the trees, the dust, the sun-resembling fruit. It was the dread of losing all this that distressed Kate and me, thinking we might have to eschew this order of inherent sunshine because it wasn't always accompanied by dependable offers of medicine.

In Malcesine, across the lake from Lawrence, we were where Goethe, sketching the castle that's the town's delectable marker, was arrested as a spy: and had the greatest difficulty in persuading his captors that the practice of sketching old ruins for the pleasure of doing so was widespread, and the more obviously unrelated to espionage in that they *were* old and *were* ruins. The town's apologies, two hundred years on, are everywhere, in squares named after him, statues and busts.

We'd remember Malcesine partly for the belts. They were on offer on a tremendous scale, forming curtains as they hung outside a shop, dangling in dense festoons from revolving stands – once a great cave of them we peeped into: on the analogy of a snake pit, a belt pit. You couldn't imagine the sudden massive lust for belts that would lead to the purchase of a fraction of these. They hung among bags, and leather jackets, alongside vast trays of wallets, and armies of shoes: and the air had a bright brown smell that was the smell of new leather. And that reminded me that cobbling was one of my father's skills. At lightning speed, blowing brads out of a mouth bristling with them, he would with one unfailing blow hammer each home into a sole he'd shaped and pared with his special knife. The smell of leather had become the smell of my admiration for my father's handiness, acquired as part of the response he and my uncles made to the need to do so much for themselves. Like the rest of them, he could sew, he could build a brick wall, he could cut your hair, he could glaze a window and repair a broken tool so that it was better than new. For that smell, he was as omnipresent in Malcesine as Goethe.

You climbed to the top of the castle tower, your starting point one of these acts of contrition (a bust), and looked down at the slim tower sketching itself black on the turquoise water, and looked towards the head of the lake, to see a whole city of windsurfers crossing and recrossing on what appeared to be a floor of pure light: with the tiny wings of their sails, a soundless scudding of insects. And you looked across at Limone, which when Lawrence was there was the poorest village on Garda, but is now one of the richest in the whole of Italy – its fortune an ironical one, made by visitors drawn by the very trappings of its one-time poverty.

10

Lawrence had been much of the time over at Villa, a village near Gargnano. So we took the ferry. It was a day offering views only of what was close-up, against a background of mist, a wonderful grey or silver blankness. Any bright colour was amazing against that background. We made three stops on our side before a slow beating across the lake: in the middle of which we were in a silver nowhere. Somehow, tourism had made nothing much of Gargnano. We lunched (the mist, virtually in an instant, lifting and vanishing as we did so, as if it was needed for use elsewhere), and then set off for Villa – easily identified in the distance by the scraggy neck of its church, as described by Lawrence. About an hour's slow walk, we thought: but to make sure, I asked a passer-by if we were going the right way. Yes, he said: but we shouldn't walk along the main road, the Gardasane, circling the lake, that has virtually no pavements: we should go down *there* – and he pointed to a road leading closer to the water. An hour? I asked. An hour! he exclaimed. No, ten minutes, if that.

And indeed Villa was almost upon us: and it was quite another, somehow less likely, thin-necked church that was Lawrence's San Tommaso. So here we were in the midst of a vivid geography I'd imagined at first reading, fifty years earlier, and barely modified since: clearly getting all the distances wrong. And parts of it were recognisable. Here, leading in the direction of the church from the lakeside, were labyrinthine passages that had caused Lawrence to claim that Italians, known as children of the sun, were in fact children of the shadow. I paused to read his account of them again. 'Going through these tiny chaotic backways of the village was like venturing through the labyrinth made by furtive creatures, who watched from out of another element.' I was dismayed, face to face with these backways on what had become a burning day, by the prosaic thought that the real impulse behind their design might have been the wish for respite from glare and heat. Lawrence described the bafflement of trying to reach the church, which was always visible, but to which none of these passages seemed to lead. To us now the way we should take seemed clear enough. Here already, as we climbed away from the lake, was the Gardasane, which cut through that world of wandering paths and passages, so that the village Lawrence had known had been growlingly bisected; and here, surely, was the winding staircase of an alley at the end of which, at last, he'd found the church. As we did. Yes, here it was: 'the platform of my San Tommaso', 'a platform hung in the light', suspended above the village 'like the lowest step of heaven, of Jacob's ladder'. He'd looked to the lake, and there 'was a blood-red sail like a butterfly breathing down on the blue water'.

[177]

We turned, and looked at the lake, and there it was, a solitary sail: though this one was sky-blue.

We sat on a bench at the edge of the platform and read Lawrence's account of being there, eighty years before. As we'd come through the village I'd begun to feel that eighty years were hardly the measure of the distance between him and us. Now that feeling deepened. The stone of the church had been politely plastered: the 'sun-bleached stone wall' edging the platform had been replaced by a green-painted railing: and though the splendid cobbles had mostly been preserved (such a gift the people of the lake had for making cobbled handsome-nesses to walk on!), areas of it had been replaced by crazy-paving. 'My San Tommaso' had been made, generally, genteel.

It was on this platform that Lawrence met an old woman whose distance from him, the distance there'd been in 1912 between a young man just out from Nottingham and an Italian villager, together with the way as it seemed to him that in the end she simply cut him out of her consciousness, made him run up the steps beside the church to further curving climbs between walls. He wanted to reach a flat place at the top of all this climbing, a place with olives, and a cascade and a stream, where the village schoolmistress had told him he'd find snowdrops. We began this climb ourselves: but soon Kate was out of breath, and turned back to the church. I'd go on, I said, trying to reach Lawrence's upland meadow. The sun burned. Another road, not as busy as the Gardasane, but still busy, cut across the path. As I stood there, puffing, a middle-aged man, perhaps a gardener, came towards me, pushing a wheelbarrow. He grinned and stopped. I made a pantomime of problems with my lungs, and he was clearly ready for an amusing exchange about ageing, and want of breath: but I couldn't find enough Italian words, so we mimed wryness and sympathy, and parted. And soon I had to give up, and make my way back to Kate.

So I sat with Kate on that platform it had once been possible to think of as the foot of Jacob's ladder, and worried at the mixture of melancholy and shock we'd felt that afternoon. The shock lay in having been made so sharply aware of the immense, estranging distance, so very much more than eighty years, that lay between

Lawrence's Villa and this one we sat in. A symbol was the Gardasane and its traffic. Through the village had been cut what was not merely a wider, more businesslike and infinitely busier road than the Villa of 1912 had ever dreamed of, but also a means by which the entire world was given access to the lake. That was what had happened, and it was obvious: but the experience of the day had made it unsparingly evident. The difference between then and now was that now the world was everywhere. No old woman in Villa today, confronted with a visitor from Nottingham – or Barton – would disdainfully cut the other out of her consciousness as being too alien to be bothered with. As to Lawrence's feeling that the muddle of roofed backways reflected the nature of the villagers, furtive and nocturnal, it was impossible to walk through today's Villa and judge the truth of that. It was impossible even to feel Lawrence's bewilderment, trying to find his way through the labyrinth to that church so scraggily evident to the eye. All such feelings depended on the Gardasane not being there, on there being no huge intrusion by a world that was, ruthlessly, a world of signposts. The mystery of such a place, which lay in its having grown so slowly to be what it was, and not feeling it had to make itself understood to a stranger, had been blown away by the world's entry upon this scene as upon every other, and by the sense we now had that there was more we shared, willingly or not – by way of films, radio, television, suffocating quantities of news from every corner, the use of universally available and hugely trumpeted products – than was peculiar to us. The poignancy of the day had been that we were at the site that had inspired such a singing text, to find that not merely the singer but the song had gone for ever.

Nothing to do but take the ferry back across the lake. 'It was as beautiful as paradise, as the first creation,' Lawrence had written. And though it was now a scene of our exhausted knowingness and what Lawrence had foreseen as 'strange devices of industry', it was still that – still, as the ferry made its curious roaming zigzag of a crossing, paradise.

Oh, I thought, reading as we went, it's what Lawrence does with his sentences, too – making the weight and knit of them suggest always their subject-matter: so that he doesn't have ready-made formal shapes of sentence into which he drops most of his matter. For him, a sentence was a sensuous response to the needs of his subject.

But then I thought: Damn it, how could he, with his damaged lungs, make that climb, on a day as hot as this, and I could not. And then I thought: Of course, he was twenty-seven, and I am seventy-two!

Though it is never easy (as I must remember to say to Harry Frost), confessing to age as the cause of such defeats.

I I

Harry Frost, I'd discovered, was a member of another tribe of which I'd lately become aware: of those who, critical of this or that aspect of things, addressed themselves to the pinnacle. So, if Harry's annoyance had a political source, he wrote to 10 Downing Street, his letter imagined as a fist coming down courteously but arrestingly on the Prime Minister's desk. If it was a supermarket that had displeased him, a letter went straight to Lord Sainsbury – this one thought of as an encounter on some staircase in the Upper House that might lead to a (not disrespectful) clutching at the other man's lapels. 'They are better out than in,' said Harry of his feelings. One of his aunts had spoken very strongly about the danger of bottling things up. To his mother's annoyance, she had tended to commend Harry's tantrums.

There'd been a moment he treasured during his recent stay in hospital. A few days after his hernia operation he'd been shuffling down a corridor when a passing nurse exclaimed: '*Your urine is fine, Mr Frost!*' 'The strange thing,' he said, 'is that I blushed with pleasure. I knew it was a compliment, but it took a minute or so for me to see what sort of compliment it was.'

I said that reminded me of the buried urinals I'd been suddenly aware of walking over as I made my way a few minutes earlier to the Friar's Holt. They were our local contribution to that rejection of the idea of a public convenience that was one of the meaner marks of our time. Before they were buried, or sealed off, some time in the 1950s, you made your way down – oh, I'd clatteringly, whoopingly done that thousands of times in my childhood, and, gravely, many times more in my youth! – to a cavernous space that was devoted as much to conversation as to urination. First because you were often with a friend: and then because it was usual enough to find you were acquainted with your neighbour, man or boy. I remember being horrified once by the discovery that I was elbow to elbow with our headmaster, Percy Chew. Surely there must be a school rule that forbade you to piss in the company of this great man? I tried to deafen myself to the headmasterly stream: it seemed outrageous that I should hear it. He said, as I remember, only: 'Ah, Blishen!' I wish now, of course, that I'd not missed the opportunity to reply: 'Ah, Chew!'

On another occasion I found myself next to one of the school governors, Mr Petty. He was a man almost entirely given to being quite unpleasantly aloof, so I was startled by his friendliness, his wish to know what form I was in, his clearly giving himself room to take in my twelve-year-old presence, his lack of all inclination to dash in and out, as people usually did. We seemed to be settling down to a long exchange of affabilities on his part, and baffled murmurs on mine, during which it was difficult to know at what point one could bring the actual business of the occasion to an end. I remember his saying that he would look out for me on the rugger field, which puzzled me: I being a perfect example of the sort of boy you didn't look out for on the rugger field. This because, if I was there at all, I'd be for the best part of the time invisible, buried deep under some vile, collapsing scrum.

When, as today, I remembered that the urinals were still down there, merely sealed off, as if they were a disreputable sort of tomb in ancient Egypt, I had this odd feeling that we were down there, too, Percy Chew and Mr Petty and a drunkard who would prop himself against a wall and denounce me and my friends as snobbish little sods and ask us to agree with him that they were bloody silly little caps we were wearing. And Ronnie Cole who (as I suppose a practical illustration of that point of view) had been my great friend till I went to the grammar school and then was my friend no longer. It was as if we'd been malignly transformed into quite other persons by this single twist of my fate. And Ray Bolton was down there, with whom I had discovered music and politics, and who was likely still to be around, somewhere. (Sometimes I found it unbearable that these old intimacies, belonging to a time of life when nothing was banal, should have been so utterly severed. If I met Raymond Bolton, in his mid-seventies, wouldn't Ray still be discernible, wide-open in the closed man? Shouldn't the boys we were meet again, at least once?) And of course down there, under the pavement, was Geoffrey Dewdrop (whose real name I could no longer remember) who was with me when a man demanded to know if we'd ever seen one as big as that, and Geoffrey, a schoolmaster's son who regarded every question as an opportunity to give an answer, said, sincerely: 'Yes, my father's.'

Mr Petty – wasn't he a bank manager? Harry asked. Yes, I said. I thought of him sometimes, the absolute bank manager of his time, a man who in his very movement about the town, slow, supervisory, watchful for raised hats, suggested a model of solidity that would never be overthrown – I thought of him when in some television commercial it was proposed that banks were subject to fits of rapturous benignity. I was willing to bet that never in his life had Mr Petty been or feigned to be rapturous, or benign – separately, let alone together.

But then it was like Villa, 1912, and Villa, 1992, wasn't it? That's to say, same name, but different substance. The bank Mr Petty had been a pillar of was so different from the bank that appeared in a television commercial that there must be a case for a new coinage.

Harry said here we were again, being old men. And there was a point, wasn't there, when it suddenly became impossible to deny, to oneself or others, one's ancientness. Well, I said, I'd always held, a lazy formula, that we were immortal until we were forty, when we became aware that we must die. But in fact the essential sensation of being endless, of existing in a state of endlessness, went on very much longer. You didn't *really* bother with intimations of mortality until quite late – till this sudden moment, perhaps usually in your mid-seventies, when you realised that the element you existed in was now not that of endlessness, but that of ending.

Anyway, I said, I'd had a thought lately that would perhaps frighten Harry as it had frightened me. It had followed from the tendency of the credits that unrolled on the screen at the end of a film or a play on television to become longer and longer . . . and longer. My problem was that, because of an appalling politeness I was cursed with, I found it impossible not to watch to the end. When my fellow-cinema-goers, or televiewers, were shaking the drama off and turning to other things (the former causing that tremendous clatter as seats across the cinema celebrated the moment of relief from their great burden of bottoms), I would remain seated, not knowing how to excuse myself from being told the name of the least grip, best boy or hairdresser.

Wasn't it likely that something like this might happen when you were on your deathbed? You'd be half out of the seat that you'd occupied for . . . eighty years, I proposed . . . Harry pleaded for ninety . . . when you'd become aware that the credits were beginning to unroll. The cast alone would occupy a small eternity. 'And the acknowledgements!' said Harry. In the part of the world he came from, almost any woman who had a relationship with the family, of almost any kind, was deemed to be an aunt. Harry had had aunts as I had had uncles. The credits claimed by his aunts, real or honorary, would take hours, he said. 'And,' he added, as gloomy as if it wasn't nonsense we were talking, 'you'd have to wait for ever to find out who'd been directing.'

There was nothing for either of us to do but buy the other a further pint.

Part Four

I

To console ourselves for the loss of that Greek holiday, we went in February to Tenerife; and on the second day, walking harmlessly in a rose garden, Kate slipped and broke a leg.

Absurdly, we thought afterwards, we'd felt safe because we were among roses. If the world was going to be good to us, this was where it would happen. A rose garden was the last place to offer further tactless demonstrations of our fragility; and nothing we could see, that charming morning, had any worse aim than a balmy sort of decorativeness. The mountain the island was famous for, looking like a strayed Fujiyama, appeared to be rising directly out of a garland of morning glory. There was the smallest of lakes; and suddenly from a shrubbery at its edge came a peahen, seeming an extraordinarily narrow device for transporting a few very long white feathers, its tiny head having a sour, distempered look. It clearly hated being in the light, despised itself for being visible, and appeared only, scuttlingly and with a rattle of quills, to vanish. Kate turned at my call, and was moving in the direction of my pointing finger when the soil she was treading on seemed to break up: she slipped and fell, one leg oddly-angled under the other, crying: 'No!'

I lifted her, knowing this cry meant something bad had happened: but she said she was all right, truly she was all right. She could stand, though it was difficult to take a step. Well, she *could* take a step, of course. She was on the brink of declaring that her leg was all the better for the fall, any other declaration being, on that scene, at that time, impossible. But it was dragging rather than walking. Her horrified face spoke for her. She'd strained a muscle, she said. We found a rough table, meant clearly for picnics; and there, under a cheerfulness of bougainvillaea we soon found difficult to bear, we sat, and decided to have lunch. Kate tried to smile, but couldn't easily. We were joined by a tiny stray dog, all eyes as the peahen had seemed a few narrow feathers; it made a cushion of itself at Kate's feet, suggesting an anxiety matching hers. The air was sweet, and over to the left was a small, daft grove of cactuses, fat balls of prickliness growing out of the ground on no apparent stalks; and a number of thorny batons. Among these wandered a cat (the gardens had a corner for lost animals), its raised tail another cactus.

Kate thought she could walk, but let it be slowly, to the entrance. And there we sat, waiting for the free bus that had brought us. Once we had to leave that, there'd be the long walk along the seafront to the hotel. The sun was directly above; we were dazed, not sure what was happening. And then there appeared an improbable taxi. In no time, what we'd dreaded as the long agony of the return became gratefully swift. I supported Kate with her alarming leg across the Plaza de la Iglesia, and so into the hotel. Making her way up and down steps was a particular nastiness; but we were back in our room, she was on the bed, she was dozing. Then she was awake, and saying we should perhaps ring the doctor. Somehow, yes, it had become necessary that we should ring him.

He came within ten minutes. His examination seemed to lead to comfortable conclusions : she could bend, flex, stretch. 'You must go at once,' he said to me, 'to the Clinica San Antonio. I will ask reception to order a taxi. There must be an X-ray.' Glad of Kate's deafness, I asked: 'Is it serious?' 'It is serious,' he said.

And there we were, transformed by one unlucky step from contentedly idling holiday-makers into an anxious couple in a taxi, being taken, as it turned out, eight kilometres to the clinic, a neat, small, preoccupied building at the top of a hill. On the way I said: 'If they decide you ought to stay overnight, don't worry.' Kate's eyes filled with helpless tears. 'We are doomed not to have a holiday,' she said.

In reception was a tall, thin young woman, darting between a computer screen on a desk to an inner office, and a ruefully frowning young man who, on another screen, was committing a large number of documents to the mechanical memory. A large man in a green coat, hugely moustached, came in and out: laughed, barked.

Then it was our turn. We handed over the doctor's letter: and our insurance policy. The document that ensured us free treatment was politely returned; this was a private clinic. At last someone came to take Kate away. Seeing, as she was helped through a door, the pained askewness of her steps, I wondered that we could ever have talked of strained muscles. Then I was in limbo. The rueful young man, answering the phone, staring aghast at the computer screen as if all the information it offered was catastrophic, suddenly said: 'I'm new here – but I suppose that is obvious.' I tried to read the book I had with me, *Tom Jones*, but it was like blundering into that shrubbery the fatal peahen had come from and fled back into: such a suddenly unwelcome density of words. Above the young man's head was the slowest clock in the world. I had despaired of anything relevant ever happening again when a doctor appeared, another overhang of black moustache, and beckoned me into a room, where the thin young woman acted as his interpreter. He produced X-rays. *There*, he pointed, was the fracture. It was high on the fibula. What he would do would be, that evening, at eight o'clock, to operate: he would pin the bone together. As one does when uncertain that language will be understood, he made the point exaggeratedly with mime: Kate's fibula was to be reunited by the use of crowbars, marlin spikes. Recovery might take . . . seven days? Ten days? Possibly two weeks.

I went to find Kate. In a white gown, white-faced, she lay in a small room alongside a woman who looked like tragedy itself, her face stormy. Kate said wanly that she thought she was in shock. One wasn't ready, having been in the process of growing into the foolish ease of holidaying, to become abruptly someone in a strange room waiting to be operated on. Whatever happened, she said, *please*, I was to do those things we'd have done if this hadn't happened. I thought to be required to do that would be punishment and not pleasure, but smiled as unwoefully as I could. The other woman raised herself on an elbow. She was German, spoke no English and seemed to my rattled ear to be outlining some doomsday future for Kate and herself. Then I realised that she was urging me, passionately, to take with me Kate's wedding ring, bracelet, watch. '*Alles Schmuck!*' she cried. All jewellery must be removed. She lifted herself high on an elbow, and there was an appalling impression that she knew things about jewellery too awful to be spoken. Kate said: 'I've explained that I don't speak German, but it seems to make no difference.' I said, in my schoolboy German, that Kate hadn't the language. The woman fixed Kate with a dark glare and addressed her, presumably on this matter, in German of very great complexity.

And then I had to go.

2

The fact is that I'd never had dinner before in a hotel given over to the idea of holiday when my companion, who should have sat smiling at the other side of the table, was having a broken leg operated on eight kilometres away. I felt helplessly tragic. The Mackenzies stopped to speak. They had seemed, at first meeting, the most frowning of Scots; he was grumbling then, like a man born to it, about many small dissatisfactions. He grumbled now, about the hilliness of the little town they'd visited that day. It was the town at the edge of which Kate was now ... I bit my lip. It was absurd, Mackenzie seemed to be saying, for a town not to make some attempt to be flatter. He knew from personal experience that towns could be flatter. And our day? he asked, clearly thinking that Kate was upstairs putting the last bewitching touches to her appearance. Everyone in the dining room (except me) bore evidence of such last bewitching touches.

I wanted to be cool but couldn't be, and was aware of having some horrid relief from saying: 'Well, it wasn't a very good day. My wife broke a leg ...' Then I felt in disgrace, having offered so dark a remark when the Mackenzies had paid good money for a fortnight free of much milder glooms than this. But they seemed, if anything, cheered by the awfulness of it. Their sympathy, I felt sure, was real, but clearly they tended to feel that the world was recognisable only when it provided some daily quota of harsh happenings. She, it turned out, was a nurse, and though she could have nothing specific to say about Kate's particular case, she managed to suggest, in a kind and sensible way, that she had not only been medically involved with many broken legs, but had known most of them to mend, very well, very well indeed. The head waiter appeared: having heard of Kate's misfortune, he gave my shoulder a manly squeeze, and then, in a less manly fashion for which I was grateful, patted my cheek. Whereupon the Lucases drew alongside. They had fairly recently married, late in life, both survivors of former marriages. They were plainly satisfied by this arrangement, but had not yet synchronised their conduct as to exchanges such as they now had with me. He would make his contribution and she would make hers, and they would be about to move on: when the notion of something extra to be said would occur to him, and he would dart back to say it; and she would stand, waiting, her smile a little fixed; and he would rejoin her: when she would think of something that might be added, and come to add it: and he would stand, waiting, his smile patient and impatient at once. I was sorry, again, to answer their chirruping enquiries as to our day with such a glum announcement: but after they'd expressed their amazement that such an event could occur on anyone's holiday, such unlikely bad luck, they were quickly reminded of similar occurrences that they'd been involved in or had simply heard of: and when they'd moved on, he darted back with an irresistible addendum, and after that she darted back with one of her own: and then I was left, as I soon felt it might be expressed, to dine with my absent wife.

In the night I woke to hear Kate breathing in the empty bed beside me. The breathing was distinct and real, and I was wide awake and sober. I was soon aware of a hotel as a maker of unaccountable sounds. The corridor creaked with the footsteps of persons who plainly were not there. Rooms to left and right, and above, snapped, hissed, moaned. Elaborately, somewhere along the corridor, someone squeezed the life out of someone else. The bar-ristorante across the street closed, and the last of its staff, man and woman, made their way home, first pausing outside the door they had just closed (with an astonishing furore of keys turning in locks) to quarrel hideously: he could not be saying less than that he meant to cut her throat, and she could have been making no other reply than that she would cut his first. They moved off, their slaughterous disagreement increasing in shrillness as they made their way from street to street, until, a perfectly audible half a mile away, they suddenly laughed, and could not stop laughing, the sound of their merriment dying out at last, at heaven knows what distance.

Numerous clocks disputed the hour. I tried to think of something cheerful and, as happens when this attempt is made, thought instead of something disturbing. It had happened the evening before as we stepped out of the hotel into the strolling world. Here was that public space, the Plaza de la Iglesia, raised above the walk that passed the hotel: broad stone steps took you from one level to the other. At the top of the steps there was something white – as startlingly white as the newest angel on a tombstone: and as one became aware of it, and of there being a crowd staring at it, something happened (later one saw it was always someone dropping money into a box at its feet), and it came alive: which is to say too much ... it *moved*: with a flowing twist of body and flutter of hands it shifted into a new pose, with that scarcely apprehensible flurry dropping from utter frozenness into utter frozenness. The eyes were closed (they were never open): the small face denied that it was ever that of a living creature. And people gathered, in strangely large numbers: many of them, as you knew from their postures and their muttered remarks, obscurely annoyed, perhaps at being so mysteriously compelled to stare. Perhaps also (I felt as we stood there, waiting for the next quite beautiful dissolve from pose to pose) because we could not understand how anyone was able to remain so motionless, so long: and because a usually quite clear difference, valuable to us, between what was alive and what was not, was being laid under question. It (to say *he* was never quite possible) would have nothing to do with us, except when responding to a coin in the box: and the response then was minimal enough to suggest scorn of us. You overheard dismissive murmurs: people expressing their impatience, and their refusal to succumb to any fascination that was being exerted. They had no intention of lingering, they said, and lingered.

Here, I thought, was another ominous clown! The previous evening he'd seemed curiously, chalkily disturbing to us both: and as I'd made my way into the Plaza a few hours earlier, alone, after dinner, I'd shrunk from the impression he gave of a . . . tombstone with a tic. I thought too well of his performance really to dismiss him with such a phrase; but . . . Oh damn it, just now I could do without this melancholy clown.

I lay in bed exhausted: and reflected suddenly that the consolation for Kate, already taking effect (surely she'd have come round after the operation?), lay in the idea of the story she'd have to tell when she got home. Whereupon it occurred to me that it was, of course, a story I also looked forward to telling.

It struck me at once that each of our stories would, in almost every vital detail, be at odds with the other. I thought then of the harassment it would be to me to have to resolve not to correct Kate's version: and the weariness it would be to her to have to resolve not to correct mine.

Marriage in the end being, as much as anything, a union of rival storytellers.

3

Kate's bed in the clinic was empty, had never been slept in. The tragic German woman chose not only to be more tragic than before but to speak in a dense fashion far beyond my reach. Was Kate elsewhere, I asked. She shrugged her sombre shoulders. Had she had her operation? The stormy eyes increased hugely in size and storminess: she sighed, and spoke what sounded like a couplet or two from a funeral ode. I went back to reception. 'Where is my wife, please?' The distracted young man had forgotten that I had a wife, clearly had no recollection that anyone I might claim by that title had ever been admitted to the clinic. Someone over his shoulder, sounding perfectly unconvinced, suggested I try the lounge, or the garden. Absurd though they were as places to find the injured Kate, I searched them both. She was not there. In the corridor a woman, trailing a vacuum cleaner as if it had been some inconvenient pet, paid great attention to my attempt to give Kate an identity, which consisted largely of slapping my leg. For a time she obviously thought I was eager to know where I could go to have my leg slapped: but then I remembered the word *frattura*. Ah, she said, *frattura*! I should try Room 107.

And there Kate was, looking extraordinarily cheerful. In place of the leg with which I had been familiar for nearly half a century, she had an immense crude tube of plaster. There had been no operation. Not that anyone had told her there'd be none; but eight o'clock had gone past, nothing happening: and then she'd been woken from sleep to be told that at midnight would come the man with the bucket and the cement. Kate said it really wasn't easy to endure that. Reason assured her that there was no advantage to them in enclosing her in cement and dropping her in the sea. Yet when your idea of what was going on (that you were having a happy holiday) had become suddenly a wholly different idea (that you were in an extremely baffling hospital with a smashed limb), the silliest thing became credible. The man arrived at midnight, as promised, and was clearly not hostile: and cement was quickly redefined as plaster. This had been applied liberally, from the top of her thigh to her ankle, had taken some time to dry, and had imposed upon her the duty of making sure, every so often, that she could wiggle her toes. Failure to wiggle her toes would point to disaster. But she was jubilant: now, they said, she might be back in the hotel tomorrow. And if that was so, even if she was on crutches, we could be in the sun together and . . . could generally be together. *Good!*

She'd been transferred to this new room because there was an Englishwoman in it, and they'd thought she might prefer that to being in with that other morose companion: who was unmoved by the knowledge that Kate did not speak her language, and addressed great amounts of ominous German at her until Kate decided she must pretend to be asleep. Her new room-mate was taken aback by her arrival. 'I thought I was having a room to myself!' She seemed a vain woman: in her mid-sixties, with a hoity-toitiness about her, a constant manoeuvring of an unnaturally golden-headed profile. She was there for sudden great difficulties of breathing: they were taking X-rays every half hour. She was on holiday, too – eight weeks in a villa – and was nervously furious, as if she'd been not so much admitted to hospital as kidnapped.

I'd come by bus, to the little town of Santa Ursula: and then, the San Antonio evidently being at an uncertain distance, taken a taxi. Now as I left the clinic I knew where the town lay, two miles off, and turned in that direction. I felt cautiously happy, thinking there might be only another day of this dismal separation. The sun was high and hot. Far above me was the always attendant mountain: far below, the rarely absent sea. My way lay through this *calle* and that, genteel-seeming roads, gardens formally hedged with bougainvillaea and hibiscus. Suburbanised bougainvillaea, hibiscus trimmed like privet. Every house had its dog, its occupation to rage at any passer-by, hysterically rushing this way and that behind the hedges, and from gate to gate, glaring incredulously, barking to the point of bursting, until the next dog hurled itself into place and took up this apoplectic duty. A tower clearly in the town made a mark to march to. Absurd to an English imagination, in February walking through warm dust, wearing sandals, shorts, a thin shirt! There were little stretches of hill to be climbed; I sorrowed, as resignedly as I could manage, over my labouring lungs and aching legs. It was in the bones all the time now, this readiness to ache: in those of the feet, for example, so that there was this web of complaint stretching across the surface of a foot, from heel to toes.

And now I was in the town, though not a part of it that I recognised. Such handsomeness, everywhere, of old houses, many with those balconies essential to the Canarian style – so commodious, so strong, that you could imagine whole households collecting on them. And such fine walls, mostly white: every house bearing the shadows of its neighbours, an elaborate exchange of geometry between house and house. The schoolboy in me named the angles of shadows A,B,C,D.

Where these white walls joined and turned they were held together, as it seemed, by broad brown stitches of stone. It was a time of day for sleeping indoors, out of the sun and I felt I might be required to account for myself, trudging almost alone among those marvellous rectangles, varieties of triangle, rhombuses (if I was right in remembering what a rhombus was), punctuated by shutters, many of these clearly very old, looking not so much varnished as treated with season after season of honey.

I came to what must be the summit of the town, and saw nothing that promised the possibility of a bus back to Puerto de la Cruz. I asked a young couple poring over a guidebook where the bus station was. They didn't know, they said, but it sounded like the new town, which was over that way. So I walked in the direction they'd pointed to, and suddenly the nearly silent handsomeness gave way to a busy trumperiness of shops and offices and cafes: and almost at once, the bus station. It was an extraordinary abrupt shift from world to world.

As abrupt, I thought, as the shift from relaxed holiday-making to these new perplexities: most of which could be reduced to the question: how could I be sure, given that they'd forgotten the room she was in, that what was happening to Kate was what ought to be happening to her?

4

Almost the best thing about the town, I thought, wandering dolefully through it that evening, was that, whilst it had sweated furiously to entertain its idle guests – made, for example, handsomely, a false foreshore of little lakes and pavilions – the deepest pleasure felt by those guests (you easily assumed the depth of it) lay in watching the ocean at work. You had this town that had methodically filtered out every serious activity, every suggestion of the strenuous and close at hand but beyond its defences (which in places amounted to fabulous quantities of huge square concrete blocks, thrown down with an appearance of colossal carelessness under the sea wall) was the utterly unfrivolous energy of the ocean, which came charging in, a mile of it at a time, converted itself into a furious white scroll, and went on to dash itself against blocks, rocks, walls, with the most immense quiffs of exploding water, in the imagination breaking the necks of everyone who watched, but always tamed. To watch it was to watch a tremendous force constantly baffled, yet to know that the human triumph was a perfectly hollow one. The explosive ocean represented everything that made a mock of our clever fragility.

All this was best in the early evening, when the explosions of water were filled with light. I loved then to stand where I could see, along the sea wall, the lines of those staring out, matched by the huge long inward gallop of the ocean. So much staring in this place! At false statues, inviting doubt as to what was alive and what was not; and at all that activity of water, at once encouraging and destroying the notion that to be alive had any touch of safety in it.

As nine o'clock struck I happened to be watching the statue, and saw it bring its astonishing imposture to an end for the day. It rose, and began to remove its robes. This it did with the fastidious elegance that marked its performance, but now that elegance seemed to be devoted to another, very deliberate drama. Out of the chalky fineness of the costume a young man was to be extracted, distant still from his audience: joining them, in a sense, since he was revealing himself as one of them, a living creature, a youngster in brown slacks and cream shirt, but still intensely private. He did not look towards us. He folded every item of his dress with great but practised care, so that it took less time than seemed promised by the thoroughness of it. Then he moved across to a small fountain that stood at the edge of the steps. Here, with the same swift carefulness, he began to remove his make up.

And I found myself crossing to speak to him.

I'd not meant to do this. He clearly wished to be alone, and had been at his exhausting work for several hours. But suddenly I needed to know if the effect his performance had had on me was an effect he intended. I asked if the act was his own invention. No, he said, in a very English voice. He'd seen someone put on a similar act in . . .

Barcelona. I said that, because it seemed to make uncertain the distinction between what was alive and what was not, I'd found it disturbing. Was it disturbing to him? No, no, he said, sounding impatient, so that I wondered if others had asked the same question. He simply closed his eyes and enjoyed the freedom of his thoughts. If anything disturbing was found in it, that was a matter of my response, not of his intention. He was fairly brusque about this. I thanked him and left, feeling warned off. I understood easily enough that he might have wanted to get away: and that the act might have been no more than a means by which a young man with certain gifts would set out to pay his way through the islands. But I wasn't sure that I believed his dismissal of my questions. His performance was so much more intense and beautiful – and scornfully austere – than it need have been. His self-isolation from those for whom he performed was so striking. And in bringing his work to an end that evening, and turning himself back into a living man, he seemed only to have changed from performer to performer. Surely there was much more here than met the eye?

Or was this another aspect of being in your seventies – that far too easily you found things ominous?

5

'The number you have just rung does not exist.'

It was a number I had been officially given: yesterday it had responded instantly to my call. I ran through all the alternatives. They were either declared not to exist, or did not reply: though there was a long ritual to go through before you could be sure you'd had no success: a certain patient rhythm of ringing, at last replaced by an impatient rhythm, which in the end signed itself off with a gasp. I'd never before hated so many harmless numerals. Silly speeches built up inside me: 'This is my wife with a broken leg I'm trying to ring! I'm trying to ring a *hospital*! What if there was an emergency? I have never before encountered . . .'

Ridiculous! The only thing to do was to get the bus, and then walk through the sunshine to the *clinica*. My route as I made my way out of town took me past the Social Security office. This brimmed with faces that expressed a gloomy frustration: scores of men and women, a mass scowl. I felt wretched going past, a tourist in shorts . . . Then I was on a stretch of open road that led from the stub-end of town to those *calles* with their barking bougainvillaeas. In roadside fields, ragged leaves: here and there a hand of bananas wrapped in blue plastic, to prevent it from ripening too soon. A tree with a leaf that was four and a half inches long (I tried absurdly to be exact in case I remembered to tell Kate about it), broadly striped green and white: an unripe tiger. And fat grasses, charcoal-grey. On a broken wall at the edge of a field, a sudden black-sprayed word: ANARKIA. It seemed such a huge, philosophical word, out there on the ragged dusty edge of town.

Kate's room-mate was tense with impatience: she didn't want to be there, she hated the constant X-rays: even lying in bed she seemed to be pacing the room: not smoking, she seemed to be smoking. She said she found Kate's patience and absence of rage extraordinary. Kate's eyes told me she was not patient at all: it was simply that she seemed so to her congenitally agitated companion. But she'd woken in the night thinking: 'If only . . .' If only on the fatal morning we'd left the hotel five minutes later: or arrived in time to catch an earlier bus to the rose garden. Any little difference of timing would have done! She'd resolved not to think 'If only . . .' again, and had closed her eyes and invented instantly a dozen further examples. And she'd thought how important it was to avoid this approach to things, which might paralyse you with the perception that at every commonplace moment of every commonplace day you were making cumulatively and some-times instantly regrettable choices.

No one was to be found who could make a single solid statement about Kate's condition and prospects. Everyone would be wonderfully available, very much later. I was asked to leave Kate's room while it was swept and dusted, and found myself part of a kind of flotsam of relatives: realising that I'd blundered into yet another fact about this condition of being old. Everywhere, in clinics like this one, there were persons appalled to discover that, when you were surely at your most invulnerable – someone devoted simply to being at ease, in some place dedicated to delighting you, traditionally beyond the reach of all serious displeasure – you could be frighteningly struck down. Would her leg have broken had it been a younger leg, Kate wondered.

I ran into the middle-aged daughter of an old woman who, merely standing on the balcony of her hotel room on the last evening of her holiday, staring out to sea, had fallen and broken her hip. But it was not enough, they said, to call it broken: it had disintegrated, it would take many of the clinic's crowbars and marlin spikes to hold the fragments together. As if this were not bad enough, she had soon become the centre of a quarrel that might, the daughter felt, be a medical one, but might be a quarrel about money, the disputants being the clinic and the insurance company that had covered the old woman's holiday. The first move, by way of the clinic's agitated telephone (which seemed to horrify those in reception when it merely rang), came from the insurance company, which demanded that the old woman be flown back to London for the operation. The clinic retorted that to move her by air in her shattered state would be dangerous. The insurance company in its turn retorted that it would provide her with a profoundly qualified nurse to watch over her on the flight. The clinic was inclined to think that a nurse was neither here nor there. However qualified, a nurse could not prevent the hip from disintegrating even further from the inevitable bumps and jolts of travel. The old woman's daughter was involved in these exchanges, and found herself being spoken to, as it were, out of the corners of mouths by representatives of the insurance company. For goodness' sake, they said (relying on the slow and formal English of such representatives of the clinic as had their ear to the phone to ensure that they were not understood), Spanish surgery was frightful: if the daughter wanted her mother to come out of this with any sort of hip at all, she must insist that the operation be done in London. As Kate lay in the next room with her plaster tube, this argument was still raging. What, asked the daughter, was one to do, having to make a decision where the vested interests of each of the pleaders were obvious enough, but where there might be for her mother a vital difference of medical fate?

I went to see the old lady herself. She seemed to be filled with resigned amusement. 'You're alive,' she said, 'until you're dead.' The daughter, having been at first appalled by the disarrangements that followed from the accident – a matter, for instance, of their cats having been farmed out to neighbours whose willingness to be of use was based on the belief that a finite fortnight was involved – was now given up to what I could only think of as a variation of her mother's mood: in her case, it was a sort of resigned anxiety. She was almost comfortable with it. There was nothing else to be.

And there was a woman whose husband, a busily public man somewhere in Yorkshire, had suffered some complex reluctance of the heart: he was more astonished, she said, than alarmed: he might be in his seventies, but this was not his sort of thing; and he was most concerned with the need to keep the news from his friends. It was not in keeping with their general style, that they should be bothered by the knowledge that he was in acute danger in a Canarian clinic.

The cleaners leaving the rooms (and, so far as I could make out, instantly turning into doctors and disappearing) there was nothing more to be learned that day about Kate's future. She was deep in a book. As long as I'd known her she'd been a happy slave to fiction: even when we first met, and were moving among such romantic allegations as that my merely appearing made her forget everything else, she'd look up from a book and take a distinct moment to identify me. But the novel that had her in thrall at the moment, much though she was enjoying it, left her sad, restless. Out there were the sun, the sea, all the coloured busyness of flowers and fruit ... In here, uncertainty, failure of information, and her desperate room-mate. Parting from her I felt less like a visitor taking leave of a patient than a so-called champion who'd singularly failed to bring about the escape of an imprisoned friend.

The next day was no better. All those who might be doctors seemed to be engaged in answering the tireless telephones in reception, and one or two people I'd suspected of being the director of the clinic or his deputy were mowing lawns, or trundling oxygen cylinders along corridors. Kate had been given crutches, but had not yet been encouraged to use them. Her room-mate gave an account of herself that suggested she was being X-rayed nonstop. It was difficult to avoid the suspicion that the popularity of X-rays had something to do with the way the cost of them plumped out a patient's bill.

Wonderfully, in the evening I managed to get through to Kate on the phone. She was tearful. There'd been a message from our insurance company: she should return to the hotel as soon as possible. This was clearly to the advantage of the insurance company: but by now Kate felt it was to her advantage, too – she'd begin to mend at once if we were together again, and if she began to have some grasp of her own fate. The trouble was that the clinic insisted she must not leave it. She had to learn to use her crutches. They thought she was more tired than she should be. They talked of X-rays. What should we do?

6

My thoughts growling round and round in my head, in pursuit of an answer to this question, I walked out of the hotel into the gentle air of the evening. There in front of me was the living statue. It was a quarter to nine: as I knew, he packed up at nine o'clock. Money was being dropped into his box: but he remained frozen. Puzzled, people dropped in more money: there was no response. There was beginning to be unease, a suspicion that he might have lost the power to return to life. Had he become what he pretended to be? A ridiculous thought: but how to be sure? More money was flung challengingly, nervously into the box: and still there was no response: and now a kind of irritation, becoming anger, was to be felt in his audience. He himself had ensured that the rules of the game were well-known: what did it mean, his having apparently decided to disobey them? It had always been possible to release him, but now he was refusing release. His deep fixedness had become something people were desperate to destroy.

Some moved close to him: peered into his face: shouted or laughed close to his ear. Feeling seemed so strong that I was afraid he might actually be assaulted. Meanwhile, that phenomenon of his great stillness, startling when it was a matter of a few minutes, became oddly difficult to credit or endure as it stretched towards a quarter of an hour. And the faint likelihood of scorn there'd always seemed to be in his performance – wasn't that now clearly present? Wasn't he implying, that chalky figure with the closed eyes, that he'd given up the pretence that our pesetas were worthy of response? By way of his spectacular stillness and silence, wasn't he rejecting us?

People couldn't decide whether to go or stay. On top of everything else, he'd taken the power to make that decision from them. He'd deprived us absolutely of our power over him, and partly of our power over ourselves.

And then the church bell sounded the hour. In an infinitely private fashion, as if it was nothing to do with performance, or audience, or time itself – opening his eyes but not using them to stare about him – the statue quietly quivered into becoming an actor ready to disrobe.

I woke up in the morning bristling with nervous determination. The next step must clearly be thought of as bringing about Kate's escape from the clinic. Its reluctance to let her go, I thought whilst shaving, was what might have been shown by a spider to whom an appeal on behalf of a captured fly had been made by some unimpressive relative. This wouldn't do.

Oh, it wouldn't do, I thought, walking through the *calles*. The dogs barked and I was furious, being unable to bark back.

Kate, about to set off down a corridor on her crutches, with which she felt she had no hope of coming to terms, said the doctor who might possibly have been in charge of her case had been given out by an attendant of uncertain status as saying Kate could go if it was understood she'd have to solve for herself the problems of using a bathroom, and dispense with the constant attention the clinic gave her. I made my way at once to reception and announced my determination to remove Kate to the distracted young man whose name, I'd gathered from listening to him frequently on the phone, was Alfonso. Very well, he said. I asked if five o'clock would be a good hour for us to go. Yes, five o'clock would be a very good hour. His replies seemed shame-faced. He knew, I thought, that they were without value, being unconnected with reality. He would speak to the director, he added, his appearance of shame deepening. It was a pivotal feature of life in the clinic that the director was hardly ever to be spoken to, having always just left or being expected at any moment to return.

I went to find Kate. She was being tormented by a thin pale woman, in a pink dressing gown, who'd turned the use of crutches into a display of athletic ease. She frowned over Kate's worried lurchings; suggested improvements in a rush of Spanish: and sped ahead of us to show how easy it was. See, one could virtually pirouette! She had a sharp smile that she turned on when she expected Kate to profit from her advice, and switched off when it was clear Kate wasn't doing so. She'd hold my eye with hers, censoriously sympathetic. Any other wife would have been better than this one! And she'd put on another whirlwind demonstration. At any moment, we thought, she'd show us that only the feeblest creature would find crutches an impediment to turning cartwheels. It was Kate's nature to be grateful, and she gave a strong impression that that's what she was: but she said, 'She hasn't a ton of plaster to carry about!' And, in fact, if what the doctors had had in mind was that Kate should be cruelly unbalanced, they couldn't have done better. To protect a fracture in a single limited bone they'd given her a cast from thigh to ankle that would have provided reliable support for the corner of a small house.

Somehow, we got into the garden. Here was what Kate, in her over-heated room, tormented by the impossibility of believing anything anyone said, had been longing for. Here was the reason why I must bring about her escape. Here were open air and gentle sunshine and, beyond an hibiscus hedge, an astonishing blue meadow that was the sea.

I left her sitting in one chair with her monstrous leg supported by another and returned to reception. Alfonso (was anyone ever at once so handsome and so hangdog?) said he must ring Kate's doctor before clinching things. But, I said, surely it had been agreed that, barring the formality of his speaking to the director, things *were* clinched. Earlier he'd told me that he'd spent five years in an office in Holland, and now he made a face that I read as saying that he wasn't unfamiliar with this idea that declaring a thing to be clinched meant that it was clinched: but that he begged me to understand that this was territory in which to say a thing was clinched had another meaning, that the thing was *not* clinched. As a final hurdle (the message of his face being that even this might not be the end) I must myself have a word with the director. Kate's doctor turned out not at the moment to be answering her phone. As for the director, he was out, but –

He would be back at any moment, I said.

At any moment, said Alfonso, self-consciously feeble.

I raged back to the garden, joining Kate for half an hour in her astonished delight in there still being such things as air, sunshine, the sea. Then I raged back to reception. Alfonso reported the doctor's verdict: that Kate seemed very tired, and to have to stop for breath after a few steps with her crutches: and that the doctor had hoped to X-ray her afresh and in some perhaps decisive fashion that afternoon. I said there was nothing there to make us alter our decision: so might I immediately see the director? Alfonso's incredulity was obviously even greater than mine when, as I spoke, the director drove up to the clinic entrance. Making his way to his office so as to waste no time, as I guessed, before he made himself once more unavailable, he hardly paused to listen to me: but cried out that there was no problem. 'No *problem! No problem!*' But I must ask reception to prepare the necessary documents. I rushed to tell Kate the good news, and immediately set off for the little town, and the bus, and so to our hotel: among other things, to make sure that the wheelchair had been delivered.

Without a wheelchair we could do nothing. But the representative of the travel company that had brought us here had been certain she could borrow one from a local clinic. *No problem!* She was a good-natured young woman, but I'd observed that she seemed in some quite honest fashion to believe that affable cries made up for lack of attention to detail. All the same, it was with confidence that I presented myself at the hotel reception. This was not a matter in which even she would have thought empty chirruping was enough! But the receptionist made a blank face He was a man of severe, scholarly appearance, who'd always made me uneasy about asking for my key. Who do you think I am, that stern face seemed to ask. A hotel receptionist? Now he murmured '*Wheelchair?*' as if I'd uttered the most provocatively irrelevant word I could think of. '*Silla de ruedas*,' I ridiculously offered as an alternative: having looked it up in our little travelling dictionary. He began pulling folders down from shelves, and riffling through them: consulted his computer. His frown intensified. Then, with an exclamation, he got up from his chair, went through a door, and vanished. I was left feeling that a hotel receptionist who had long survived the inanity of guests had at last cracked. Asked for a wheelchair, he had seen everything, and gone. The minutes that followed were leaden. I would have to go back to the clinic and tell Kate that the attempt at rescue had failed. Once more, sea and sun would be snatched from her!

And then the receptionist returned. He was smiling. His face expressed the most tender pleasure. He beckoned me round to the corridor behind reception. And there, a massive, tremendously welcome antique, stood a wheelchair. It had every appearance of being the very first of its kind. I adored it. The receptionist clearly adored it. It had been, he said, the wheelchair belonging to the present, and ageing, proprietor's mother, long since gone, and had been stowed away in some remote lumber room. He didn't say, but I understood, that his computer had known what no other inventory would so rapidly have revealed: that it existed, and where it was.

Back at the clinic, I asked Alfonso if the doctor's report was ready. He said she was in the building, and he could swear to it that she was writing reports: but I would need to wait .. thirty minutes. When he said thirty minutes, I asked, what stretch of time had he really in mind? He made comically contrite eyes. Because, I said, it was a matter of *mañana*, of everything always happening tomorrow, wasn't it? Yes, he at once confessed: and worse here in the Canaries than in mainland Spain. I hated these stereotypes of national behaviour, I said: but what was one to do, when such a stereotype insisted upon itself so blatantly? But why did he contribute to it? Because, he said, thirty minutes might be easier to say than . . . perhaps an hour, or two hours, or . . . In this case, what realistic assessment had he to offer? An hour? he ventured. If it were longer, I said, I would wring his neck.

I'd become, somehow, indignantly fond of him.

Kate dressed: and hopped her way awkwardly to reception: and suddenly the doctor's report was there, and Alfonso was in a flurry of papers and consultations with his computer: and we signed and countersigned and attested our way to freedom. Everything done by Alfonso, who'd known in Holland what was meant by everyday competence, and everyday punctuality, and everyday avoidance of what to many Canarians was obviously the spice of official existence – the never precisely saying what you meant, and never exactly meaning what you said – everything Alfonso did was an apology: no one could have magicked Kate more deftly into the taxi he'd summoned, or made himself more responsible for baggage, crutches, documents, and for Kate's exhausted companion, who'd collapsed gratefully into confusion, disbelief, relief.

And so all the dogs behind all the bougainvillaeas barked us back home.

7

Well, back to the hotel: which behaved like home. Since moving about it from our old room involved flights of steps, we were given a new one, that involved none – except, unavoidably, down to the dining room. On this first jubilant evening a team assembled itself, with high-spirited winks and nods to bear Kate to our table: the cook, a huge man who could have tucked half a dozen Kates and their casts under his arm: and one of the waiters – yet another clown.

This was an erotic clown: a small man, with a bottom that was somehow outrageous – if you thought of him as having been assembled, then his other parts were chosen as adjuncts to these suggestively rounded buttocks – he circulated in the dining room like a little devil out of a painting by Hieronymus Bosch. He was so primitively bawdy that you knew he could not be acceptable to many of the guests: especially to those women who, majestic in their casual wear at breakfast, left you groping for words to describe the duchessy selves they brought to dinner. The waiter, so dartingly omnipresent that to say he was here, there and everywhere didn't cover it, would be saucy in every grand ear, would give a breathtaking impression of pinching every haughty bottom, would frankly peer into every supercilious corsage and speak warmly of what he saw. Somehow, his performance was a complete success. I suspected that many of his matronly targets recognised him as a creature out of their own depths. He existed beyond the reach of such responses as shame and embarrassment. If the living statue was unadulterated gravity and grace, the waiter was beautifully his opposite: unadulterated grace and grossness. For it was a sort of grace he had, in that his movements, his perpetual grins, his dartings and whisperings, were all part of a style, a way of being always consistently the little warm foolish man he was. Oh well, he was out of the *commedia dell'arte*. In another embodiment he would have sported a kapok-packed phallus and had a string of sausages round his neck.

He – or someone so like him that there is no point in distinguishing between them – had certainly waited on Samuel Pepys and Captain Cocke in Covent Garden: and now he waited on Kate, sketching out, largely with quick wriggles of his body, the thought she inspired in him: that her leg had been imprisoned in a cast only to frustrate admirers such as himself, who nevertheless had the breathless pleasure (parts of him performed plump manoeuvres too rapid to focus) of waiting for its emergence.

8

So, having gone to explore an island, we ended up exploring the Plaza de la Iglesia: the hotel standing on the edge of it, and there being too many hazards, steps, cobbles, slopes, to make a much longer journey by wheelchair desirable. Fortunately, it was one of the pleasantest public spaces we'd ever known. It had been laid out, as we learned from old photographs, exactly ninety-five years earlier, in a far barer town: eighteen then scarcely discernible palm trees, a pattern of paths and flower-beds: and, in the centre, a well-meaning heavy concrete basin, modelled on the clumsiest open blossom imaginable: and in the centre of *that*, a shiningly green swan with its head pointing upwards at the end of its fully-stretched neck: it gave out a lazy trickle of water, and had for nearly a century been in mid-gargle.

I'd push Kate to one of the benches and lift her huge leg so that her foot rested on the end of the bench: and there we'd be, in the gentlest warm air, among poinsettias – every flower-bed a red lake. First, we'd recover from the athletics in which Kate's handicap involved us. The clinic had been right about bathroom problems, and how difficult they'd be to solve. It was a feature of the rooms in the hotel that you stepped up into the bathroom: a shallow step, but enough to make things awkward for someone whose leg, enormously heavy, could not be bent. With a guilty sense of coming late to it, we were beginning to admire the principle of flexibility, as built into the human frame. Why had we not been grateful earlier for the ability to fold a limb! Why had we never paused to praise knees, or ankles! As to our relationship to each other, this had developed perfectly unfamiliar aspects. There was a sense in which Kate had been transformed into an ill-designed object requiring to be heaved from one position to another. She consisted of a central mass provided with a system of aids to movement, one of which, by ceasing to be flexuous, had made it necessary to think out, in respect of the others, in the abstract and in advance, every manoeuvre that was called for. There were times when Kate wished she had only one arm, or that her remaining leg had been attached to her at some quite different point.

When it came to getting into the bathroom, we had worked out a strategy that called for skill and determination on her part, and at which she grew better and better. Off the bed and onto the wheelchair: across the room to the bathroom door: up on one leg, and grasping the door-frame: and from then on, such a combination of swinging, reaching, seizing and steadying, hopping and squirming, such defiance of the unbalancing effect of that immense amount of plaster, that I was often compelled to break into applause. It was odd, after nearly half a century of association, to be Kate's admiring audience as, breathtakingly, she made possible the washing of her face . . . and so forth.

Then there was the wheelchair itself – for which we were so grateful, but which was made to be pushed by a giant, with muscles of steel. It was always on the point of running away, it was not much inclined to be steered, it was often in the mood to turn left when I (and, even more fervently, Kate) wanted it to turn right. I imagined it, in the 'thirties, being taken through the town, with the proprietor's grand-mother in it, by two (at least two) strong men, chosen after several days of interviews and trials. Now it served to underline the truth that no relationship is composed of absolute trust. Kate did not feel safe in my hands. I did not feel she was safe in my hands. I was made ridiculously sharp by the fact that Kate did not feel safe in my hands. She was sometimes overtaken by what I thought was the rage of the helpless. I sympathised with her and hoped she would come to no harm, and was outraged by her nervousness.

It was always a good moment when we came to rest at one of the benches in the Plaza, and I placed our copy of *Collins Gem Spanish Dictionary* under her heel (which curiously made her comfort complete), and she looked at the sky, counted the palm trees, renewed her amazement at the poinsettias, took out her book –

And was, as often as not, interrupted by our two small French friends.

They were, in fact, tiny: Gabrielle and Maurice, they told us: curious, in the first place, about Kate's leg. With a sort of diffident insistence, they seated themselves beside us, and began, at once, to tell us about their experience of broken legs, about themselves, about the French political scene. At our feet little sparrow-like birds (perhaps sparrows), with pale downy ruffs, nervously stretched for crumbs or insects and nervously fled: and the resemblance to Gabrielle and Maurice was marked. They bent towards us with some assertion, tinily intense, and then drew back, out of reach, smiling. You might disagree, their little bodies seemed to say, but this was what they believed.

We had a fair amount of French, but only if it didn't come too fast. However, from our knowing any at all they soon assumed that they could talk freely, and at speed, and did so. They were, curiously for such small modest people, whisperingly, smilingly, in some gently vicious fashion, hostile to *le socialisme*: in their exchanges with each other, intended for our enlightenment, the word occurred again and again, pronounced with an effect of hissing and accompanied by tiny grimaces. I tried to make it clear that we didn't share their hostility: but it was not something about which they were ready to have things made clear. They smiled fondly – ah, we joked, we joked! No such nice people, with such a nice broken leg, could be a friend of *les socialistes*! I spoke to tease them of their dying president. '*Pauvre M Mitterrand!*' Their fond smiles became a stockade, behind which, glancing at each other, they declared: '*Nous ne l'aimons pas! Nous ne l'aimons pas!*' To clear up what they evidently felt was the sort of misunderstanding that might arise between decent people on holiday on an island in the Atlantic, and so not quite in their right minds, they asked me to say a few words in praise of Mrs Thatcher. Out of the vast vocabulary of detestation I had accumulated over a decade and a half, I chose a term at random: '*Une vandale!*' They smiled their unhappy appreciation of this English joke. Then they rattled on again, so that we were always half a dozen statements behind, could not with the faintest certainty pick up numbers or place-names or words denoting relationship : and so grappled with the idea that they had fifteen, or fifty, grandchildren, seventy sons who might be nephews, but could perhaps be daughters, all of them living in Caen, or Cannes, or perhaps in some *coin*, some corner, possibly of Paris. At the end of a lengthy declaration, shared out between them, they'd beamingly seek the appropriate response – amazement, amusement, distress, approval, we had no idea what it should be; and so we smiled in a fashion we hoped would do for comedy and tragedy alike: and as Kate said, felt the awful oddity of being tormented by a couple so small, so warm, so unacceptably pleasant.

At last I'd make some excuse, though excuses were not convincingly invented when we had such a limited reason for going anywhere. Sometimes I'd push Kate to a corner of the square that was usefully masked by trees to stare in the window of a shop that was full of nothing but effigies, larger or smaller, of Don Quixote and Sancho Panza. I'd think at once of Ben and myself. Not that either of us was much of a Quixote or a Sancho; but that two men who'd carried on a conversation for sixty years couldn't fail to be affected by the queerly moving process that emerges more and more clearly in the second half of Cervantes's novel: the sanchification of Don Quixote, you could call it, and the quixotification of Sancho. Apparent opposites, they dissolve into each other. It had certainly happened to Ben and me, in those encounters of our old age. I had caught him talking yieldingly, in my manner, and had detected his surprise when I retorted inflexibly, in his. It was one of the ironic pleasures that the end of long novels, or long lives, might provide. Meanwhile, I gazed at the tallest of the shop's Quixotes, seven or eight feet tall, a long bristling bone, and thought how thin, almost on that model, I'd been once, and how, if only mildly, sanchified I was becoming. It was easy to make the comparison from my reflection in the window; and I saw from Kate's reflection, her mirrored eyes fixed on mine, that she'd made the point herself.

In the gaps between tree-trunks and passers-by we'd see that our tender French persecutors were on their way, and sneak back to our bench.

9

Getting into the dining room for dinner, Kate said, she felt too much like, say, a girder being swung into place on a new bridge to undergo the experience at breakfast, too. So I was to load a tray for her and take it to our room. This the erotic clown would not permit. No, *no*! Such labour was his! He returned to the dining room on the first morning, beaming, and gave my shoulder a congratulatory squeeze. 'Saw your wife!' he cried. '*Very good!*' Kate said she had never been so aware of the inadequacy of a nightdress, and never so cheerful about it. He seemed to worry deeply about the awkwardness of the wheelchair, and (as I discovered) was behind the sudden appearance of the hotel handyman, who replaced the tyres and strengthened the brakes. The waiter also added to the autographs on Kate's cast (mostly the work of passers-by in the Plaza): an immense red heart, in a general atmosphere of arrows and tears: with a name appended that may or may not have been his: RAMON.

I fretted enormously about our return home. To get back to the airport, Kate could not board the usual coach. In the plane, she could not confine herself and her girder to a single seat. Were the numerous agencies in charge of our destiny aware of our needs? Were they aware of each other? Was the travel company leaving it to the insurance company, and was the insurance company leaving it to the travel agent? Every reassuring message contained some discouraging omission. Kate thought I was over-anxious. I thought this was a situation in which there was no such thing as over-anxiety. And when we were told we'd been switched to another flight, which could offer Kate the space she needed, and that the switch would make it necessary for us to leave the hotel in the middle of the night for the three-hour journey to the airport, my confidence plummeted. I'd wake at some glum hour and all the lights would go on at once in my head: every desk in the administrative block would be instantly occupied: every issue would be rehearsed, every event retraced, every conversation played back, every doubt embraced and inventively magnified. I would try to oblige my thoughts into fuzziness, casting around for some topic that was wholly unimportant – surely, something distant in my childhood. Instantly my earliest and most innocent memories took on a ruinous intensity.

But when it came to it, the reason for alarm lay elsewhere.

In the harbour throughout our stay there'd been a boat on chocks, the front half of which had been cut away and was being replaced. It was never surrounded by fewer than a dozen men, most of them expressing by their appalled poses their failure to understand how anyone could set about replacing the front half of a boat in such a fashion, or anyone else could propose alternative methods that were not the alternative methods favoured by themselves. Somewhere in the middle of it all was a man doggedly at work, for the boat grew steadily more complete; but it did so hemmed in by this perpetual distempered seminar, with men laughing harshly, throwing up their hands, stomping away and stomping back again, and sarcastically assaulting each other's shoulder-blades.

Then the day before we left we'd seen men putting up huge notices of the carnival that was to begin the next week. There were three of them, and a very large ladder; but there was a tremendous team of advisers and critics, derisive as to the hammer used, and the nails, condemnatory of the ladder, and boilingly at odds as to whether a notice was, or was not, straight. I understood why those two from the bar-ristorante had seemed, as they locked up in the middle of the night, to be on the point of murdering each other. It had probably been some mild difference of opinion as to how to turn the key in the lock, or what to do with the key once that was done. In the *clinica*, come to think of it, it had been much the same. Scorn was the natural local response to anything suggested or done by someone else; and this scorn was a treasured source of energy.

Now it was five o'clock in the morning, and Kate and I (everything amazingly having happened as promised, and at the times promised) were being rushed through the intestines of the airport. As an afflicted person, she was only fleetingly subject to the normal severities of taking to the air. Passport control had waved us on, astonished that we should even offer to display our documents. Security had electronically examined Kate's plaster, but by way of a sort of cursory good humour. Then, under a lingering moon, we were at the foot of the steep steps that led up into the plane: and Kate was being transferred from her wheelchair into a high skeletal chair, a papal chair as imagined by Francis Bacon, into which she was to be strapped. There were four men to see that this was done. For them, the science of helping the handicapped to board an aeroplane was in its early, controversial stages. I followed Kate, her face pale and appalled, as they took the chair by a series of terrifying argumentative lurches halfway up the steps, where they seemed resigned to disagreement, and to acting, for the completion of the ascent, on four simultaneous rival schemes. It seemed to be by pure luck, and not from any scruple they might have had about tipping Kate onto the tarmac far below, that they got her into the plane at last, and unstrapped, and carried to her various seats.

Three, as it turned out.

I O

The specialist in the fracture clinic looked busily askance: 'We'll soon have that off!' he said. The technician with the miniature chain saw said he had seen worse, but not many. Far too much of it: not close enough by half at the ankle. And no underlying bandage, so that its removal would involve a painful act of depilation.

But Kate rejoined me, hugely smiling, as if they'd given her wings.

Part Five

I

'The fighting for beds here,' said the man who'd come to take a sample of my blood, 'is dreadful.'

Suddenly the offer of a bed, that unlikely marvel, had been made – but for the day before this: and ringing early, as required, and being connected with a bleep, I'd been told it had vanished. I was back at the start of the game, having again, before I could make a first move, to toss dice until a six turned up. I'd abandoned hope of feeling anything that day but doleful rage when the phone rang. Could I come in tomorrow at eight? Oh, I said, I'd come in the middle of the night, if asked. Well, said the weary woman at the other end. Light breakfast only, then.

I was to stay in the dayroom until the bed was vacated. 'At least it'll be warm,' said a passing nurse. Three or four persons came in with the general mission of establishing my date of birth. The anaesthetist, a lean, easy man, seemed to be briefing me for a not unamusing game to be played later in the day. Given my asthma, he'd recommend a spinal anaesthetic. I'd have a sedative in the ward an hour beforehand, which would calm and relax me: a second one in the operating theatre if I wanted it. That sounded splendid, I said: and somehow, it did. The consultant came in, with his cluster of vaguely smiling attendants. There was something ambassadorial about them. Nothing had changed since we last talked? No, I said, hoping I was right. We'll meet later then, he said. All these courtesies seemed appropriate to some quite other activity.

Patients went past the door, each carrying a transparent handbag, as it seemed, of (largely) blood, mounted on a frame: long scarlet tubes vanished under dressing-gowns, and the imagination winced. There was about these portable devices something at once mincingly respectable (that suggestion of a handbag) and shamelessly coarse.

And then I had my bed, in a bay with five others. 'They're very nice in here,' said my neighbour: who'd been, he said, until recently the most healthy man aged seventy-two in the world. Then had come, in succession, his need of a prostate operation, and the discovery that his liver and kidneys looked alarmingly odd (as he seemed to think of it) under inspection. He exchanged ruefulnesses with a large handsome elderly Indian whose catheter had been withdrawn but who couldn't control his pee. 'Oh God, oh God,' the Indian kept murmuring, but most affably. Groaning, he smiled fondly at me as I was checked for this and that. The man who came to give me an electrocardiogram said suddenly that he was a composer, really, and would probably return to composing. This sort of work, he said, wasn't a patch on that.

For the others, lunch arrived: it seemed to be based on a general determination that things should be minced. The afternoon ticked away, the Indian smilingly uttering his desperate cries. I was given my gown, one that in respect of the need to tie it at the back would have presented no trouble at all to a contortionist: and a pair of white stockings, tremendously tight, that would keep the blood circulating and prevent clotting. There was a curious exasperating daintiness involved in trying to pull on these last without giving yourself cramp, or tipping yourself backwards so that you became a helplessly bawdy spectacle.

Then came the sedative: and a period when you were struck by how ordinary you remained: this belief merging into a sense of things being agreeably blurred, with quite rapid transitions: so, being in bed, you were at once on a trolley, and simultaneously in the presence of the anaesthetist, with whom you were having amusing exchanges though it wasn't clear what these were about. And here was the surgeon, who'd converted himself from the familiar severe figure in a suit to a person unwise in his choice of fancy dress: the whimsical-seeming green mobcap especially did nothing for him. And immediately you were on the operating table, staring at the great lamp: in which were inset seven large turquoise-tinted bulbs, which provided a pleasure of small twitches of colour as movements were made by the, surely very large, population of the theatre. There was now a need to present your back to the anaesthetist, who was feeling his way among your vertebrae. There was discussion, appearing waggish, of your spine: and a sensation, as the injection took place, of having been struck smartly. 'Midsummer Night's Dream,' I said to the anaesthetist, and either he or I chuckled, understandingly. 'Try lifting your legs,' he said. I made confidently the usual demand on the machinery, to meet with blankness. I had no legs. There was this rather amusing, strangely heavy absence of legs. I could hear murmurings beyond the ramp: and in the air there were small pingings. I think I said 'Benjamin Britten' to the anaesthetist, and at least fifty of his hundred or so assistants agreed with me, the coloured patches in those turquoise bulbs twitching beautifully as they did so. The anaesthetist offered another sedative, but I refused it, feeling simply a general satisfaction at having provided the subject matter of all this activity. Almost at once I was in bed, and under a compulsion to check on the part of me that had gone missing. It was as when the anaesthetic in your jaw is wearing off after a dental operation: then you feel you have immense cheeks and lips, now I felt I had the most grotesquely enormous buttocks in the world. I moved, and my deeply outraged cock protested: the catheter, connected to my very own handbag, standing on its frame beside the bed, had snagged unbearably. I devoted myself to reposing, as motionlessly as possible, upon my great comic bum.

'That abomination, the catheter,' Oliver Sacks once wrote. You'd never thought of the channel through your cock as a passage for more than a hairsbreadth of anything. After a prostate operation you discovered that this most delicately limited channel, your ultimate intimacy, had been obliged to accommodate a tube a quarter of an inch or more in diameter. It was as if through any stretch of domestic piping they'd run an Underground train. It became important, lifting your handbag at the start of a journey, to bring about perfect simultaneity of that and any other movement you made. You were, of course, post-operationally weary, and delicate adjustments were not what you wished to have to make. 'Oh God,' murmured the Indian, smiling across at me. 'Oh God,' I murmured, smiling across at him.

There was this other oddity. Your penis (to use the last term you ever felt honestly inclined to apply to it) had always been a shy and modest adjunct: given, of course, throughout your career to spasms of remarkable immodesty – but still within a context of some notion or other of the private. (I thought again of Pepys's Captain Cocke, that gentlemanly paradox.) It had been part of a whole culture of the hush-hush. Of course you'd never seriously claimed not to have one, but you set store by not being required to acknowledge its existence in any outspoken fashion. And here you were, in an environment in which what had to be done for it could not be done without the treatment of it as a physical fragment as perfectly blatant and everyday as it could be. You'd spent your life thinking of your cock as a special item, the possession of which was on the borders of the scarcely allowable: and here it was, a quite ostentatious victim of urinary disorder, and no more secret than your elbow.

I had this other problem. Perhaps because of the tensions springing from anticipation of an operation, added to the switch to a new way of life and a new diet (inexorably centring upon mince and minuscule jellies), I was suffering from an adamant refusal to co-operate on the part of my crumpled colon. I had this crumpled colon, I told my advisers, unable to remember the technical term. Yes, they said: and arranged for the use of suppositories. A nurse packed them into my now deflated bottom. You had, if you could, to hang on for twenty minutes, resisting what was held to be the desperate urge to dash away earlier (somehow cautiously managing your handbag). I waited twenty blank minutes and had to confess to an absence of the urge to dash anywhere. 'Don't worry,' said an absent-minded nurse. I was not worried: I was in a state of uncontainable indignation. I wanted the recalcitrance of my colon to be the subject of a scathing editorial in *The Guardian*.

Kate appeared, looking like an actress who, in a film studio, had strayed from one film set onto another perfectly different. To my fellow-sufferers her arrival was a satisfactory event, as to me were the arrivals of their wives, daughters, miscellaneous friends. I tried to attend to what Kate said and not instead to speculate on what they might be thinking of her. There were these persons groaning around you, fellow-jugglers with handbags, and suddenly their characters were extraordinarily expanded by the arrival of, especially, wives. It was as if to what you'd got to know of them enormous footnotes had been added. A wife could make her husband unrecognisable. There was a young man who had suffered some abominable disloyalty on the part of his bladder, and who lay rather beautifully and silently all day on his bed, wearing only boxer shorts, and whose wife, suddenly present, was a sort of Russian boyar, as to her round false-fur-trimmed hat and very short false-fur-trimmed jacket: given that this boyar had long legs of sturdy charm: and was moved, on arrival, to throw herself upon her husband, as a sort of inhabited eiderdown, and remain there throughout the visit, sometimes murmuring but more often adding her silence to his. I longed, but thought it improper, to observe how, between them, they managed the handbag and its lashings. They had a pagan splendour about them, were Tristan and Isolde in this battered hospital in the heart of London, and in a setting notable for what you'd have thought to be the offputting presence of urological gadgetry.

I told Kate about my strange notion that the scene in the operating theatre had been connected somehow with *A Midsummer Night's Dream*, and she helped me to work it out. Of course: they'd all been wearing green: and of course, there'd been those quivering smudges of colour, and that fairy music, those pings, which I'd been told were the sound of cauterisations following on cuts: and, of course, at my head I'd had an entourage of jovial and helpful attendants, the anaesthetist and his assistants, and at my feet another, the surgeon with *his*: and, of course, they were Moth, and Mustard-seed, and Pease-blossom. It was evident enough who I had been.

'No Titania?' asked Kate.

It had been a surprisingly exhilarated operation, but I thought, No: there had been no Titania.

*

[223]

She was an agency nurse, a Jamaican, who'd married an Austrian and lived in Vienna, but was in London for a course in business management: she did occasional nursing to add to her income. She seemed to be wearing high heels, though she wasn't; and was altogether, and oddly, given that mix of a background, rather a dainty English lady in manner: kind, friendly, but tinklingly proper. She was the only nurse who made me think there was something distasteful in the prominence in the proceedings of my private parts.

I thought there was in her, when it came to nursing, some sort of fluster, an anxiety under her politeness. As she came to remove my catheter at six in the morning she looked preoccupied, and I didn't care for the way she began to talk self-encouragingly about what she was doing. 'The first thing we do is – *ah*!' The catheter is held in by a bubble of water, and the first thing we do is to use a valve to draw this off. 'Oh,' she cried now, this having been done. 'Oh, I don't like that very much!' She excused herself, her politeness suddenly absent-minded, and went to consult a staff nurse. The staff nurse, her frown businesslike, took the water away to measure it. It was not as much as it should have been. She tried the valve again. 'Oh dear,' said the agency nurse. There were more frownings: and then the staff nurse said: 'I'm going to try to get this out. Are you ready?' No one is ready to have a half-free catheter tugged out of him, and six o'clock is an early hour for it; and I wished the agency nurse were less of a mournful chorus with her cries of 'Oh dear!' There must have been a tug: there was certainly a fearful pang – 'the shrieking of mandrake roots,' shouted the anthology of bits and pieces in my head: and I duly shrieked: and there I was, woefully, liberated.

Post-operationally, I suppose, we're all daft. Even at my best I might have failed to interpret the mechanism of the shower correctly: but now, with a kind of unsoundly cheerful hysteria, I was wholly baffled by it. There was nothing (a wheel, a cog) that appeared to be capable of being turned, or having its position varied. This was paralysed machinery. Naked, a man lately rid of a catheter and set free from a handbag, longing to go home, and resigned to peeing blood, I cried out in ludicrous anger. Beyond my curtains I heard someone enter the bathroom: and poked my head out, willing to canvas anybody's aid, *anybody's*. This was a cleaner, a woman with a mobcap more convincing than the surgeon's. 'Do you understand these showers?' I cried. I think she didn't: but she simply had an important gift in respect of unfamiliar machinery – she knew you could afford, and indeed needed, to be brutal. She advanced and was extremely brutal to a ... wheel to which I'd given some hopeful, but in the end hopeless, attention. Water gushed. 'Oh don't get wet!' I cried. But the shower-head was hooked harmlessly into place at a low level. 'That's it, dear,' she said.

And I thought how easily the tremendous delicacies of our existence could be displaced. A hospital was where the body as a theatre of dismays and disasters was taken in everyone's stride. Even the fastidious agency nurse, discerning the night before that I was fearful of dragging at the catheter, for the subtle distress caused, had a brisk, sensible solution to suggest that overrode all that shyness and retirement behind curtains on which ordinary life rested. The catheter, she said, could be fastened to my thigh by adhesive tape: and she went off to fetch such tape, and tied the tube down, breathing busily, daintily. I thought, being incorrigibly made up of literary and artistic allusions, of Venus attending to the thigh of Adonis. Well, yes, there was in all this a touch of myth. I could imagine a painting by, perhaps, Uccello, of the cleaner and myself, in that baffling bathroom: a famous story – he'd done his best to make the shower work, and had failed, and she had appeared in a cloud of cleaning fluid, to make things straightforwardly possible. Uccello had made such use of perspective as a bathroom permitted – perhaps more: the washbasins were at the other and very remote side of a tiled desert.

The painting of the cleaner's mop was particularly admired.

2

I thought, as I walked with Kingsley Amis through the labyrinth of Broadcasting House, of the case that might be made for giving the elderly a medal or two. I'd have the Prostate Cross, of course, and the Cataract Medal with Bar, and the medal for gallantry in face of the possession of an inordinate colon. But my chest would appear naked, surely, alongside my guest's, with his many valorous ribbons.

'If I'd known it was going to be a route march', he said, 'I wouldn't have come.'

The route march was from the front of Broadcasting House to the back: a longish distance, full of traps in the form of double doors, but not involving a truly epic journey. However, by this stage in his life the man I had several times threatened to expose as being secretly decent and having a furtive liberal outlook had unserviceable feet, as well as a reputation for disgruntlement to sustain. Ruth Rendell, who was the other contributor to this edition of *Couldn't Put it Down*, was experiencing no obvious difficulty on the trek to Studio 16.

I'd first encountered Amis in the joyful way many did, in 1954, when I opened *Lucky Jim* and (something I couldn't remember ever doing before) was committed to laughing in public: helpless and, in the obvious view of my fellow passengers on the train between Barley Wood and Finsbury Park, insane fits of pleasure, the worse for seeming to be caused by reading a book. In the following year I published my own first book: which led to my second encounter with Amis in November of the year following. From Swansea came a letter. 'I can't think how it happened,' it said, 'that I didn't read *Roaring Boys* until yesterday, but I must now lose no time in thanking you for writing it. I found it tremendously funny and very serious and moving, really most admirable in every way – I do congratulate you. I look forward to re-reading it frequently for a very long time. Yours sincerely, Kingsley Amis.'

I don't easily see how such a letter, from an already immensely notable writer to an obscure beginner, could be described except by such words as 'kind' and 'generous'. It is how I thought of it then, certainly, and continued to think of it during the years when Kingsley Amis's view of the subject matter of my book underwent a famous change. I had attempted to make a case for saying that the abilities that might have been brought to bear on the general scene (and on their own destinies) by such children as those I taught could hardly be guessed at, since society and the education it offered (this was a secondary modern in a battered corner of North London) did not begin to take them seriously. It became very much the idea of things that Amis did not entertain.

I found myself, as the years passed, tormented by the notion that the distance between the generous tone of the letter from Swansea and the increasingly ungenerous opinions of the novelist was too great to make real sense. We met from time to time. I interviewed him about his books for radio, and once at length, in public, about his work. I always enjoyed his presence, his sour affability. His manner promised amusement, and often provided it. And now, here we were, in Studio 16, and he was being wonderfully blank about one of Ruth Rendell's choices: Trollope's *Small House at Allington*. The novel began, he said, with five thousand words of description of a village. It was really what he was never in need of, a five thousand-word description of a village. It was too much. He'd wanted to go no further, and had gone no further. But didn't he feel there might have been rewards, the five thousand words surmounted? Oh, no doubt. Rewards, he was sure. But no, it was not the sort of bother he wanted to take.

I'd not expected him to like Ruth Rendell's second choice, and he didn't. It was a novel by the American, Paul Auster: in fact, a little nest of novels, all versions of the same mysterious tale: the opening version being deliberately naive. If you started out with an actual dislike of experiment with narrative, there wasn't much enjoyment to be expected from it. Amis famously had that dislike: embellishing this consequence of his not feeling any need of experiment himself with arresting mockery of those who did. Having admitted that he'd not read beyond the twenty or so pages of the opening version, he brought his gift for expressing outrage to bear in mocking Paul Auster. It was a performance by Disgusted of Hampstead that for all its unfairness had the effect on me that my fellow passengers in the train from Barley Wood had once clearly deplored.

Amis's agent had made it plain to the producer of the programme that he would feel unable to do it unless there was whisky to follow. The days when the BBC's drink cupboard was at hand to satisfy such urgent appetites were long over: so the producer had bought a half bottle on the way to the studio: and after the recording it was carried in on a tray, with glasses. And, talking, Amis opened the bottle, poured himself a draught, and firmly screwed the cap tight again. After a moment I said: 'Would you mind pouring me a little whisky, please?' He made his large eyes larger, and marvellously baleful. 'I thought,' he said, 'you were a Perrier water man! Indeed, I thought you were very much a Perrier water man!' But he surrendered the bottle.

After he'd gone, we saw that he'd dropped Trollope and Paul Auster in the waste paper basket. And he had taken the bottle with him.

Some of the stories we have to tell are irremediably unsatisfactory: like the story of my acquaintance with Kingsley Amis – a route march across forty years from a gesture of great kindness to a small bizarre scene in a BBC studio.

3

But then, lately, unsatisfactory stories seemed better than satisfactory ones. That's to say, you tended out of your memories to have made narrative glibnesses, tales that became smoother and smoother and more and more neat and complete. And *stale*! I'd think: How horrible it would be, to die *stale*! What seemed to please me now was whatever cast doubt on what I'd thought I knew – whatever made the satisfactory suddenly less so! Changes of tack! Developments unexpected and awkward to explain! A favourite anecdote shown to be gravely inaccurate, some confident old belief blown to smithereens! Why, if that sort of thing went on steadily enough, you might become . . . faintly . . . young again: even if you couldn't hope to be, as the young were, plumped-up like cushions, oiled and agile, their heads still such a long way from being grossly crammed!

Our younger son, Dan, threatened with redundancy, asked himself why redundancy should seem a threat, when he'd lost his appetite for being an electronics engineer. For heaven's sake, he told himself, his delight had always lain elsewhere: with music and woodwork. Why, instead of waiting for the blow to fall, didn't he dismiss himself from his old trade, and seek admission to a course in making musical instruments and a grant to maintain him while he was doing it? And this he did: saying in respect of his experience of being unemployed and then minimally maintained that it was interesting to discover not only that you couldn't afford to have this or that, but that you didn't seriously want them, anyway. One of his earliest achievements was to copy one of the three surviving Stradivarius guitars: a beautiful honey-coloured ghost of a beautiful original.

He hadn't waited until he was in his seventies, I thought, to begin to stave off staleness.

And then we were in Canada, visiting my cousin Bobby, a sociologist who in his retirement was busy dynamiting his past. (Why the devil had he elected to become a sociologist! Was it too late to become something else?) We were there partly for the leaves, it being autumn, and Bobby had driven us into Vermont, where every downhill drive was a plunge into a honey pot. A colleague of his offered to show us the leaves from another viewpoint: that is, from the air, by way of his small plane, a Cessna. It was, he said, a sort of aerial Austin Seven. Kate was delighted. In the first place, she increasingly considered herself an airwoman who, damn it, had neglected to become one. It was a matter of foliage again, really – she'd always loved the notion of turning herself into a sort of steerable leaf. And anyway, her first car had been a terrestrial Austin Seven, which she'd bought for £35. Her father, a tremendous dismantler and reassembler of cars, whose own typical car might have been summed up as a bull-nosed Rolls-Ford, was scornful: she'd paid £30 too much, he said. The car was given to leaping, and she called it The Flea.

We'd never been in a tiny plane before, and were much moved by the struggling insistence with which it fought, growled, shrugged and stuttered its way into the air, and clung there, disputing the inclination the air had to return it to earth or to send it spinning or to open sudden emptinesses under it, and by the way it reacted to every breath of that fitful element. You were doing your best to counter the air's tendency to cough, sneeze, gulp, hugely puff, or do all these things at once. As we found a level of air in which the tiny thing was at home, growling its way round a steady spiral, so that we were able to give our attention to the mobs of trees, the reds and the oranges and the persistent greens, our host wondered if Kate would like to *take over the controls*. It was a phrase that flung us back into the 1920s. In fact, in that struggling machine in the air over Ontario, in 1993, we were back where we began, Kate and I – with machines that struggled, and that had to be brought under control.

Kate did not hesitate. She said later that you were able to feel what the thing wanted or needed, that it taught you what to do with it. I thought it might have been more difficult than that, but felt the extraordinary happiness of Kate's own feeling: that she was, at this late moment, doing something dramatically new. Her knuckles were white, she wore an astonished smile. Our host said bad weather was ten miles off, now eight miles, now five miles, and we must go down: and Kate reluctantly abdicated and we went down, to bright leaves and lakes, sideways against the wind, a cranefly.

4

I was at the shadowy top of the stairs, and on the landing, where it shouldn't be, was a light, a small bud of light. Whatever was carrying it was moving up towards me. In its purpose there was a cold intentness. It was cold and implacable. It was also stupid, in the sense that it was uninterested in discussion or debate. In any other crisis, one would be able to protest, make a case, attempt to affect the menacing thing by expressing indignation or rage. But this was not to be appealed to. Looking back, I can find words for the qualities it had: but at the time I was aware only that inside me there was a dreadful, useless, consuming hysteria. It came up, and I leant down and began to beat at it. It was made of wood. It had a round blank wooden head, which I struck so that it fell sideways, and it had sloping wooden shoulders, and I called desperately for Kate, but there was no strength in my voice. Then there was an amazing crash, and Kate was crying: 'What on earth was that?' My eyes were open, and I could make out a pale rectangular shape that in a moment would be familiar, but now was strange indeed: and it was part of a disposition of things I couldn't make out at all. Then everything rearranged itself: and the pale shape became the low bookcase to the side of my bed. Part of its unfamiliarity followed from its usually being topped with a lamp and with books for which room couldn't be found on the shelves. Now it had been swept clean. The crash had been the noise the lamp and books had made as — with a force that later, when I'd turned the light on and seen what had happened, I found extraordinary — I'd hit out at them and sent them scattering far across the floor.

Later I remembered a verse of W.E.Henley's that had long haunted me:

> Madame Life's a piece in bloom,
>   Death goes dogging everywhere:
> She's the tenant of the room,
>   He's the ruffian on the stair.

And later still I remembered that plaque in Covent Garden that says: NEAR THIS SPOT PUNCH'S PUPPET SHOW WAS FIRST PERFORMED IN ENGLAND AND WITNESSED BY SAMUEL PEPYS 1662: and how, every time I noticed it, I recalled the very great dread I'd felt as a child, watching Punch and Judy. I couldn't for one moment feel that the knockabout was funny. It was murderousness, plain and simple, and nowhere a trace of contrition, mercy, or doubt. Not a hesitation! Unhesitant mayhem! Those wooden puppets, that wooden truncheon, that wooden gallows! And what I thought was proposed was that, with the slightest shift of intention, the world might turn out to be like this. Under the thin delusive warmth of flesh and blood, mere homicidal wood! . . .

We were trapped on the M25 at one of those moments – it was the greying end of a day – when a mysterious failure of flow occurs. You are bowling along and suddenly there is universal congealment: in front of you, as far as you can see, hundreds of cars, vans, lorries, designed for rapidity, inch forward and halt, inch forward and halt. There is no escape. You are a creeping captive, and there is no certain end to it. It *will* end, in a resumption of flow as mysterious as the failure of it: but God knows when. And meanwhile, the greyness gathers, the terrible fretful patience of the imprisoned adds another layer to the atmosphere, enormous amounts of poison gather, and (if you are old) you begin to ache. You become aware of being bent at hip and knee, and that these joints have become only theoretically suitable for bending: and you are desperate to stand up.

And I saw that in the slow lane tall lorry after lorry had the appearance of a pale upended coffin.

I'd told a friend, a subtle man who'd been famously athletic but lately had had a serious stroke, about Ben's saying that he wasn't coming to funerals, not even his own. 'But he'll be there,' said my friend, surprising me by his vehemence: he sounded like a boy in a playground, anxious to prevent a playmate from thinking he'd hit upon a foolproof scheme for escaping the consequences of mischief they'd both been involved in. 'He'll be there, *in his box*!' And I remembered my father towards the end of his life using the same naively disgusted phrase when he looked at a photo I'd taken of him – one that made obvious the way the flesh of his face had been drawn tight against the bone. 'Now I know what I shall look like in my box,' he'd said.

This friend was a man of some sophistication, with a habit of ironical speech: which made his use of the phrase more surprising. He was a tall man, a great strider, before retirement a senior official whose weekday suiting had never done much to disguise the informal sportsman, and I saw now how the effects of the stroke seemed to have made him hollow, a man with all the appearance of sturdiness, still, yet emptied from within. His outdoor face, made for the expression of vigorous intentions, was dismayed and shrunken.

'Well,' he said. 'So long as we keep our sense of humour.'

Poor man, I thought. It was what he'd clearly lost, and with fair reason. He hadn't liked Ben's black joke, he was revolted by the comic ease with which a coffin could lose whatever grim dignity the word gave it and be reduced to that single scornful syllable. You ended up in a *box*. Ugh!

I worried at times about my own frivolity in these matters. Lord, I hated the notion of a coffin, too: that dreadful ... *box* that had such an unsuitable air of flashy novelty about it, such varnish for a supremely unvarnished occasion. A coffin was a *gauche* thing! You really wouldn't be seen dead in one! But it seemed to me (who'd been so unamused that in my dream I'd engaged in demented fisticuffs with the ruffian on the stair) that comedy was ungovernably present in every twist of the story. And being aware of that, I thought, didn't point to courage on your part, as was assumed by those who supposed that the presence of amusement meant the absence of fear. At best you could claim that comedy thrust itself upon your attention at every sinister development.

No, not courage: only, perhaps, one of the livelier forms of cowardice.

5

When I found Oliver Cragg's Christmas card, after the phone call from someone who said she was a friend of his, I saw he'd written on it: 'Another year with no contact.' And in a heap of papers on my desk I found a letter he'd sent that summer. I thought how I must always have read his letters with careless affectionate haste. I'd not noticed, certainly hadn't remembered beyond the moment of reading, that Oliver had said he'd been counting the people he'd known who were dead. It had been a silly thing to do, he supposed, and after he got to a hundred he'd given up. 'I was afraid would find I knew more dead than living.'

His friend had said she was sorry to ring with bad news, but Oliver had died suddenly the day before. Would I mind if she told the minister at his church to phone me for a phrase or two for the address he'd give at the funeral?

Oliver was seventy-six. It was fifty years, almost to the day, since he'd arrived at our house, having hunted down the only other local conscientious objector he'd been able to trace who was bound for farm work in Essex. He was small, with a very white face, a quick stuttering manner: a member of some sect that held that everything that was going to happen and everything you ought to believe was to be made out by measuring the Pyramids. Existence was a jealous acrostic, a cryptogram.

We'd been apoplectic together in ditches and hedges and on thresh-ing machines: he infuriatingly anxious that I should see the world as he saw it: I enquiring, maddeningly, how a man so generally shrewd could believe that under the staggering complexity of things was nothing more than a half-witted parlour game. About Oliver there was something Rumpelstiltskinish: he'd hop with rage, and aim his elbow at my ribs, laughing wildly, the white face becoming a scarlet one.

But he was crack-brained only nor'-nor'-west, and we'd become close when the wind was in other directions, incompatibles glad of each other's company during the long, relentlessly physical days, weeks, years of digging, cutting, burning, raking, lifting, dropping, heaping, scattering.

Since we'd resumed our more natural identities, we'd met very occasionally: exchanged quite rare letters: and sent Christmas cards, all of which bore some legend like that on Oliver's last, not yet a week old. Well, you thought people would always be there. At your leisure you could repair the damage caused by years of not quite getting round to arranging a meeting.

The minister rang. Oliver had mellowed into Methodism, though I didn't believe he'd ever lost his hope that everything had been arranged beforehand, some great and not unaffable organiser having turned out before any of us was up and littered the place with codes and clues. 'I'm told you knew our dear friend fairly well at some stage,' said the minister, unenthusiastically. I thought he was aware that I was the wrong sort of person to consult, and his calling Oliver their dear friend was meant to warn me off. And I could think of nothing to say about him that would have seemed to relate to Oliver as, in that protective sense, the dear friend. I could think only of such things as his telling me that he much preferred a woman's breasts to any other part of her. Supposing myself a sophisticate, because I'd read novels, I was then to be thrown by almost any pointer to sexual realities: and I was greatly taken aback by this assertion from my mild and weirdly pious friend. I could say too – fondly, but it might not fit into the tribute the minister had in mind – that he was very vain, unable to bear looking stained or careless: which, given our occupation, set him enormous problems. I recalled him as he'd been in his version of agricultural dress: corduroy trousers tethered at the knees with string: a jersey deeply injured by contact with thorn. Oliver, c1943, at the side of a ditch, scrubbing away at some stain, some very minor muddiness. He'd catch my eye and smile in a melancholy fashion and mutter (invariably): 'Oh my!' He was always a nervous mutterer, given to bringing great sighs up from his boots. 'Ha ha!' he'd say sometimes if you looked in his direction, and make his shoulders shudder, as if you had caught him at some barely decent moment. For him, peeing was a severely sensuous luxury, and as he peed he would exclaim: 'Oh *mother!*'

It turned out once that he'd had an immense growth on his chest, in the end as large as a cricket ball, and he'd said nothing about it until it burst when he was cycling from London to Cold Clapton, having hung around so long after a weekend's leave that he'd missed the car that took the rest of us back to our labours. He often hung around in this manner, being (as I at length deduced) unable ever easily to leave his wife. At the same time he was inclined to plan immense acts of desertion. So, once, we mapped out with enormous thoroughness a cycling trip to Wales, and taught ourselves to ride a tandem, which a friend was willing to lend: and at the very last moment, within an hour of our agreed start, Oliver had rung to say some obstacle had arisen at home – would I go ahead on an ordinary bike, and he (on an ordinary bike) would join me later. I realised then that, as he could not bring himself to confess to the existence of a possibly lethal cricket ball emerging on his chest, so, while our planning was going on, he'd quite failed to inform his wife that he meant to leave her in order to travel by tandem to Bangor and back: and that the last-minute announcement of this scheme had led to protracted negotiations incompatible with his being with me at the hour, the day, even quite the week so firmly agreed. Oliver lived in two worlds, in one of which he had committed himself to embark upon no project of an independent kind, while in the other he was enthusiastically dedicated to doing whatever he liked, whenever he liked.

He'd been a gallant, too, in an absurd fashion. Someone might have asked a landgirl to pass a sandwich to him, and she might have done it ill-naturedly, and he'd stand there holding this surly sandwich and say: 'This will taste the sweeter for having been in your fair hand.' It was an unfailing response to contact with any woman – dangerously, at times, farmers' wives or daughters. The banal floweriness of what he said on these occasions was so daft that I can't remember offence ever being taken. Well, much about my old friend had been embarrass-ingly crazy: and yet he had some quality, some naive warmth, that made it difficult, in the end, to think of him as merely ridiculous.

This was the sort of thing I knew about Oliver, and it was of no use for the ministerial elegy, devoted to Oliver by the diligent Methodist. I muttered a few pieties and the call was quickly over.

The gathering in the church had no obvious common character, except what was suggested by white hair. We sat for a long time, nothing happening, and I thought: Oliver's late, as he always was. Then I decided the cremation must be taking place beforehand: we were waiting for the family to arrive from it. There'd be the three daughters and their husbands and several grand-daughters: as if nature were deferring to his gallantry, Oliver had sired, at first and second hand, only women. His wife had died of a long cancer, ten years before: and I imagined how he'd have devoted himself to florid flirtations with his girls and *their* girls and the ladies of the church. These last were all around me now: women to whom Oliver would have passed cups of tea and sandwiches with a bow, one of his ornate speeches, and then the shiver of his shoulders, and his muttered 'Oh my!' Perhaps only I knew that he might have found their breasts tantalisingly adorable.

Then I thought how being burnt, as he was perhaps being at this moment, would have incensed Oliver. It would rank as a major example of those impertinences he'd always been sensitive to: of the order of someone running into you and then running on without apology. 'Cheek!' he would say. I remembered him on a hundred occasions making this queerly inadequate protest when he was a shilling short in his pay packet, or a sudden order had been circulated that we should work overtime on top of our usual overtime. Once, when we were walking back to our lodgings in Cold Clapton from the Saturday night cinema in the nearest town, suddenly half the German Air Force was above us, so that the blacked-out farmland and the lanes we walked along seemed to shake under the pulsing, ill-intentioned growl of engines, spread across the entire sky, and the indignant crack of anti-aircraft fire. 'Cheek!' said Oliver.

I thought that being burned, anyway, would seem to him like the apotheosis of those stains and smears he'd spent so much time rubbing out of his clothing. His vanity would be offended. We'd learned, working together, much about each other's vanity. I'd said once, as we sat side by side in the cab of a lorry, that more than one person had remarked that I looked like the actor, Leslie Howard. Oliver was furious. Ridiculous, he cried. He'd often – very, very often – been said to resemble Leslie Howard. He'd reached out and seized my chin with a cruel sort of anger, and wrenched my face round so he could look at it. 'You like Leslie Howard!' he cried.

And now the church stirred itself, whispered, coughed: the family had arrived. There was an affably resigned hymn, that I did not recognise: weighing life against death, it came down in favour of death, for reasons only hazily defined. Then the minister spoke. I had prepared myself not to recognise Oliver in what he said, but wasn't ready for his portrait of an anti-Oliver. Well yes, kindly and warm and jolly: Oliver might, with a sort of loose truth, be so described. But what was this about his being always a helping hand, so that his friends could only be pleased that he had gone ahead: to make things ready for them, said the minister. I thought desolately that he must have in mind some image of Oliver, in the great church hall of the hereafter, putting out the chairs. But the Oliver I knew would be the last person one would ever send on ahead, for any purpose at all. He would never arrive. Oliver was infinitely distractible. I remembered foremen who'd sent him back to our tool chest for this or that, and then endlessly, ragingly, would look for his return in the direction in which he had vanished: Oliver reappearing at last from the opposite direction, without the tool he'd been sent for, full of the vaguest sense of having failed in his errand for the best of reasons. And then the minister spoke of Oliver's sense of humour. They would miss, he said, his wit. He had delighted them all with his unfailing wit, and it would be horribly missed.

And there I was, fifty years after that little white-faced stammeringly eager man had arrived in our living room in Barton, exposed to my father's candid discouragements – 'You don't look as if you'd last six months on the land – any more than this lad here! Good God! I wouldn't take you on, either of you, if I was a farmer, for all the tea in China!' – and Oliver had just been reduced to ash: and I was quarrelling scornfully in my mind with the minister's assessment of this man with whom I'd shared such bizarre years. Oliver had never been a wit! He'd have been horribly alarmed, finding himself being witty! What he was – the exact word for him, I thought with sad affection – was a wag. He'd set out to be droll. As those years in the open air turned his white face to an irremovable brown, he'd set out to be droll. He'd been droll and waggish, often with ghastly effect, when addressing foremen, officials of the War Agricultural Committee, farmers who had never in their lives allowed themselves to be amused.

It struck me, as the church prepared to sing itself out of Oliver's presence – though I supposed it was his absence, really: made that, for me, the more intensely because of the minister's portrait of some perfect stranger: but Oliver, I guessed, would have been happy with the minister's view of him – that he'd lived dangerously, with those gallantries and outbursts of waggishness, so often ill-directed. He'd had, I thought, this other attribute, that he was quite fervently keen to discuss whatever he saw as an odd turn of events. Being dead would certainly be such a turn. 'You remember you were counting your dead?' I'd have to say. 'Was I? Oh my!' 'One more now, Oliver!' 'Funny, isn't it! I mean . . . that's funny!' He'd give his attention to a farmyard smear on his sleeve. 'The minister said you were a wit, Oliver. But you never were a wit, were you? You were always a wag.'

At once he'd be Rumpelstiltskin. I'd feel his elbow in my ribs: he'd laugh wildly: his face would become amazingly red. Then he'd cry: '*Cheek!*'

6

The fact is that the death of friends is, *strictly*, beyond belief.

We were in Northern Ireland and our son Tom was on the phone to say he had a message he'd rather not have to deliver. Maurice Lee's daughter had rung him . . .

Once, as we walked in his stony Yorkshire fields, Kate had pointed out to Maurice that his shoelace was undone: and then had realised that she could have chosen no better way of ensuring that it remained undone. Maurice had an enormous disinclination to take, on his own behalf, precautions of, as he thought, a petty kind: which covered a huge range of precautions. Leaving his car, he never locked it. Of late years, having a severe heart condition, he refused to lead the limited existence such a condition was held to enforce. He did not know how to live cautiously. He'd been in the Resistance in France: and Brian Redhead once, taking it that we both had shown courage of one kind or another, I in having been a conscientious objector, had invited us to debate the matter on his programme *A Word in Edgeways*. 'Courage?' said Maurice at some point. He was not aware of having been courageous. In fact, he remembered a moment after he'd been dropped in France. He was cycling down a lane, on a gloriously sunny day, equipped with his false identity – and with the suicide capsule that in no time he had lost – and the thought struck him: 'What a lucky fellow

I am, to be having my summer holiday at the expense of George VI!'
The last thing Maurice ever did was to invent romantic tales about
himself. If he said that was what he had thought, then that was what
he had thought.

Visiting friends in France recently, he'd found himself in the middle
of the night in the grip of what seemed clearly a fatal attack. Oh, fool,
he thought: having sat up late over dinner, nibbling – an habitual
punctuation when talking – pieces of cheese. Cheese late at night – in
his state, a direct route to death. So he crawled out of bed and tore a
sheet out of his notebook and wrote a letter of apology to his hosts.
Such an ass! and worse – making it necessary for them to deal with
the corpse, on top of the shock of finding it! For such thoughtlessness,
would they forgive him!

The next he knew was that it was morning: he was astonishedly
alive. He tore up the letter.

And now, entering the empty house after holidaying with friends,
he'd had a massive attack that must have killed him at once. He was
discovered by visitors.

And there was no way of believing that Maurice had ceased to exist.

There's this difficulty: that we have never thought of our friends as
anything but alive. And death being another matter altogether, we are
left in a no-man's-land of feeling. Our friends cannot be dead, because
that has never been a description of them. We have to find a new
description of them, but do not see how we can, since it must be one
that contradicts everything we know and feel about them.

How could there be a forever-silent Maurice? How could there be a
Maurice who did not arrive at the side-door by which he always
admitted himself to our house, a great gust of an arrival? What sense
did a Maurice make who could no longer enter with laughter, make
the whole house prick up its ears? What sense did a Maurice make
whom you could not embrace?

We do not know how to understand a friend who is no longer there,
and will never be there again.

And Rufus rang, saying he'd been reading Homer, because he'd been commissioned to make a radio drama out of the *Iliad*, and how poor the characterisation was, a man was said to be brave or a coward and that was that, and how obvious was the narration, and how bad the translation he was reading. All of which amounted to this: that Rufus, fresh from six years of work on Shakespeare, was beginning to shift nests, to this one that of course had been occupied by many before him: grumbling his way into it, with a contemptuous tossing of twigs and exasperated rearrangement of leaves. Rufus was greatly given to extreme acts of literary espousal, and extreme acts of literary rejection. They were little rages, as I'd thought, of over-adoration or over-disdain that provided him with energy he needed. He hadn't the sort of engine that ran best at moderate pace.

How was he? This discomfort in his chest – part, he thought, of some general digestive discomfort. Yes, yes, he did mean to see his doctor.

Which he did: and cancer was found at once: and, offered a choice, he chose an operation. And the operation went badly wrong. I took him *Wodehouse on Wodehouse,* Rufus never having taken against that writer's writer, whatever his need of energy. His eyes were huge with alarm, and with anger at being imprisoned here, in this ward for those who'd undergone acute surgery, and with the desperation of being away from his wife, and his music, and his books, and his dog. They came to take him to X-ray. 'When in doubt, X-ray,' Rufus murmured, bitterly. It took three people five minutes to get him on the move, given the immense amount of machinery he was attached to. I waited for his return. He said, then: 'I wanted to say to the man pushing the wheelchair: If I gave you £500, would you push me straight home?' It would have been an uphill mile, and then a little way round the corner. When I left him his huge eyes were fixed on me. I was the rescuer who had failed to rescue.

It was the last time I saw him.

Bleak expungement. A person you love and whose teeming life is part of the teeming life in you, is, in no time at all – in far less time than such a huge alteration of things would seem to require – obliterated.

How could there be a forever silent Rufus? How could there be a

Rufus who did not materialise at the end of the telephone line, floating your name enquiringly and, when you answered, sighing with vast satisfaction. Oh good, you were there. Oh good, talk could begin. How could there be a Rufus who was not to be spotted with relief and pleasure at a party? He'd once invented two delinquent eighteenth-century schoolboys, called Bostock and Harris: and when I saw him across the room it was Bostock gleefully glad to encounter Harris: though it might have been Harris immensely pleased to encounter Bostock.

As to telephoning, he communicated in no other fashion. I hated using the telephone, as an intrusive instrument, a ruthless buttonholer. Rufus adored it, as a sensible means of almost always being able to be in the company of a friend. I had warned him that when the time for commemorative volumes arrived, there would be one called *The Collected Letter of Rufus*, and I had the letter concerned: which he'd sent me at the unimaginable stage in our acquaintance when he didn't know my telephone number.

How to believe that within weeks of his devastatingly crushing report on the work of Homer, Rufus would be silent ash?

Beyond belief.

Facing the hospital from which none of us rescued Rufus was a building that had provided an annexe, for subversive subjects such as art and metalwork, for the school I'd written of in *Roaring Boys*, calling it Stonehill Street. It was part of a ferocious phase of my existence, and I was astonished, visiting Rufus, to observe that it was being converted. 'Converted', with its suggestion of profound spiritual mutation, seemed the exact word. The old Board School that had been the scene of so much educational hurly-burly and hope and distress was now gravely scaffolded, and a very large notice announced:

27 DOUBLE-HEIGHT APARTMENTS
OF EXCEPTIONAL STYLE AND SPECIFICATION
CREATED THROUGH

THE SENSITIVE RESTORATION OF A
FINE LATE VICTORIAN SCHOOL

In its own way, this was also beyond belief.

7

'Her nerves were so bad,' said my mother once, who was given to beautifully missing the target of a word, 'that they gave her tantalisers.'

I'd thought often that this was a fair summary of my own elderly condition: but it seemed even truer of Harry Frost's. Beset by hernias, capricious blood pressure, inascribable flutterings of vital muscles, rebellion of knees and elbows, fits of dizziness (notably occurring when he happened to be in the shopping precinct), he was tantalised almost beyond endurance by the streams and rivers of knowledge and enquiry that every day invited him to embark upon. I told him (in that matter of his seeming to be medically affected simply by entering the shopping precinct) that I'd read that after the building of the colonnades in Covent Garden, large numbers of girl children were named Piazza: and that I felt we should enquire into the question: how many of Barton's children (boys or girls) had lately been christened Precinct? Harry said this was ridiculously interesting and he really didn't want to know. He was engaged, anyway, in this debate by letter with the Duke of Edinburgh on some detail of conservation. The correspondence, as he described it, was remarkably one-sided: but he was working towards stinging the Palace into more than formal replies, more than one sentence long.

I took the opportunity to confess to our recent visit to the Palace. Well, that was to make the wrong sort of statement. What had happened was that the Palace had requested our attendance at a garden party it had found it was laying on. Our first response was one of indignation – surely they knew our views? – but then we thought it must be a bizarre experience not to be missed, rather like wandering for an afternoon into *Alice in Wonderland*. And so we found ourselves with others gathered at one of the gates, men and women who'd weaved their way among the sensible everyday users of the pavements of Victoria, trying to appear at ease and accustomed: which was difficult in such more-than-best suiting, ties so expensively sombre, shoes so gleaming: dresses so flowing, hats at once so discreet and ambitious. I was in brown, having no black: and brown was obviously the colour not to be in, the cad's colour. I could hear my father, somewhere, uttering his unforgettable disgusted snort. Again the bloody boy hadn't bothered to get it right.

The gate was opened, and we strolled towards the lawn, windingly past a small lake: all of us absurd, pretending to be at home, anxious not to give a hint of our real condition: which was that of puzzlement at being there. Such affectations of poise mixed with sly uneasy glances this way and that! The lawn was two or three score of lawns run together, with a band performing in every corner: so that in mid-lawn there were collisions of Johann Strauss, Arthur Sullivan, Andrew Lloyd-Webber. There were tables and chairs, far too few for the ever-increasing company, so that there was much dashing and seizing and some elbowing, undignified acts that were performed as if they were dignified ones. I noticed there was a remarkable number of soldiers in versions of the hat worn on this imperial frontier and that by soldiers pictured in the comics of my childhood. There must surely be several dozen colonial wars still being fought of which we were told nothing?

Along edges of the lawn were marquees, in which at a signal tea was to be obtained. The signal was given and, in a moment, and again with no discernible decline in the general dignity, persons strolling on the lawn or at watchful ease at their tables became people queuing, their postures predatory. Tremendous numbers of tiny sandwiches were borne here and there. I noticed a small mountain of them being delivered to a woman whose dress was beyond rational understanding. The designer of her hat can have been given the order only that he must make her incapable of seeing or hearing. Her gown, of the sort of yellow that is desperately anxious not to be mistaken for any other colour, was split downwards from a huge button that, as it was placed, could have one intention only: to provide rapid access to her private parts. She talked with loud vivacity to half a dozen men who were certainly invisible to her, each of whom came to her flowing yellow elbow with as many canapes as a plate could bear, and often more.

It was, the whole scene, much like the Mad Hatter's tea party, on a huge scale. Though there was no actual sporting of price-tags, like the one in his hat, there was an overwhelming air of their being present. And at a late stage, from the distant haunch of the palace, came three figures. The Queen, tiny, apricot, was to the fore: rather behind, and to her right, a thin stroke of grey, her husband: and to her left, much deeper and at a wider angle, her heir. Before the crowd closed on them, I had a tremendous notion of their being arranged for cricket. If she had been carrying a bat (and at this distance I could not be sure that she wasn't) any careless or awkward contact with the ball might have sent it to the close slip to her right: or, more thrillingly, to the one on the left, whose positioning was obviously based on long study of her weakness against the bouncer.

8

Ben had gone five thousand miles to see his villagers, and on his return rang with a terrible tale he could hardly tell for laughter (and for those tears that, now as sixty years earlier, laughter, especially if inspired by disaster, caused him to shed). In the street, in the midst of a ceremonial occasion involving elephants, he'd been approached by a pious man with pamphlets, and had uttered a local word of quasi-obscene dismissal: to reinforce which he'd taken a dramatic stride from road to pavement without noticing that at this spot the pavement was raised higher than usual. He'd tripped and broken a rib and bled profusely onto a brand-new tropical suit. I said I hoped the man got a pamphlet out of it about the retribution to be expected by those who refused to consider buying pamphlets. Ben said that whatever fatal moment awaited him, he now knew it would be absurd and would cause

laughter in which he would be sorry not to be able to join. Was I
intending to die absurdly? I said everything pointed in that direction.
For the past six months I had had non-stop indigestion. Dr Rowe had
hit back with tablets that had no effect at all, and a consultant had
prescribed others that seemed to favour the condition rather than me.
That was enough, said Dr Rowe: and another consultant laid on a
gastroscopy. This turned out to resemble an attempted act of murder,
carried out by a group of amiable people, the method being to cram
mouth and throat with what felt like linked stretches of metal tubing:
one amiable person clamping her hand over your mouth, presumably
to prevent your disgorging its dreadful contents. At the end of it all a
telescope descended into your stomach and the consultant was able to
make a tour of inspection. He had found the stomach grossly inflamed,
and given to bleeding where the telescope touched it: and had taken
little bits of it for a biopsy, which had discovered nothing. So now I
was on a diet of fiendish capsules: and having been at the point where
I hated eating and drinking, and would happily have done without
either if possible, I was now very slowly deriving a miserable satisfaction from a limited number of bland dishes. But a morose stomach
was a poor companion. The second consultant had told me that
medicine was constantly changing its mind about practically everything, and I had this sensation of being toyed with.

What I'd gained was vast respect for Dr Rowe, who stood in the
middle of all this changeability, and all these difficulties of matching
conditions and consultants (some of whom were scornful of general
practitioners, as if a door had been scornful of its hinges), and who
had drawn me a rather beautiful picture of a stomach which suggested
that if you stumbled over one somewhere you might well suppose it to
be a set of bagpipes. And, oh yes, I'd had this secondary cataract,
which made you think there were mobs of traffic lights where in fact
there was only one, and the name over a shop became a tangle of
names. This had been dealt with by laser, a pleasant young woman
aiming at it with a contrivance that clicked startlingly, as if you were
being stapled.

I put down the phone on a weeping Ben.

9

Our youngest grandson, William, had fallen into an anxious habit of saying: 'You might die . . .'

We were in Whitby, weekending. A problem, especially in the company of children who'd recently shaken off the weakness, was simply that of staying awake in the afternoon. The loss of consciousness, then and after dinner, was very much closer to being seriously stunned than to what one might have expected sleep in old age to be – a drifting off into gentle unawareness. It was intense, as if the head had been taken into the not particularly good-natured grip of a very large dark hand.

Sleep was the pool you were drowning in, and every day you drowned a little deeper.

And dreams became more frequent and fragmented, and worse. It was like being taken over by mocking storytellers. But mockery was only part of the intent of this invasion: which of course wasn't an invasion, you'd reflect, since the apparent intruders were probably the mind's true inhabitants. The worst of it, as it seemed to me, was that there was no way, awake, of telling the stories told by these zany scriptwriters. The techniques of conscious narration did not begin to cover the twitchy shiftiness of these tales told in the sleeping head. As some sort of storyteller by profession, I felt this to be the ultimate offence committed by my dreams: that they suggested that a feature of the essential truth of things was that it could not be told. We moved with some sort of confidence through the conscious day because we had developed this plausible technique for seeming to make sense of it. But sense was not made, and in the end could not be made. In the end, in the involuntarily honest privacy of our beds, we were confronted by ourselves as we really were, creatures swarming with nonsense.

We were walking as night fell by the black water of the harbour, in which the reflections of the lighted windows of flats on the other side had the appearance of watery buttonholes, and William said:

'You might die . . .'

You might (his argument went) be squashed by almost anything. Almost anything might fall from almost anywhere onto your head. You might, from standing in almost any spot, like this present one, fall into the sea. Falling into the sea, you might be drowned.

You might, he said from the neighbourhood of my elbow (he was about the height I'd been in 1924), at almost any moment be struck by lightning. So you might die?

'Yes, William,' I said. 'I guess you might.'